STRANG

Laura Fish was born in London in 1964, of Caribbean parents. She has lived in Southern Africa and Australia, and has held posts as a Creative Writing tutor at various universities including the University of East Anglia, where she recently completed a PhD in Creative and Critical Writing. Her first novel, *Flight of Black Swans*, was published in 1995. She currently holds the RCUK Academic Fellowship in Creative Writing at the University of Newcastle.

LAURA FISH

Strange Music

VINTAGE BOOKS

London

Published by Vintage 2009

2 4 6 8 10 9 7 5 3 1

Copyright © Laura Fish 2008

Laura Fish has asserted her right under the Copyright, Designs
and Patents Act 1988 to be identified as the author of this work

Quotations from the correspondence of Elizabeth Barrett Browning
reproduced by kind permission of the Provost and Fellows of Eton
College, The Henry W. and Albert A. Berg Collection of English
and American Literature, The New York Public Library, Astor,
Lennox and Tilden Foundations.

First published in Great Britain in 2008 by Jonathan Cape

Vintage
Random House, 20 Vauxhall Bridge Road,
London SW1V 2SA

www.vintage-books.co.uk

Addresses for companies within The Random House Group
Limited can be found at: www.randomhouse.co.uk/offices.htm

The Random House Group Limited Reg. No. 954009

A CIP catalogue record for this book
is available from the British Library

ISBN 9780099507987

The Random House Group Limited supports The Forest
Stewardship Council (FSC), the leading international forest
certification organisation. All our titles that are printed on
Greenpeace approved FSC certified paper carry the FSC logo.
Our paper procurement policy can be found at
www.rbooks.co.uk/environment

Printed in the UK by CPI Bookmarque, Croydon, CR0 4TD

No one is born fully-formed: it is through self-experience in the world that we become what we are.

Paulo Freire, 1921–1997

Author's Note

While this novel is inspired by historical events and person-ages, it is a work of fiction. Elizabeth Barrett's narrative includes extracts from diaries and correspondence with her family and friends. Some of these passages have been edited considerably and alterations have also been made to grammar and punctuation.

10 January 1845
New Cross, Hatcham, Surrey

I love your verses with all my heart, dear Miss Barrett, – and
this is no off-hand complimentary letter that I shall write . . .
I can give reason for my faith in one and another excellence,
the fresh strange music, the affluent language, the exquisite
pathos and true new brave thought – but in addressing myself
to you, your own self, and for the first time, my feeling rises
altogether. I do, as I say, love these Books with all my heart
– and I love you too . . .

Yours ever faithfully,
Robert Browning

Prologue

Kaydia

CINNAMON HILL ESTATE
14 February 1840

In blue light Mister Sam lies, sickly face sweating yellow. Hips, shins, spine – him body curl up making spiral-shell shape.

Lifting him into bed don't go easy. He retches, shudders, gasping for breath. But I can't feel pity. Did him lips touch my cheek? Did him hands stroke my body? How we did share four-poster, I'm thinking, when he fills my soul with grief? Grief and deep dread.

Mister Sam moans weakly. Spit strands link lightly parted lips. I dab him mouth dry on my grey skirt, wrench mattress straight against wall, tug shoulders forward, wedge lace pillow beneath him head. Neck floppy, him head lolls back sliding into softness – Mister Sam mustn't go. Not yet. He told me to wait at bedside. But I choose to run because I can't cure bad fever like this.

I go from blue bedchamber to tell Pa to fetch Doctor Demar. Sea's facing me. Silver-pink clouds. Cordia flowers bright and orange speckle coarse blades of grass, buckle beneath my bare feet.

Below great house I pass overseer's house by sugar works, barracks for bookkeeper, masons, carpenters. I pass trash-house, plantation path sweeping round and down to coast road. I reach wharf planks. Ship's sails flap as rigging grows taut.

Pa's heading for main wharf hut. Striding along wood strips cool-like he gives me a glance. Him face kinda snarl up like a dog's but inside him starts laughing. Pa slams hut door shut in my face, grey-green gecko shoot down wood shafts.

Pa's refusing to open up. I knock to tell him Mister Sam's worse again.

Pa don't know why Mister Sam mustn't go. Not before a will's made.

I run back up coast road to plantation path. Evening air comes cooled. I turn, looking for Pa. Orange sun ball perches, fuming, on blue ocean rim.

Pa squats beside sugar winch now. Running faster onto coast road, towards wharf hut. 'Pa,' I shout, approaching him back. 'Pa, fetch Doctor Demar fe Mister Sam.'

Pa stretches bony arms; legs slowly clamber down from plank wharf, wade into clear shallow sea; water laps round him knee. He leans against strong sour evening light, angry ocean blue. He don't speak. My head's burning. Pa, you can't see?

Wet up to him waist, wading onto shore, Pa's soaked overalls stick on him body. Waves wash my feet, shifting worry lines on yellow sand. Pa bends over, wrings frayed trouser bottoms. Salt water trickles into star shapes on sand.

Pa shakes him feet, saying, 'Yu hot wid fiah. Wot yu waan?' Then he strides back onto coast road, salt water running from clothes.

Pa's spirit unleashes like green-bronze flash of gecko. 'How come yu come on such a day as dis? Yu don't know wot day is it?'

I say, 'No.'

'It Friday's birthday.'

Inside I'm moving so I say, 'Wot bout May's or Mary Ann's or mine? Yu don't know wen dat is?'

'No.' Him voice leave no questions. But I look at him, questions whirling round my head.

Fast I run to plantation path to Pa's brother, Dick. Because he my uncle and knows about Pa. Dick's bamboo hut's raised off soft sandy earth, keeping cool. Each dusk Dick stumbles back from masonry, chipped, grey from grinding stone. Dick's humming, 'Hi! De buckra, hi!' Having no more work till Mister Sam sends orders, he sits on top-step edge, waiting, watching like he knows why I come. Dick, him eye walking up and down, spying from under hat brim, says loud, 'Why yu flee like devil chase behind yu?'

'Yu cun tell why Pa's mad at me? E treat me like me not a dawta. Pa's same Pa to Sibyl an me.'

Dick's strong hand, bathed in white stone dust, wipes silvered streaks down sweat-polished cheeks. 'Because yu are of one blood an still e treat yu bad, ave noting more to do wid im.'

'But we living in same place.'

Dick sighs long. 'Me cyaan say wot mek Pa wot e is.'

I think it's a nigger I see on horseback for him clumping so quick up silent slope swerve.

'Yu betta go back to de great house,' Uncle Dick says. Standing up, wordless, he turns round. I feel him wanting to break talk off. Him feet siss then, edging away.

Conch-blow bellows *Fuuuuffuu-ffuu* like it struggles free from a monster's heart swooping through air, roaring towards quietly hunched tamarind trees edging plantation path. I'm staring past Dick at hut's outline, washed-out sky – there's space for sky between branches, leaves – and as conch-blow hurries into it, Dick's cold words close in on me.

Dusky air falls silent. Waiting for something. Someone. Darkness steadily sweeps across deepest blue fading to deeper black.

Duppy was on great-house track? No, its body too thick, too bold. Must be a nigger. Then I'm running down plantation path hill to coast road, running round wharf-hut back. Pa's shape's a smear behind grimy glass. Wharf room holds a stale wood, stale fish smell. Where boards don't overlap Pa's smear shape shifts, fusing with rough-edged planks. I run to hut front, thump hut door. My shadow don't follow me round any more.

Door opens. Earthy floor looks sameway but a gap between we widens. My armpits tickle, tingling.

Pa says I'm a bully coming back again, he getting ready to fetch Doctor Demar and because I've come back he won't. Says I'm to serve and save white buckra. Pa says, 'De devil widin yu.'

I'm struggling to tell what is it. 'Eeee? Me cyaan ear yu.'

'Don't be renk. Mek me tell yu.'

'Yu's dawg. It mek yu too ugly.'

'Don't ax me. Me cyaan go now, me busy. Me head a-hurt me.'

Sibyl walks in. Then I can't throw insults at Pa. 'Sibyl. Sibyl,' I'm calling to she, because she also don't know where's we mama. Rebecca Laslie's we mama for sure. Sibyl's face answers silent. Empty. She don't understand sickness I live in. *Me was back*

because me was smashing an tearing, wanting to be rid of wot's in
me belly.

Pa says, 'Yu behaving white again.'

Inside I'm warring. I'm saying to Sibyl, 'E too hard,' running
out. Running from wharf. Running back to great house.

Chapter One

Elizabeth

3, BEACON TERRACE, TORQUAY
13 November 1838

My dearest Miss Mitford,

My beloved father has gone away; he was obliged to go two days ago, and took away with him, I fear, almost as saddened spirits as he left with me . . . His tears fell almost as fast as mine did when we parted, but he is coming back soon – perhaps in a fortnight, so I will not think any more of them, *but of* that. *I never told him of it, of course, but, when I was last so ill, I used to start out of fragments of dreams, broken from all parts of the universe, with the cry from my own lips 'Oh, Papa, Papa!' . . . Well! But I do trust I shall not be ill again in his absence and that it may not last longer than a fortnight . . .*

Just weeks ago I swooped down on my dear brother Bro in a storm of emotion which quite wore me out, hence my recent removal to Torquay; yet this detail need not be revealed in correspondence – it is safer to say a blood vessel burst during one of my coughs and I fell gravely ill, which is also true. To have stayed in London would, Dr. Chambers said, have been suicidal, so here I must remain.

I hang by a thread between life and death, and can feel with each morsel my weight increase. Bro says I have grown vain. But I am bloated with guilt. Any desire to eat left me in March last. Since then I have shed weight as a snake sheds skin. In but three months I shall be thirty-three yet my anxiety increases as does my weakness. My new doctor, Dr. Barry, believes blisters and leeches will remedy this. I can't see how such a miserable treatment will effect the shedding of guilt and anxiety. Doctors can be full of absurdities.

This doctor forbids me to write *anything*! Especially poetry. Which is good, for I never can write when ordered to, but when refused, *that* is when I can. And do. It is a mercy Bro is with me in this conspiracy. I would not dream of sending my verses to anyone without first passing them under his keen and critical eye.

Although this morning Dr. Barry caught me in the act – I was mid-way through 'The Sea-Mew' – and I have sworn not to write again, already I know what I shall write next. And there is another poem I am thinking on while I sit watching over this mesmerizing sea.

14 November 1838

Kind Papa has written permitting my sister, Henrietta, to stay permanently during my confinement to this room. Bro is to remain too – *I* shall see to *that*. Dearest Georgie travelled here with us but Papa says he must soon return to London. Weaving a tapestry of comings and goings my other brothers – Stormie, Henry, Daisy, Sette, Occy – circulate as regularly as their other engagements will allow; as will my sister Arabel. Hopefully Sam is sailing back from Jamaica – he is a constant cause for distress. Papa himself has promised to visit every two weeks.

My beloved Arabel, do pray *write, & don't wait for me to do it . . .*

. . . Now mind! – you are not to fancy that I am in the least worse if you hear of any more blisters. Dr. Barry made up his mind from the first I believe that he wd. give me plenty of them – & the better I declare myself, the firmer became his resolve . . . he really does take most incessant pains, & everybody says with a corresponding ability, to do me good – and doing good does not always mean, in this world, giving pleasure. You see, I had made up a hope of my own, encouraged by Dr. C's permission, to manage here without medical visits, & to trust simply to God's sun & air as the means of accomplishing whatever mercy He intended for me. So that I had the less ready patience for certain persecutions – & for not being allowed to write or read or eat or drink or go out or stay in, or put on my stockings, without a certificate from Dr. Barry. And really it has come to this.

Now fancy — on the occasion of my writing-case being accidentally visible —
'Have you been writing today, Miss Barrett?' 'No.' — 'Did you write yesterday?'
'Yes.' 'You will be so good as not to do so any more!' — And again — 'You
have observed my directions & been idle lately, Miss Barrett?' 'Yes.' 'And
within these last three weeks you have never written any poetry . . . Well then!
I may as well take my leave! I have told you the consequence. You must do as
you please; but if you please to do this, neither I nor anyone else can do anything
for you.' And then there are flannel waistcoats up to the throat — & next to
the skin — & most of the most disagreeable things you can think of besides . . .
provided that you happen to be particularly imaginative whilst *you think!*

My bed is shaken with vibrations! The steam packet departs.
Soon Crow, the maid, will knock with my tray, for that dreadful
hour, eleven o'clock, is close at hand — as are letters to me from
Papa and Arabel. Bro's rowing across the bay to the steam packet
will not have been wasted.

Every morning at eleven o'clock I am made to take asses' milk
and soup, and a meal in the evening at six. Oysters or macaroni.
At these times I have no appetite; this surprises me not, for ever
since my eyes first opened I have felt hunger only for books. Though
oysters have on occasion proven reasonably palatable.

Bro's footsteps are upon the stairs.

'No mail today?' I ask. Bro shakes his head, licks his pale dry
lips and rubs his wind-chaffed cheeks with an open hand. 'Dr. Barry
left hours ago. Why did you not come to see me immediately after
the examination?'

'I was afraid of what he might have said,' Bro replies, 'and I've
been working below with water-colours.'

'Dr. Barry said I look as though I carry the world's burdens
with me and should worry less. He also gave his opinions concerning
the situation on West Indian plantations, saying that although the
apprenticeship system was in ruins it should never have ended
early.' I feel a spirit of rebellion rising in me like flames from a
burning torch. 'Was slavery not immoral?' I ask in a tone more
heated than I had intended, but even my strident pitch belies the
true feelings within my heart, which are more fiery than Bro would
suppose. 'The emancipationists should have just waited, Bro, for
apprenticeship to end, and done nothing?' Bro looks blankly at the

sea. Has he no sense of guilt? Not one breath of sorrow? 'People will continue to be hurt and it's no one's fault if we do nothing. Is that it?'

'Slavery's over and they are free,' Bro says finally.

'Many died cruelly. They needed our help.'

'They are dead. There's nothing we can do for them.'

That West Indian planters caused such grief is incomprehensible. I long to seek forgiveness for them yet I know not how. 'I'm not good at being alone, Bro, and I know you are here. But I *feel* wretched and miserable. I *feel* alone.'

Bro sinks heavily into the armchair opposite my bed. He takes from his pocket a small rectangular card. He emits a sort of lassitude as he turns the pale blue calling-card bearing Annie Shropshire's neat copperplated handwriting, and paints, with his eyes, her lively, determined, innocent face. He prickles with frustration. Something truly terrible happened between them.

'Papa said you attract all the wrong women.'

Bro's blue-green eyes are ready to turn to anger. 'Papa could not, would not, even join me in my room for tea before he left for London.'

'He was busy with business in the study. You know what happened, Bro. Papa had re-arranged his plans and was going to catch the stagecoach a day late for the sake of wishing us all a hearty farewell. Suddenly he changed his mind and almost flew from the house when an article on increased taxes for cargo imported at the London docks appeared in *The Times*. He barely said farewell.'

Quietly Bro stands and turns for the stairs.

Each farewell I endure feels like a preparation for death. A morbid notion to be sure – one that leads to a much exaggerated response – I am prone to faintings and uncontrollable tears when anyone I love departs. Good-byes remind me of leaving dear Mama for the sake of my own poor health. To live without a mother's love is to live without hope. Is that why my family avoids involving me in good-byes? Is that why, when Bro went to join Papa on business in London four years ago, what I was told would be a two-week separation ended with him sailing to Jamaica without any farewell?

Bro had to assist our uncle on the estates before the slaves' emancipation, how well I know *that*. The ship that took Bro away to

Jamaica, away from me, was the *David Lyon*, the ship in which I now have shares. That is a curse if ever there was one.

I lie on the bed in this chamber, with the shadow of my distant father – in girlhood I thought only of how to win his smile. Counting memories, I stumble across some forgotten treasure. Hand in hand, I – in a little white muslin dress and frilled pantalettes – am running with Bro; slipping, slithering in and out of the sheets of sunlight shooting down between parted leaves.

'Ba,' Bro says, 'let's not play hide-and-seek.' He has reneged on plans we made at luncheon, and at the last minute.

I return stubbornly, 'Yes, now. Before the school bell rings.' We race across the cobbled yard, under the great clock tower and along shady gravelled walks, round lily ponds fringed with bullrushes, past the home farm cottages, past the dairy and gun-rooms, by haylofts and back to the lake – a fine sheet of water fed by springs and well stocked with the fish it is our pleasure to catch – past cascading streams, over the Alpine bridge, by the summer-house and ice-house, which is under construction, the walled garden, the hot-house's massive flues where peaches, figs and grapes ripen, around the cinder shed, back through the gateway to the stables and harness-rooms, past the cider-house, brew-house and cellar to the laundry, and hide in the knife-and-shoe hole. We hear the bell and the governess, Mrs. Orme, calling all the way from the south gate, and tear down the subterranean passage, through the ornamental shrubbery to the chapel and school-house. Bro gazes from the school-room window to the lawn where at the weekend he played cricket with Papa and Sam; beyond, the obelisk of Eastnor Castle peeps above treetops.

Bro was aged two and I three when Henrietta was born and the family moved to Hope End in Herefordshire. After Henrietta came Sam, Arabel, Charles – nicknamed Stormie for being born during a thunderstorm – Georgie, Henry, Alfred – who we nicknamed Daisy – Septimus (Sette), Octavius (Occy). At Hope End we lived in a world of our own.

How can life be so treacherous as to take childhood away? But since he first moved on this earth Bro has always been my sanctuary. My adytum. It is true I was jealous of him when he abandoned me at Hope End to study at Charterhouse – how the tide turns.

Although Bro is wanting in his sense of direction and purpose –
particularly passion – my love for him increases with each hour he
spends at my bedside, with each passing day. We were jointly
baptized, Bro and I. Never was there a truer love between brother
and sister. The invisible sun burning within us feels as comforting
as the distant lowing of cattle strolling across hills, past trees bent
inland; the pale yellow sunlight streaming across moving waters
reaching forever away from me.

Dearest Arabel,

Will Georgie really go . . . I am sitting up in bed wondering & wishing
perhaps vainly about it . . .

15 November 1838

This afternoon, vain or not, I have felt particularly anxious, though
dear Bro will say unduly, about my appearance. One can put up a
mirror to oneself but can one turn the image back to truly see
how one is viewed? Can a woman see herself from her own reflection? I have long been displeased with the plainness of the face
that peers darkly from my glass. I am small and black. (Black, I
imagine, as Sappho.) A thin partition divides us; why do I regard
the woman who watches me with distaste? She has a searching
quizzical look, slightly remote and mischievous; the features, wasted,
compared with my sister Henrietta, who sits quietly sewing by the
window overlooking the bay, and certainly *is* very pretty – there
is no nose to speak of; the brow, furrowed and pain-worn. I take
objection to the hands for they are the fairy-fingers of an invalid.
The mouth is large, obstinate, projecting – she is full-lipped – and
has dark eyes, deep and calm, and long thick ringlets, again, dark
brown, almost black, which Crow must brush very, very soon lest
they lose their silkiness. Funny though it seems when I think on
it, the droopy locks resemble Miss Mitford's dear spaniel's long
floppy ears.

17 November 1838

Darkness is lowering. The garish red sea, framed by my two
bedroom windows, is shot with a jealous shock of yellow from the
last light of a fast-disappearing sun.

Yesterday evening when Crow brought my opium draft I wore the silver locket inscribed with *Edward & Judith Barrett of Cinnamon Hill*, a family heirloom given to Papa by his mother and brought from Jamaica by Bro to be passed down to me. This evening the locket has vanished. We have shaken out the coverlets and the *couvre-pied* warming my feet, searched beneath the bed, under the carpet. Crow swept all four corners of the floor and emptied the small box of sharpened pencils by the oil-lamp on my bedside-table; she even scoured the stairs lest somehow the locket was transported down there.

I am naked beneath Papa's accusing gaze. All is undone. My relationship with Papa, with the great-grandmama I never knew. Gone.

A vivid sky of dazzling silence casts shards of ochre light which invade this space I already know too well. Gilt-edged scrolls on red-cushioned chair backs glint amber; the family griffin crest glows gold; the sofa's elegant claw feet shine sharply, waiting to pounce. Never has fear gripped me more firmly. An undefinable fear. I am inside a glass bowl surrounded by distorted bulging serpent-like furniture. Loneliness gnaws at my stomach like hunger as I reach across the bedside-table for my writing-case.

A sentence resounds in my head: *Ba, pull yourself together. Climb down from the bed, do away with the chair, and walk along the cobbled street!*

Crow once supported me to the door. She steadied me each time I stumbled, and when it became evident I could not walk alone, she wept into my hair, hiding her face. That was so many days ago I can barely remember. Opium colours my life here. Dresses my world in radiant crimson. Yet I want to cross this vast desert unaided, I want to walk once more.

Now, if I can practise sitting myself up, then spend time swinging my legs over the side of the bed until my toes reach the floor, I can begin the process of hobbling, or crawling should it come to that, to the door.

For a while I stare into the fire. The acrid odour of burning coal snags in the back of my throat. Flames can change their character, making extravagant shapes, but the wild forms into which they bloom only wither, fading to feebly glowing embers.

Even the carpet is hard and hostile. I find the courage to stand up. I am groping, unstable at the window-sill. Someone is watching me – not through the window, for one cannot see up into here from the street. Torrents of sound gush in my ears like water flooding from sluice-gates. I turn my head – am thumped on one cheek – feel warmth on my face, and open my eyes towards the hearth, which holds the blackness of a grave. I must have fallen. I lie, unable to move, and the dark figure that haunted my thoughts disappears.

Footsteps approach. 'Ba, are you all right?' Henrietta's voice.

A biting wind dashes up stairs, awakening me fully to the perplexing view of Crow's and Henrietta's green and red slippered feet advancing across the spread of carpet weave expansive as the blue heaving sea.

'She must have attempted walking,' Henrietta is saying.

Once more I feel faint. In my dream I see the woman again – a dark shape flitting across the doorway, down the staircase where the wind whistles, and out into the hall. She is standing at the door to her life beneath the black pavilion of sky; branches sway like waving arms. She launches into the blustery night. Ebony ringlets swirl round her head, stream across her face. The fire lights easily. She is burning a house of memories. Flames, like some great beast, shoot through a bedroom similar to mine at Wimpole Street; a blazing heat consumes the chaise-longue, the armchair; drawers crowned with a coronal of shelves to carry her books. She moves past sheets of crimson merino paper. Smoke streams round the window where a box full of deep soil is fixed. The scarlet-runners, geraniums and nasturtiums are charred tentacles about a great ragged ivy root with trailing branches so long and wide the tops fasten to a window of the higher storey, whilst the lower feelers cover all the panes; her face; arms; legs. Ivy tendrils mesh with her wild matted hair.

As Crow and Henrietta peel me from the floor, the admonition resounds again: *Ba, pull yourself together. Climb down from the bed, do away with the chair, and walk along the cobbled street!*

18 November 1838

When Bro came to my bedside at his usual hour this morning worry was written across his face. 'Crow, Henrietta and I find ourselves faced with a deuce of a dilemma: either we lie to Papa and hide the fact that you not only stood but are walking, or we live in blatant denial of who you are.'

'This act of which you speak entailed such appalling suffering it would be preferable to be dead,' I return. My thoughts are in harmony on this matter. But I long for contentment and a sense of peace without a draught of that dusky-brown drug. In my cloudless state of mind, I have discovered I think not less clearly, as I had feared, but with *more* precision. I have entered into what Papa and Henrietta call my 'rebellious state'.

Seating himself in the armchair, Bro stretches out a closed hand. 'Is this what you were looking for?' His hand opens gently, as though protecting flower heads. The locket and chain make a small silver mound on the opened flat of his palm. 'Henrietta found it beneath you by the fire-place.' Bro's words come soberly, 'You must try to live your life less cast down by the weight of sadness.'

He folds his fingers back over the locket and leans forward, talking with greater intensity. 'When I was in Jamaica, the number of Africans on the estates given to committing suicide had greatly reduced. The governor allowed them to air their grievances. In the newspapers I read of thousands of ordinary folk rallying in London's streets against the apprenticeship system. One churchwarden was reported as saying the traffic in human bodies and blood had injured the perpetrators as much as their victims, and was a disgrace to the religion they professed to preach, and to our nation – in fact, all those concerned had been plunged into an abyss of iniquity.' He pauses, clears his throat, and shows his sense of contrition by turning his eyes to the floor. 'Papa wrote to me of what you and Arabel did. Why do you fight Papa? Why do you fight your illness when what you need is rest?'

I think back to the churchwarden, an ardent emancipationist closely linked with the Society of Friends, and his merry band of children with their peaches-and-cream complexions of the moors. His enthusiasm was contagious.

The chapel door had flown open. Papa burst in. He bristled. His face a ghastly white. Needless to say, he heard that Arabel and I had volunteered to sign a petition to end the apprenticeship system on West Indian estates.

'Did your ancestors work for you to throw their achievements back in my face?' Papa demanded, quite on fire. To the warden he exclaimed, 'We won't need your help eating dinner tonight!' With Arabel and I, protesting, in tow, he marched through the arched doorway, proceeded along the road to the gateway of Belle Vue, our rented home, went straight to the dining-room, knocked back his gin aperitif, snatched the ham we were all to have eaten for dinner from the table, charged along the grassy path running behind the house, and threw the ham to the neighbour's dogs. After Papa blew that meeting apart he demanded we attend a different chapel and wrote banning the warden from Belle Vue.

Like a great wave despair rolled up, ballooned within my heart and burst. How the apprentices must have prayed for freedom's cool breeze, prayed to do whatever they pleased. A furnace of guilt smouldered within me. Sour hatred permeated through those Belle Vue walls which were more frail than even I have become – I feared the entire house would collapse under the weight of the atmosphere. Arabel scowled and moaned. I hid my emotions. But that night Arabel and I did not eat – we shared in the apprentices' suffering. Papa got no pleasure out of that whipping. Yet his expression of desolation purged my sense of injury. I determined never to cross him so again.

I say to Bro, 'I don't want to fight Papa. I'm scared inside. Afraid of who I am.'

'We mustn't fight him, Ba. There's more to this than you know. News reached Papa from the West Indies last year,' Bro says, 'news Papa has kept from me, news which gives cause for much more grief. Papa was advised that Sam is swayed by very bad influences and in conflict with church ministers, overseers, attorneys, even the Chief Justice of Jamaica, Sir Joshua Rowe, for hosting parties which have become notorious across the island.'

A few years ago, sweet Sam proudly announced in a letter to Papa that he was serving as an ensign in the St. James and St. Elizabeth Militia. Mention in our uncle's will of his approval of Sam's 'general conduct' implied that incidents concerning Sam had recently occurred which were not favourable. This was a great worry and brought tears to my eyes. Bro has now confirmed our uncle was alluding to some disgraceful behaviour. Yet Sam's rise in rank and the overall tone of the will persuaded our dear, ever-forgiving father to pay expenses Sam ran up on an American voyage. We none of us have been certain of Sam's whereabouts since March last when Papa wrote to Sam that he didn't know whether he was still in Jamaica, or preparing to leave, or determined to remain. Needless to say Papa, Bro and I are worried sick.

27 November 1838

Double the usual opium dose tonight has not relaxed me in the least and leaves me wondering whether I should take less, or more. Slanted up against piles of cushions and pillows, taunted by screaming gulls, I am unable to find comfort and unable to sleep. I am troubled by a dream I had last night in which all the passengers of a West Indies vessel, except two rescued by Bro, were drowned. I fear I have dreamt this before – that makes my heart tremble and I fear it is a portent of something terrible. Sweetest Sam, I pray the angels in heaven are watching over you.

The woman in the mirror has returned. I hadn't seen her for days but have felt her presence outside the door. I've been aware of her moving about my midnight candle and amongst shadows clipped by dawn. I've sensed her creeping into my thoughts, smelt her in lavender-scented sheets. Tonight she stands in shadows on the far side of the room.

She is superstitious. I can tell because the way she stares at me is the way people gaze into a crystal ball, deeply, as I examine my own reflection in the mirror Crow holds before me now.

I have tried to talk to the woman but I can't speak when I cry. Crow comforts me like a child in her arms. The other woman cries too. But not in the same manner as I. She does not weep.

Then this small-boned woman with thick ebony ringlets, moving smoothly past the window drapes in a dress of magenta-coloured velvet veiled in black lace, vanishes into the wintry wind.

Am I possessed by fever, or drowsy from over-intoxication? I swelter yet am shivering, bound by sheets sodden with perspiration.

Whirling before me now is a wheel made of my brothers' and sisters' faces: Sette, Occy – noisy, smiling, fit and fair, they seem to be teasing me; eyes half closed, lazy Daisy's dozy grin lurches towards me fast and smooth; Sam's witty smile; Bro's features come with a glow bright as a halo; absorbed, angled forward, Henrietta's face peers at me, eager with her fondness of music; Arabel's face, shaped and focused as though for sketching a rural scene; Henry's frowning heavy brow; shy, tongue-tied Stormie. Mama's face escapes me. It is barely thinkable that that good-bye at Hope End was to be our last. Mama died without me. Georgie's face is almost the image of Papa's, although Papa's expression is not peaceful but fixed with horror and pain. Rushing by the faces blur and re-emerge as poets: Homer, Wordsworth, Keats . . . *Milton's eyes strike piercing-dim: The shapes of suns and stars did swim Like clouds from them, and granted him God for sole vision . . . And Marlowe, Webster, Fletcher, Ben, Whose fire-hearts sowed our furrows when The world was worthy of such men* . . . Features I know grow violently vivid then fade then protrude and merge into family again. Moving on and on the wheel splits open; inside is the face I know as well as my own, shrinking back on itself – tear-streaked; torn and dark, caged like a bird – a poet's, fragmented, in exile from herself.

From far away words come to me, my family seem to be calling or is it the poets' voices stretching faint across a bitter-sweet sea? Each night since Papa's departure as I fall asleep I long for waves of calmness. Waking, I find I am still crying for Papa, then, seeing a blue sea mist rise as the dawn sky slowly changes, am left wondering how he could have left me.

The effects of the losses poor Papa has undergone are taking their toll – dear Mama's death; the loss of his own mother two years later, a severe blow of which he remains unable to speak; financial losses and difficulties on the sugar estates which caused the mortgagees to foreclose; the shame of selling our Hope End home; the loss of his own good health when he was struck down by cholera; then the death of his only brother in Jamaica almost twelve months ago. Sometimes when Papa looks at me with those kindly fierce penetrating eyes my stomach turns to jelly, and I cannot meet his gaze.

And I am becoming so distraught that I can barely *think* of Papa. The stark blueness of these November skies simply heightens the awfulness of his departure.

Though the wind howls, and I am plagued by sounds of crashing waves on rocks below the casement, though I do not know how to reconcile my turmoil, I do still long for peace ... *all my favourite passages in the Holy Scriptures are those which express and promise peace ... in the midst of thoughts and feelings given to be too turbulent.*

The sea, sadness, death, roll into one hell which envelops me. I cannot believe I will live much more. And I fear that if much more goes wrong I shall go mad! – Such thoughts are, to Papa, but phantoms of the mind. Yet from a play of thoughts and words what is not becomes reality. No, I am *not* mad. I am cut off from the world. Maddeningly.

29 November 1838

Bro comes to sit with me at his usual hour. I read Arabel's letter to him – dear Georgie has promised to visit – good news is here at last. Arabel says all Georgie is waiting for is Sam's return.

'Sam ignored Papa's directions for a cargo of West Indian rum to be thirty per cent proof,' Bro explains. 'Consequently, Papa is subject to pay very high taxes on the large shipment.'

'Is Sam not due to dock in London by the end of this month?' I ask. 'That could be any day.'

Leaving my bedside for an armchair, Bro looks horribly grave.

Sam has not docked yet – for *that* I am grateful. Dear, merciful God, mend my heart for feeling this way, forgive me my unkind thoughts but more tales of Sam's escapades now will not do.

There is a rapping on my forehead, as though someone is trying to get in. Or a fearful storm is brewing. The sea changes under the early-evening light from green to blue. Can anyone do more than *exist* in an unbearable world devoid of happenings?

A lump rises from my chest, hurting my throat when I swallow. Bro has just insulted me. Accusing me of being quixotic. Until now I have always accepted his opinions in the end. But are we in the same league?

Bro stops reading *The Times*, looks down on me.

Cautiously he stands, moves as though the floorboards might bite his feet; his face is lapped by a pristine blue reflected off the ceiling – the transient quality the winter sun gives the water, quivering, trembling. Because of Bro's harsh words I am so sad I do not think it will be possible for me ever to look at him again. He has always been somewhat vacant, as though he would prefer to stand on the edge of life. I once thought him more solid and profound in his opinions than I. But I was not mistaken about his greatest flaw: satisfaction with mediocrity.

30 November 1838

'Where are you going this evening?' I ask.

Strolling from the landing to my doorway, 'Nowhere,' Bro replies curtly. 'There's an article here concerning the Poor Law Amendment Act and declaring poverty in England is a crime.' Bro settles in the armchair opposite my bed.

After he has finished reading I say, 'The Reform Bill opened many opportunities for change.'

'It constituted a major historical event.'

'What is history? Events I am told occurred, but that was, perhaps, only one person's view. There is still much room for improvement. Workhouse orphanages are appalling. Do you remember that cartoon of a woman, manacled, giving birth, in the forefront naked children being beaten? Do you not then conjure up in your mind visions of chimney-sweeps and rag-pickers forced to start work before dawn and finish well after dusk, children who never see the sun but on the Sabbath? Picture an infant of four, dying, wedged in the bends of a chimney. Imagine *that*!'

'That isn't true.'

I say to Bro, 'In my imagination it is – which is the same, you know, as its actually being so.' My pilgrimage from this high mountain is to reach the oppressed through thought, to create those images within my mind and then live with them. 'Can we not imagine ourselves into another's skin? Can we not dream ourselves into another world, as did the prophet Isaiah? Give breath and life to histories that otherwise might not live?'

Bro's footsteps are abrupt and hard descending the carpeted stairs.

Night encroaches. The thudding in my head is more like some creature trying to escape, not get in. One is permitted to let feelings out by weeping, though to weep pains my chest and will cause my fever to rise. I fear for my health only because of the pain my loss would bring to my family. Death itself is a bridge. I fear it not.

If I do live, as I have explained to my dear friend Miss Mitford, I hope and believe I shall write better. I shall focus on that.

1 December 1838

December is upon us already. Mama's sister, Aunt Bell, whom we call Bummy, has arrived from Frocester to pass the winter here with Henrietta, dear Bro and myself. I trust Bummy's kind-heartedness in offering to come, and her presence, whilst she stays, will give a sunnier aspect to this new house. It did not always at Hope End, I seem to recall.

Perhaps I am becoming tediously sorry for myself. The Hedleys were very kind having us to stay until we moved to warmer, more comfortable accommodation, and now there is room enough for Papa, Arabel, Georgie, Sette, Occy, in fact, all twelve of us, to stay in Torquay.

> *Ever dearest Miss Mitford,*
> *. . . the difference between the Braddons & Beacon Terrace is all the difference between the coldest situation in Torquay & the warmest – & my body was so ungrateful as to require another sun besides that of looks & kind words.*
> *Here, we are immediately upon the lovely bay – a few paces dividing our door from its waves – & nothing but the 'sweet south' & congenial west wind can reach us – & they must first soften their footsteps upon the waters. Behind us – so close as to darken the back windows – rises an abrupt rock crowned with the slant woods of Beacon Hill! And thus though the north & east winds blow their fiercest, we are in an awful silence & only guess at their doings.*

Although Papa has consented to Bro staying with me in Torquay it is still clearly against his own wish. Dearest Brozie. *His presence is not* necessary *in the strict sense of the word. Perhaps no happiness IS.* Nothing equals the pain of knowing Papa does not wish him to remain with me.

And now that Crow has dispensed my evening opium I am more than weary, and good only for staring straight into the marble moon's silver wake spooling across the spreading sea.

Dr. Barry's insistence that I rise before two o'clock every afternoon was outrageous. Nay, preposterous! He visits daily. That he should spend so much of his precious time on me pains me greatly;

but he insists, and in his last letter dear Papa insisted too. Nothing could be further from my mind than to upset Papa more by trying to alter this regime. However, I rather fear all Papa's preventative measures are in vain. Daily Dr. Barry asks, 'Have you taken all your medicines?' or, 'How often have you had your opium dose?' Conversely, opium pitches me up and down like a wave.

I am glad the cold has come and that I can return to my late London habit – very useful in enabling an invalid to get through a good deal of writing without fatigue – of lying in bed until early afternoon instead of being made to rise and then, after the exertion of dressing, to take as much air as possible. Upon my arrival this physician even insisted I was sent out in the chair most afternoons. As a result I have been prevented from corresponding with friends and tempted on from hour to hour and day to day in procrastination. Utter nonsense is all I have managed to write for weeks. Lines destined more for the fire than for publication. But to please Papa I have at least appeared to follow this doctor's advice.

Yesterday Bro said he heard from Papa news of a frightful controversy concerning Sam, which Papa would not fully disclose. I fear dear Papa made a tragic mistake in sending our brother to Jamaica to be . . . 'readjusted' was Papa's exact word. Bro has previously mentioned tales from a Presbyterian minister who, with his wife, was driven by Sam from Cinnamon Hill estate on the island's north coast. In all probability, Henrietta said last night, the latest controversy concerns the freed slaves' pay at Cinnamon Hill, which differs from Papa's other estates. Sam has written Papa that after emancipation the Negroes wouldn't work so he *had* to pay less.

Again I am terribly anxious for Sam. I anticipate news of his arrival any day. I remember at Hope End – though the exact year escapes me – when Sam and Bro came home from a cricket match in an irrational and unChristian state. Henrietta told me in a much frightened voice that she had heard Sam carried upstairs. Neither Sam nor Bro appeared at breakfast. Bro, I recall, went out to shoot and Sam went to Mathon; Henrietta said that the farther Sam went the better. She was extremely angry and threatened not to speak to him for a fortnight, which was, in my past opinion, both wrong, abstractly speaking, and impolitic. For although I suffer a habit of moral dignity, nobody is immaculate; and young men are more inclined to a fault of this kind than to many others; and our sullenness would have done no more good in such a case, than Xere's whipping in punishing the sea.

2 December 1838

Looking from the window into a stormy amber cloud darkening into the vast sky, I am chilled by wintry draughts and the fast-fading light. The hills – an amphitheatre around and over-looking the bay – should offer better shelter from offshore winds.

No letters for days. Disappointment, by adding to my concerns, serves to maintain this deplorable situation. Nothing has happened for weeks, I fear, to cause stimulation, but fevers and faintings and horrible imaginings, and worse.

> *Dear Miss Mitford,*
> *Do let me hear from you when you can write* – whenever *you can. I have so few pleasures!* – *and a few words from you bring many! A true one to me was, that Dr. Mitford liked the cream. He shall have some more. How is he? How are you?* Do *go on caring for me . . .*

17 December 1838

I am *not* missing London! I can sleep and wake here very much as I could there. Although it was a point gained to be settled some-where after the torturous Hope End days that grew into weeks and then into months before Papa revealed our fate. Sidmouth; Gloucester Terrace, London; then, finally, gloomy Wimpole Street, whose walls look so much like Newgate's turned inside out; the filthy-yellow smog of London's cluttered streets; the steady stream of guests 'just dropping in' to see how one is – all were an anomaly I could have well done without. I much prefer to inhabit castles of the air located in a state of conscious ignorance. Gossip and small talk give me no pleasure, such trivia is abhorrent, as is visiting for visiting's sake. During my girlhood I cringed then started to freeze when obliged to polka or sing in a group. What is called GOING OUT is the greatest bore in this world, I share the horror of it with Papa. Pretty Henrietta is far more domesticated. She can meal-plan, play the piano, and sew and paint. I hate piano practice. I sit down discontented and rise disgusted. Sewing, embroidery, especially beading slippers, are equally abhorrent. I loathe the world of society, those people amongst whom Bummy says I should have mixed. Ladies with hourglass figures and rustling petticoats. Gentlemen with a pious pompous satisfaction engraved into faces that talk of matters dreary or frivolous. Seagulls have replaced my cooing doves. And I miss *them*, because no two doves are quite the same. I also miss the garden at Hope End. More than *them* I miss *that*.

Above all I miss contentment and a sense of peace.

18 December 1838

The stethoscope was not tried this afternoon yet I was greatly fatigued by Dr. Barry's visit. He said he could tell, when feeling my chest, that the rattle of respiration is no clearer on the affected side. Although I am spitting less blood, my exhaustion from moving from Wimpole Street to the Hedleys', then to Beacon Terrace, has not left.

Due to the view and continually crashing waves, I think of this new residence as being *in* the sea. Except for the undulating hills on the opposite side of the bay I cannot see a yard of vulgar earth when lifted from my bed to the sofa, where I am forced to remain the best part of the day. I have been unable to stand since I was removed from our previous accommodation. Yet my malady of discontent hardly compares with others' suffering; three months ago a wheel went over poor Dr. Mitford's leg.

19 December 1838

> *My dearest Miss Mitford,*
>
> *. . . I am better than I have been — for I have not been very well — & only emerged from an imprisonment of ten days in my bedroom, this day! But all the imprisonment was not* necessary *— only precautionary on account of the west wind! I hear from Wimpole Street that Mr. Kenyon is confined to the house with rheumatism! . . .*

Dr. Barry visited at noon and he maintains that the family must not think of seeing me in London this Christmas. Physically I am too weak to do anything but write. Should I so much as move a terrible pain in my left side returns and once more I am spitting blood. Please, heavenly Father, don't let anyone give this news to Miss Mitford or yet to dear Papa.

3 January 1839

We are stuck in the month of January. Bro said yesterday that when this frost thaws I must be better, or when Sam visits Torquay – which ever happens first. Sam's smile can melt the severest freeze, as will the warm glow Bro says he will surely bring from Jamaica. Sam claims, Bro remarked, that since the apprenticeship system ended he has had to work like a slave.

I agreed with Papa, even before emancipation, that the West Indies would be irreparably ruined if the Emancipation Bill was passed . . . *Papa said that nobody in their senses would even think of attempting the culture of sugar, and that they had better hang weights to the sides of the island of Jamaica and sink it all at once. I think certain heads might be found heavy enough for the purpose.*

Of course the late Bill ruined the West Indies. That is settled. The consternation here has been very great. Nevertheless I am glad, and always shall be, that the Negroes are – virtually – free.

The power of Papa's anger at the Emancipation Bill seems equal to that of his love for us. I know Papa does love us all, and that he too suffers greatly in these turbulent times. We Barretts are cursed. I long to depart from all this – to climb from the window Papa sees me through, to live with another view that is not his and suits me better.

I expect Bro wishes to see Sam as much as any of us here in Torquay. Dear Bro was up after midnight writing to Sam. *I* have a great mind to write on the question of slavery, amongst other injustices. Although as poets we have a solemn responsibility to do so, this subject is, I fear, perhaps beyond my sympathies, and even beyond the sphere of human poetry in its 'absolute unap-proachable-ness'. Some concerns are more expressible by a woman than a man; or by a man than a woman. Is this so with black and white; slave and master? Confined to this bed, my stage has become my soul, but a page filled with poetry can be a stage for life as much as a play, a novel, a tapestry. Despite all dear Papa says, I instinctively believe a woman does have a business with questions like the question of slavery. She should not write if she believes otherwise. She should slide back into the antiquated days of the past, live as a kept creature, far removed from intelligent thought and speech. For of what use is the pen to a woman shackled and enslaved if she refuses to pick it up and to slash the bands that tie her? Slavery still finds favour in many an American quarter, disgraceful though it is. I pray to God I will never think as an American thinks, or behave as they do. The moral ground they inhabit crumbles when liberty is at stake.

Papa *has* come! Good health is restored! I hear his voice below in the drawing-room.

Chapter Two

Sheba

CINNAMON HILL ESTATE
April 1838

Yawning long, loud *Fuuuuffuu-ffuu* abeng swallows Lickle Phoebe's bawling. Happily me body moves under Isaac's, moving on love. Isaac's breath in me ear smothers more gentle rhythm of sea licking shore, hungrily shifting sand deep into she watery belly.

Leaves rustle when we shuffle-drag weself from sack's warm dent. Me eyes wrestle with darkness. Blindly me fingers touch axe, hoe, billhook, all sleeping beside machete against wattle-shack wall.

Me first in line, picking a way we'd beaten, air sticky amidst waist-deep grasses, path sealed in a strange silence of empty shacks, provision grounds in hills above. But Isaac's voice thrusts out ahead of me, chanting, 'Hi! de buckra, hi!' a deep-toned song through me soul. Me file after Isaac through cane-piece gate where cinnamon treetops join in a arch, following him machete blade sprouting over him shoulder. Slowly me voice meets Isaac's, and soon all we voices grow as one rumble pouring up into sky, held by nearly coming day's yellow-grey glow.

Bad spirits, waiting to suck pickney blood, feed round cotton tree trunks. Lickle Phoebe, Harry, all them pickney run from cotton tree branches we pass beneath. Bad spirits stir, swirling round tangled roots. Branches dance and sway above sameway as arms can, fe cotton tree possess a soul. Tall grasses grapple with legs straying from cane-piece track, sliding alongside cattle pen. Heavily tools rest on shoulders now, telling me we almost on main cane-piece track.

Legs dangling, Harry swings from top rail of gate head overseer's unlocking, pushing open. Before ditch and earth rise up to cane rows is sitting place fe stillness leading to dawn.

Canes murmur a little. Overseer's hunting fe cart whip. Sitting place fills up with First Gang, fills up with exhaustion. We gang up close, talk hushed.

'Windows of great house wasn't lighted,' is Windsor's voice.

'Me call anodder meetin,' Uncle Ned hiss excited. 'Torch it. Burn it down.'

Isaac sweeps machete blade *swish*, slicing grass heads, whispering, 'We cun mashup de door den . . .'

'Yu a-mek too much nize,' me feel say.

'Me a-come wid me machete,' Uncle Ned say, pounding machete handle on de ground, each dull thud throbbing through me legs. 'Let we godeh now.'

'Slavery's ended,' Big Robert say, 'no need fe torching. All we free free.'

'Yu full-a foolishness, Big Robert,' me feel say. 'Way we live jus git worse.'

'Buckra comin,' is Isaac's voice.

'Silent!' me hiss. Suddenly we more still than cinnamon tree. No one move cept head overseer. Although we stand together, each one now alone. But nothing have life on its own forever. All we's one soul. Me fear harm Isaac want to do to Mister Sam's great house Isaac will do to himself; to me. To all of we. If me hurt somebody, is me who hurt. Me know.

Overseer's lantern searches wide round cane piece, back and forth, back and forth, back and forth him yellow lantern glow.

'Me naa do it, me radda go to me sack,' Windsor say. 'Me gawn back now.'

'We family.' Slapping de ground with him foot, Isaac pleads, 'Windsor, yu cyaan go, yu me brodda!'

Windsor stray off into morning darkness. Taking. Taking. Taking. All them that won't work take. Take what small hope we have to get canes cut, get crop in. We gang burst apart, rally together; burst apart and keep changing shape like a sea swelling up heavily til winds thrash we down again, bring we crashing down on each other, breaking gang up with crushing pain. But we'll rise, swell, bunch together again.

'Sheba?' is Isaac, gentle-soft him voice slips into me ear.

'Aha,' me say.

'Yu gawn back to yu sack?' Isaac's voice takes me to grassy hollow he settled in. Sliding sideways, Isaac makes room fe me to sit beside he and Eleanor.

'Minister say if we work hard Lord will protect we,' me feel say. Elbowing me chest, Isaac's deeply mad, him back's turned on Lord Jesus. Me snuggle against him shoulder, me weary head sinking into me neck – sleep weak – though sleep's a day away. Me hear Isaac suck in him cheek, make chupsing sounds, suck air between him teeth. Folding arms around him – Isaac, me – we wrap weself together. Tight. More tight than mango flesh clings to mango stone. More tight than ever. You reach into me heart, Isaac; you stay deep at de core of me body. But darkness of night lives in each day and we cyaan hide in forest fe everything far and near consider we prey. Me looking up to dawn star fe hope, fe buckra breaks black woman like he breaks him horse. By riding she. Long ago Eleanor warned me, and she always right. But she no look at me that day fe she telled me: 'Sheba, yu mama ded. Died in Kingstan lang ago.'

'Trouble-Too-Much ere?' Eleanor's whisper asks.

'Me ere.'

'Son, me thought yu gawn. Uncle Ned gawn back.' Eleanor snorts, 'Me no like dat.'

'Others follow Uncle Ned,' Isaac's voice say it true. 'See Bacchus, see im dere?' Isaac whispers in me ear, 'Bacchus gawn back now.' Me cyaan see Bacchus, me can sense him feet creeping alongside cattle pen near plantation path. Isaac whispers, 'Windsor, Colonel, Jane, Stanley, Sylvia. Bout half de gang lost.'

Eleanor clasps she arm round me shoulder. Warmth spreads into me skin when she presses me hand. 'Yu got cockroach?' she asks.

'Aha.'

Eleanor passes overseer's clay water bottle onto me lap.

'Jus let me fingers undo knot,' me say. Dead cockroach hides in a tight knuckle me tied in skirt cloth. Untangling knot me hear Lickle Phoebe start up bawling. Cockroach falls from cloth onto me lap.

'Unscrew top,' me say to Eleanor. She eye makes four with mine.

She skin, ruddy-black, blends with dark morning light, but beautiful smooth skin's a poor reward from God, me think, fe hardness that's she life. Eleanor takes clay bottle from me. Cockroach makes splash-plunk sound falling in overseer's water bottle.

Hungry fe work to begin, head overseer ambles aimlessly, fingers fiddling with hat brim.

Big Robert, Trouble-Too-Much, Isaac, Isaac's mama Eleanor sit firmly settled against dawn glimmer. Emily, Lickle Duke, Isaac's sister Lickle Phoebe, Harry – all them pickney fidget-fight in long grass and weed that slyly turns brown then green with sun's rising glow.

Overseer's crouching, fingers tapping on him trouser knee, then on gate rail. Slowly wooded shadowing mountains appear.

'Yu filled water bottle fe me?' overseer asks Eleanor. And me know workday's about to begin.

Weeds cling to shins, grasping like pickney's fingers. Me's here but cyaan be found. Swiftly slashing sugar stalks in cane tunnels, leaves slice arms, me feet sole cracking hard like rock-hard earth, skin sand-dry. Using machete to chop in line, stumbling in furrow, stubble knee-high, row so long gang end looks blurry; stacking, waist-deep in cut cane, cool shade only fe feet, a rash breaks me skin, lashing bundles together with string.

Shouting, 'Git a move on, yu missed some,' overseer's voice carries over gleaming green-cane sea, shouts back from mountain's raw-pink face. Overseer's sky-blue eye's gaze strong as sun's rays striking we back. Him sour groan, 'Ay,' sweeps cane piece. 'Where's de rest of First Gang?'

'Dem far away.' Isaac's shout returns like it's trapped.

Overseer's voice rings out astonished and filled with disgust: 'Yu should be grateful me don't use cat-o'-nine-tail because Old Mister he had dat whip banished.' Overseer's belly droops like corn-filled sack over trouser top. Mighty vexed he picks a spare machete, joins we cane-cutters battling in cane tunnels. Cinnamon Hill keep four top buckras: Mister Carey; Mister Sam; Mister Farquerson; Mister Sam's cousin; then there's head overseer, and overseer fe each gang. All we cane-piece workers get split into gangs. First Gang have heaviest task but all overseer and buckra feed worm of fear burrowing into we mind.

And now me back's hunched from cutting and bending like me cyaan take more agony, cyaan cut another cane. Me eyes screw tight against strong sun's blast.

Overseer stands straight and quiet, brown hair blowing in dry dry winds. Winds making lonely sounds, bashing and thrashing through rippling canes.

Suddenly me see minister climb down from him shiny black horse. He rushes, black gown flapping behind like wings. Cane-cutters mob together in a crowd-ring. Minister desperate to spread Lord's word wide. Minister struggles through mud, through rain to school-house. School-house empty. Pickney no like rain. But minister struggles same time, same place next Sunday. Him crazy?

Minister say, with pink lips split from dryness set in a saintly smile, 'You must hurry with your work because soon the burning must begin.'

Hatred bulges from Isaac's eyes. 'Lissen, Mister, lemme tell yu . . .' Me eye springs on Isaac, forcing him mouth shut.

'Trust in the Lord.' Minister's arm's raised, him tight fist punching sky. 'Let His strength flow through your bodies.'

'De field-hands oo won't work, yu say, mek de crop get in late,' Windsor shouts, pointing at minister. 'Yu must mek Mister Sam give betta pay so we all can get crop in before it's ruined by rain.'

Trouble's rough voice shakes: 'Seen a lot, seen too much. Anger mek we blind now. We need more pay.'

'If the crop is late you won't get any money,' minister say.

Trouble's hard face turns mahoney-wood black, eyes angry sparks. Breaking a path between Isaac and me, Trouble-Too-Much cries out, 'At Oxford estate Mister Sam brodda pay betta!'

'This, I believe, will pleaseth God.' Minister's voice drops. 'But pray, how did you hear of this?'

'Yu lead struggle wid empty hand,' Isaac say.

Coming in closer, Eleanor growls, 'Yu gainst we, Minister. Yu shoulda come to speak fe we at great-house verandah. Yu know we cane-cutter gang cyaan work fe noting, or fe less pay.'

Swallowing hard, minister stumbles back, licks lip cracks. He had enough a we heat.

Overseer's eye-look threatens. He that vexed he fret and fret, yelling, 'Yu lot, git back to work.'

Anger rises in me, me cyaan hold back. 'Betta Mister start at dawn, finish at dusk,' me feel say to overseer. 'Dat buckra, Mister Sam, always late start, early finish. Sleep all afternoon. At night an animal in im come out. Me tell Mister Sam, if e don't pay proper wage, sixpence, all we go.'

Isaac say, 'Dat rite.'

'You have not the right to claim more from your young master,' minister shouts, 'because you didn't make a satisfactory agreement before undertaking your work. Now you refuse to accept the two bitts your master has offered. You should have followed my advice, for is it not better to sit still than to rise up and then fall —'

'A-good, me say. Minister, a-good Samaritan, come to aid poo neger like we.' Pushing past me and Isaac, Big Robert sings out, 'Wash me clean of sin, sweet Jesus. No longer me follow Baptis chutch, me wanna be born again!'

Beckoning Big Robert forward, minister say, 'Speak louder, man.'

'We negers know noting. Buckra minister know everyting. He have a rite to be massa. Me say of de young buckra oo wrong we humble sinners ere, Fadda, forgive im, fe e know not what e do. An me pity de young buckra fram Englan, e cyaan git trew neegle's eye.'

'True! True!' chants John from back of crowd-ring.

'Silence!' minister shouts. 'This man has an important point to make.'

Big Robert's skinny chest, streaming with sweat, rises and fattens with pride. 'No longer me fear mussa but wen me yeare of de ways of de Lard me shake an shake, waan yeare de Holy Bock speak fram itself. Forebber grateful to God an me queen in Englan oo kill de slavery monster ded in Falmout chutch. Since dat day me drink no water, only wine, Mussa Minister, sah,' Big Robert say. He wipes sweat drips from him chin.

'So why have you not made yourself known to me before, if you believe the word of the Lord so strongly?' minister ask Big Robert.

'Trongly me feel is true true. But me need to be sure tis de Lard an Mussa in me heart an not de debil come to confuse me. No doubt in me mind now, mussa. Dat wot me tellin yu. Fe me wait fe a year till dis day come, Mussa Minister, sah.'

'You say you drink only wine.'

'Mussa, water's all me drink, Lard's water taste like wine.'

'What about rum?'

'Peas, ax me no more but odder pusson ere will speak gainst me if dat's de truth.'

Even harsh light seems to mock Big Robert. Me too shame to shame him more. De special kind of quiet stings.

'If odder pusson speak gainst me,' Big Robert say, 'me deserve to suffer fe me sin, me deserve flogging. Ebery bad ting me no more do. Teach me, a poo neger servant, to blong to de chutch, den we cun flog de debil out-a Jamaica an build a trone fe Mussa Jesus. All is equal in de Lard's eye, all black pusson sinner same as white mussa sinner. Dem dat lie, tief, bline to good ways of marriage certifikate fram de person minister ere. An me bin savin, savin, savin since dat day me see de lite. God bless minister an misses minister an deliver we poo neger servant fram evil. Amen.'

Minister ask, 'Will anyone else stand before God and open his heart to Our Saviour, Jesus Christ, like this good Christian man?'

'Ooebber tink me live to see dis day?' Jumping up and down Big Robert shouts, 'Me rich! Me rich! Yu mek me, a poo sinner, rich, Lard! Yu cared fe an lubbed dy wandering sheep. Wen lost, yu find me. Wen thirsty, yu quench me. Yu put out me fiah fe pum-pum. Yu fed me! Wen me sick fram flogging yu comfort me in yu chutch. Miracle werker! Hab mercy! O Lard, yu hab de power an de glory fe meking leper clean. Forgive we ungrateful chillun fe not following de Fadda's werd, Minister, sah. Me bin waitin fe dis day. God give me sweet faith in Jesus. Me nebber lissen to no debil no more.'

'Pray, fine man,' minister say. 'What is your name?'

'Big Robert. An me sendin me heart to Lard Jesus.'

'Then, Big Robert, tell your people to make good terms of employment before turning out to work again, for I must make haste to take the service at Barrett Town.'

Sun's terrible blazing eye glares at Big Robert. Grinning, pumped up like he'll burst, Big Robert swaggers past Isaac and me back to a cane-piece row, swipes up shining machete. Skilfully he slashes cane with great sweeping strokes.

Staring curiously down on Big Robert, Jancra swirls – a great bird, wings full-spread, black-feather tips cloud skimming blue sky.

Minister's horse swishing its tail while minister fixes a foot in a stirrup, flings him leg up over saddle back. He sets off galloping across Cinnamon Hill, heading fe Barrett Town.

Like pickney winning market game, Big Robert's fattened by him new prize – faith in Baptist church – making him body grow bigger, making him work faster. Him mind's crippled, me think, but him face say believing in white buckra church carry him far from hard cane-piece grind. Me look up to white clouds snaking and swirling in clear sky, and prickle blue with envy.

'God's will be done,' overseer say. Him stare's empty, and angry edge to him voice gone, leaving only hollow words. 'Jus git to work.'

Tools can so easily slash skin, slit throats, make blood stream, only we too spent from work. Machete feels like a dead weight now. Weeds twine round canes, leaves lace legs, arms, machetes. Tearing stalk's rank stench makes slow moving air sickly, cane row so bushy-thick cyaan see black snake till we chop it. Cyaan see baby boar till we step on it. Wild boar piglet sleeping in dark shade of leaves shrinks to a glimpse of pink, bobbing through swiftly parting sugar, waking sows; boars deep in cane piece dart in all directions, swollen bellies almost stroke soil, squealing through tall trembling canes go tiny piglet sisters, brothers. Between rows all that's left's a brutal trail of trotter tracks to crumple and worry bare earth. Even in sun's brightness we fearful and in need of lantern fe lighting we way. A coarse shout from cane-piece middle will scare because we know what made that sound. Is terror stalking. Faster, faster we cut, spine hurting, thinking only of empty churning bellies, not of close, loved ones; or, sight falling to trash on parched earth, love's a very true thing filling we mind, and we cyaan move on fe these thoughts are like searching fe a bead of hope that's lost and cyaan be found. Is here but cyaan be found.

Coming to row end me find young Mister Sam jogging up to main gate on him horse. Eyelids heavy on him face like a drowsy lizard. Strong hot wind strokes hair dried-grass yellow, brushes green canes. Sugar crests and sways. Jancra circles lower, lower. Current swells, crop ripples and swirls like thick manes tossing. Even de soil frown like Isaac's puckered brow. Each rift and wrinkled dent me feel beneath me tread.

Mister Sam's trouser tightly belted; shirt's too bright a white to look at, buttoned despite thick heat. Fanning flies from him neck with a banana leaf, screwing him eye against sun's heat, Mister Sam's scanning cane gently swaying, gliding flocks of parakeet, then he disappears into forest edge.

Crickets hum. Morning shadows gone. Abeng booms *Fuuuuffuu-ffuu.* We flock to forest shade. Me skin baked, raised all fassy.

Isaac say, unwrapping boiled plantain and yam tied in rags, 'Mister Sam won't give sugar or proper pay to dem dat say prayer to Jesus Christ.' Kissing him teeth, Isaac shuts one eye and sniffs sweat so it dribbles up him nostril. Isaac's words bring grief, but him eye laughs. 'Oo needs prayers more dan Mister Sam? E wake we village at night like duppy or white jumbie, crashing into small cinnamon tree, yard, even we shack, searchin fe pum-pum.'

Curled on one side in long yellow-brown grasses, Lickle Phoebe pecks at she bowl of cassava. 'Yu tink all we gonna die?' she asks in a voice half stolen by cane-piece wind.

'It dem, or we,' Isaac say.

'Me *seen* Mister Sam doin it,' Lickle Harry shrieks, 'so did Lickle Phoebe, she bawling wake de village!'

On a bandana Eleanor lays roasted coney and cane-rat Lickle Harry caught yesterday. 'Dat brought Mister Sam to a-kinda stop,' Eleanor say. She turns to me: 'Yu got more cassava, Sheba?'

'Aha.' Me set out coconut bowls brimming with cassava.

'E no duppy,' Lickle Harry say, 'e a-zombie, Mister Sam!'

Looking like Isaac's and Lickle Harry's words hold a terrible lasting stench from which Phoebe must slant away; she balls-up, skinny legs drawing into she chest.

'True, Mister Sam walkin dead man,' Trouble-Too-Much say. 'No feelin in him body, no memory in him head.'

Isaac's eyes turn sun-shot amber now it's noontime. He eats, picking meat strands from coney bones. 'Sameway as any white buckra Mister Sam have too much of de spirit rum,' he say. He fills a palm leaf with cassava. 'E like black woman's pum-pum too much. See ow e walk an ow e ride im mare like e have swollen buboes, wid sad sharp pricking pain.'

'Wot bout Big Robert back dere?' Eleanor asks. 'E snoring. E a-beached-up manatee.'

Shaking himself, Trouble-Too-Much say, 'Bway! Me thought e had sense.'

Lickle Harry giggles, shoulders bobbing up and down. 'Big Robert read de Bible *tree* time a day,' he say.

'It not so funny,' say Eleanor.

Lickle Harry folds top and bottom lip together, him mouth becoming a crease to disguise him laughter. Me smile a bit inside me head.

'If it wasn't fe Mister Farquerson, I'd be gawn,' Isaac say, eye-winking me. 'But Mister Farquerson stop me cos e not so wicked.'

Sunshine streams strong strong. Lickle Phoebe and Lickle Harry skip and bicker round tamarind tree trunks thickly overgrown with tangleweed, and me cyaan say where their energy spark from. Swiftly they take flight from tiny snakes sliding through shivering grasses, tongues switching out, in, blue-black as night.

'De two cousins, Mister Sam,' Isaac say, 'talkin wid buckra an overseer like dey're waiting fe we to run.'

Wading through grasses that spread into tamarind forest, head overseer, buckra, Mister Sam and Mister Sam's cousin go all hitched up together. Waving canes stretch behind them to blue hazy sky.

No wind blows while under sheltering trees we lie, sugar scent suffocates; forest air sits still and hot as a great thickly woven blanket-cloth; its stillness, strange and heavy. No laughter. No sighs – we practise what we've learned. Learned to talk without sound. Learned to walk on silent feet.

Noontime's long come. Noontime's fe spreading out in tall yellow-brown itchy grasses. Sunlight slants through a leafy green roof staining grasses gold where all we rest. Bamboo creaking. Sky spirits swish round branches chased by a sudden busy spurt of afternoon breeze. Dizzy blue sky sets me wondering why we have to play hide-and-seek just to be together. Me cyaan say what de matter is but when you work on night shift and night crickets screech till dark air sings and bellies rumble fe supper, squabbles break into brawls and me know you in trouble, Isaac, though me hate to look out through shack doorway to find out why. And when fighting's over you won't come to me. So me sit alone, see you in me mind, Isaac. Want to be with you in me body. You face, you strong shining eyes; eyebrows, soft lips and warm tender hands hold me face, firm voice mops tears. Lower lip juts over you chin gently ripe, full, tasting star-apple sweet.

Sitting up from crushed flowers Isaac gives a dry smile. 'See im dere? Canya see Mister Sam?' Clutching overseer's clay water bottle, Mister Sam bends double. Whistling through teeth, Isaac throws small mauve petals at me, just in case me fell asleep. Him eye flashes white and makes four with mine.

'Im badda dan any buckra,' me feel say. 'All Mister Sam waan is pass rum bottle. Mister Sam sow seed fe spirit of unrest.'

Spitting out cockroach Mister Sam pours buckra's water onto dusty ground. 'Look pon dat now,' Isaac say gleefully.

Buckra have worn faces; steady hot steel gazes, prowling up and down nearby cane piece.

'Dem in-a worries,' Eleanor say.

Isaac nods, 'Dem's too hard.'

'Mister Sam worthless,' me feel say. 'Im regret sailing fram him home, England.'

'E lie,' Isaac say. 'E have plenty money, dem's two cousin, Mister Sam.'

'Who the hell put a cockroach in the water?' Startled, looking over me shoulder, me see white sweat shining face of Mister Sam. Him jaw fixes, him eye looks raw, cheek muscles twitch. A red rash crawls up from shirt neck, up throat, spreading across pale cheeks; blue-grey wrinkles riddle him forehead like tiny wavy snakes. 'If you don't like it here you can leave. That goes for all of you here,' he say.

Isaac's face goes ragged, him furious searching eyes crave reason. 'Now we're free yu pay less. Half what we used to. Cyaan buy land or shack. Two bitts we lose fe freedom. Two bitts we pay fe wot?'

'To prevent me from reverting to the old system,' Mister Sam quickly say. 'Then I could sell your wife, or keep her for myself. I need someone to manage my affairs – financial, of course.'

'Ef yu do me beat yu.' Isaac jolts to him feet and makes him hand a tight fist tempting Mister Sam to strike. Mister Sam stands firm but him nostrils flare wide on both sides. Isaac reaches fe machete half hidden in high grass. Shoving Mister Sam, ramming machete under Mister Sam's chin, 'Me aredie,' Isaac roar.

'Isaac, don't be renk,' Eleanor say. Worry lines round she mouth come more deeply carved and show lifelong strain. Fearing what'll happen to Isaac, fe buckra say Mister Sam wants to bring torching punishment system back, me throw meself forward, grabbing Isaac's arm. At torching time, Falmouth workhouse head driver hung hundreds of field-hands. Winnie caught running away, militia troop herded she back, militia chopped Winnie with machetes till she ears and jaw almost fell off, then strung she up to hang. Caught sleeping in cane row, Trouble-Too-Much was stripped, after a flogging militia made Old Simeon piss in Trouble's mouth till Trouble-Too-Much sick. Venus got caught eating sugar cane fe food scarce. Even tho she heavy with child, she got Old Simeon's full dose – militia made Old Simeon shit in she mouth, gagged she, then after a flogging pickled she back well with salt. Memories of punishment place cling to me mind, me clawing hands try to hold Isaac back from Mister Sam.

Isaac shakes me off. He don't meet me eye. Him bony chest drawn broad and tense like a wood box – power's wrapped inside. 'Is im or me,' Isaac say, and makes to slit Mister Sam's throat.

Sweat sits on Mister Sam's hairline. No magic cure fe hatred. He stiff. Infected with it. Me not seen young Mister so sick with fury since he stop minister worshipping at Cinnamon Hill great house.

Gripping cowhide whip between thighs, Mister Sam twists leather round whip handle. Him voice snakes out, 'Lazy niggers. Here, the sugar and the works must be kept in good order.' Mister Sam don't look at Isaac, just machete blade curving up to him throat. Lines stand up on Mister Sam's neck like blue-grey threads streaking palm fronds.

Lowering him machete, Isaac steps back.

Mister Sam shudders from head to foot like unharnessed horse. 'I came here to sort these matters out for my father,' he say. 'For three weeks I've not had a full gang working.' Snapping round sameway as a makeshift thought, Mister Sam snatches me machete. A fine ridge of sand splays as Mister Sam, bending over, scrapes a line on de ground with me machete-blade tip. 'I'll show you how it's done.' White forearm hairs brush me shoulder as he steps forward, steps back, boot toe just meeting de line he scored in sand.

Isaac gives me a queer look. Buckra's face beams satisfaction, giving me a sidelong glance. Face going thinner than before, Mister Sam have staring zombie eyes. Dead with anger.

First Gang steals out from forest resting place and silently spur Isaac on. Isaac best cane-cutter. Why Mister Sam take im on? Swirling round, Isaac faces young Mister, and power we fear gave Mister Sam slips away quicker than yellow snake. Me feel white heat of we hatred fe buckra. See Isaac's hate swell up, him arm muscles ripple lively like black flame. Hate bursts from Isaac. Eyes warring, Isaac's eagerly squeezing wooden machete handle like it a friend's hand. Opening him mouth, Mister Sam swings me machete blade, slashing stalks; spiteful breath gushes out.

'Isaac chop cane wen knee-high,' Eleanor whispers to me. 'E have no problem to win.'

Drawing in a bellyful of air, Isaac swings machete blade to and fro faster than ever, 'Eh-he,' puffing breath out with all him great strength. Then all movement goes slow and ugly but most of all slow – drawn-out – suddenly. It isn't just peeled-pink colour of Mister Sam's face makes him different, makes him look like he been skinned; or him hands, floppy-white like white woman's gloves; it's everything different. Way Mister Sam holds cart whip; way he changed saltwater slaves from Africa's names; shouts; makes we pay fe what we already have – shack, provision ground; measure everything – even time he slices up, like day can be chopped into tiny minutes. Mister Sam carves up everything.

Sharp machete blades glint, slashing canes. Hot air's rising. Isaac, huffing, panting wildly works to cane-row end. Mister Sam bends with pressure, shirt clinging, sodden, to him back. We know he cyaan go on, he never going to win.

Whistling pickney clap hands, stamp feet. Face screwed up, Lickle Harry starts bottom rolling like John Canoe dancer.

'Amen! Amen!' cries Eleanor.

Like a weary pickney halfway along a cane row, Mister Sam slouches over machete blade. Jerking up its head, him horse stops munching cane; quivering nostrils flare red like he can smell a smell of dread.

Hastily Isaac tramps back across cane stubble. Speeding up me run to fetch coconut water from we noon rest place.

You me Isaac, me thinking, but you've changed. Some days flames blaze in me belly and me fear me want you too much. Fear me love too deeply. Isaac, is you now a stranger? Why? Because you beat we master? It's a trick of strength you win and you know me know Mister Sam will make you pay.

Smiling, buckra hovers, moustache drooping over top lip. Buckra's eye haunts me, making me insides hunch up.

Isaac straightens up, arches him back. He gulps sweet silver stream of coconut water with dull pride. Lord made a judgment letting all we field-hands through heaven's gate – this joy me feel. But coldness sits in me belly sameway as mangrove mud at bottom of blue pool.

Isaac sneers with cold teeth like he swallowed something sour. Huge wind gusts sway canes. Unsteady, Mister Sam leans on buckra's shoulder fe a spell. Turn this day back, me pray, when Mister Sam mounts him nervy horse, and we watch him canter sorely away.

Day feels more weary than night fe we back to we blade slashing cane; tying rows of bundles; loading mule, donkey, we head, old ox wain. Cane quivers like a heart trembling. Smooth as shadows buckra's stare slants between sugar canes, crossing me face, leaving me mind scarred sameway as cart whip lash scars can. Wind hisses overhead bringing shiver nearer. Machetes swing high. Wind comes to a standstill again. Isaac and me're dripping, cyaan hardly hold wood handle. Cyaan pause fe me eye to seek Isaac in next cane tunnel. How me do feel? True as me love's hair's black; true as earth turns deep brown when rains come. Me cling to you love like mango leaf clings to tree, Isaac, but fear fe you coils through me body.

Machete blade winks silver, bites soil. Blackened clouds rumble. Shuddering, clods flake, crumble, beneath bare rough-skinned feet. Shadows slide over we back. Heat sharpens. Canes shiver. Cart whip comes into sight. Hard me struck from behind. Whistles split me head – a head singing loud with pain *Me skull's cracked?* Me skin goes heavy.

Wrapping him arm around me neck overseer locks me to him chest. Isaac plunges through parting cane throwing himself at me. Swimming through swishing sugar, grabbing me hand Isaac trips and falls blindly, bringing we all three down. Inside me roar. Buckra dives on me again. Sinking, me stretch skywards fe air to see another buckra leap on Isaac. Buckra's hands, elbows, slide between Isaac and me, prising we bodies apart. Like slippery fish Isaac's hand slides from me grasp.

Whip tears Isaac's back, him flesh bursts open. Struggling free fe hiding me glimpse him head top. Then Isaac's swallowed by sugar cane.

Isaac's fighting spirit's all me sense when buckra round him up and me watch them push him back across cane piece.

Eleanor stares like she don't recognize she boy. Bloody shoulders lined with gashes, me cyaan recognize you either. You a sack on bendy legs. Me stare. Me stare again. You stumble-step. Eleanor approaches she son, horror in she eye.

Bashing canes aside to reach you, me caught by buckra hands again, struggle-fighting, boxing hard, head spinning, me scream, 'Isaac! Isaac! Isaac!' Across you face green canes close as buckra tears you from me.

Buckra men haul Isaac up by bloody dust-caked hands, dragging him far. Buckra's swaggering footsteps swallowed by rustling cane. Cautiously now me rise, and slowly. Buried in darkness me stand. Me want to melt into earth, be part of it like blood marks, blotted by sand. Loud as devil Isaac shrieks, ribs standing out like washboard ridges. Begging buckra men to bring him back me chase a little way, but me also want Isaac to go and never return to this place of pain.

Eleanor, Sylvia, Trouble-Too-Much have on their faces a kind of dread me seen before. Gulping sorrow lumps down she throat, shaking, Eleanor comes towards me.

Starving fe you, Isaac, me fingertips seek to feel you sticky, thinly sugar-coated skin, but only Eleanor me have to touch. Sun's rage already dried blood-soaked sand.

Buckra drags Isaac away until him shrieks sound like demon laughter and then are drowned by motionless greens, blue blue hills beyond.

Canes thrash me face. Lickle Phoebe's small hand locks, stiff, on mine. Without you, Isaac, me cyaan be meself. Me see you face, and me see you face in Lickle Phoebe's – jagged, dark brown. She face becomes a scavenger's: matted hair; starved cheekbones poking loudly from skin.

'We must tek revenge,' Eleanor say.

'Burn de trash-house!' Trouble-Too-Much's yelling. 'Fetch torch fram boiler-house!'

Isaac's gone forever. We take revenge all de more we suffer, me eye say to Eleanor. Isaac's cries, him deathly moans, don't spool away but hang in torrid air like threats, hover with scraps of dreams, of memories, too beautiful to forget. Me heart howls, *What's left of yu, Isaac? Sad pain?*

Blindly me mount hilltop where thinly grasses grow, pink sky splinters gold through tears flying from me eye, valley spreading before me's moulded into me mind: we battered shacks sitting side by side on wasted ground between parched vegetable plots lying above, and sugar mill – a monster moving noisily – below. Me know each broken plank of Isaac's verandah and wattle walls of him shack that flap on windy nights and blow away feather-light on wind puffs whenever hurricanes come or a great storm raging, stripping we of everything. Me know odd mix of pens fe chickens, pigs, tethered brindled goats, and dirty yards where pickney stay every day when too weak to work. Me know sun slides quietly red behind pointed shingle roof belonging to Cinnamon Hill great house. Me know what little we have fe it goes to make drab place we call home. All we field-hands coming over hillside feel bitter hatred fe foulness of we world. Splashes of brightly coloured flowers beside track taunt me with their beauty. Sandy paths wind down towards gold sand bay, warm blue star-sparkling sea. This a part of you, Isaac? Part of me? Soon me learned me cyaan belong in Jamaica. This island cyaan ever be a home. Although buckra say we belong, although me blend in, fit with other field-hands, although me live here since a pickney, part of me don't fit anywhere. This island don't belong to we.

Sundown's nearly done with making wattle-shack village red. Me heart searches fe you, Isaac. How close, when me don't know where you gone, you death seems.

Whispers drift into me shack on a gentle honey smell and sink deep into me belly. But no one can reach lone place life's become so sudden. Me see you try taking a step, see you falling down, Isaac. Lickle Phoebe holding me cyaan save me from falling too. Even Phoebe's still and pained face's a tormenting reminder of you.

Softly she voice drops into me ear, 'Wot's fiah made fram?' *Answer*, me heart say, *is love*, but me mind say, *No. De idea of fiah sparks fram angry hunger.* 'Me stay wid yu, fiah-maker,' Lickle Phoebe say. She sweet pickney kiss cyaan give me even small hope grain. Inside a scream slices me guts. Love's fire burns only fe me lover. Me fear me love too much.

Tools rest against wattle wall. Axe, hoe, billhook, machete. Buckra passes on him plodding horse, a glance meets me from him eye. Anger presses in on me. A knot ties tight in me belly, me saddled with memory. That thickly rolled collar of skin under back of buckra's head glows red in late-evening sun.

Chapter Three

Kaydia

CINNAMON HILL ESTATE
14 February 1840

Shuffling along main drive now Old Simeon leads a loping horse.
Slack reins trail from one hand; a lantern swings from him other
hand heading for stable block. Old Simeon's rank leg smells strong
even from here, way back.

'Where yu bin?' he shouts. 'Bin waitin on yu. Gotta let de dogs
out.'

'Me jus ax Pa fe fetch Doctor Demar,' I say.

Old Simeon wasn't born, he always lived here. Old milky blue-
brown eyes slide towards me. Greenish-white lantern glow slips
across Simeon's wrinkled face as he turns, looking to great house,
turns back, looks for stable block. 'Demar's in de house. Passed by
on im way. Junius in dere wid 'em. Mister Sam won't be needin
yu.' Snorting violently Demar's mare nods like she agrees with
him.

'Me musta missed im wen me went fe Pa,' I say. I hear Old
Simeon turn Demar's mare into a stable. Old Simeon stinks ugly
as burnt hair, rotten bones. Simeon's lamp's dying. Bolting bottom
door behind him he grunts, slings tack on saddle-room rack. Steered
by great-house hall candles he trudges behind me across main lawn.

Doctor Demar's oily black hair's plastered to him head. Rolling
shirt sleeves to elbows, Doctor Demar's all voice. 'Get the stable
boy to saddle the mare. Call the guard dogs too.'

Old Simeon hobbles into Cinnamon Hill hall, hitches up brown
overalls. Looking like Old Simeon's in charge.

'On second thoughts there's no need.' Doctor Demar staggers

towards hall table candelabra. 'I'm not feeling too good. I'll stay here until dawn.' He flops into dark wood chair, him head moving into my shadow – a darkness lurching across walls. Doctor Demar's arm sticks out at Old Simeon like a branch stripped white of bark, 'You, feed and water the mare. You,' branch swings to me, 'watch over Sam. He says he told you to nurse him. Give him water, keep him cool.'

'Mister Sam miss me?' I ask. 'E did notice me gawn?'

Sternly Doctor Demar says, 'Sam's very, very sick.'

'Ganja mek Mister Sam betta,' Old Simeon mumbles, putting lantern on table-top with a weighty thud. 'E have no need fe white buckra doctor, e need Myal man, not obeah. Trouble is yu cyaan tell difference tween Myal an obeah. Yu know wot difference dere is? Yu no good like dat Ope spirit minister man.'

Doctor Demar's whole body shivers like air's cold, or he scared of a high wind passing through tree branches.

Old Simeon's hand's a crinkled paw screwing lantern wick up until orange-white flame leaps yellow then mellows to pale jade-orchid green. 'No need fe work now,' he says. 'No need fe Mister Sam.' Lantern spits, light floods gritty maps, curling parchment, quill pens, plantation stock books loosely stacked on hall table.

Choking, Doctor Demar mops him balding head with a clean white handkerchief so skin's not so shiny-red. 'I'll take my rum neat.' He smiles a shabby smile.

Mister Sam's door's half open. Cockroaches slip behind skirting boards. Little blinkies flash emerald on wallpaper. For a moment I am still, him eye go into mine. *Even sea's lost she magic, only after rain clouds clear does salt water ripple like sunlight in attic.* My shadow drifts on chamber floor, surprised at sudden urge me feel to hold him again that close. It passed between we then – a shock – he did feel it? No other light comes, but for moon shafts spilling dull silver onto black sea, dappled, glimmering hauntingly.

Mister Sam wails, 'Oh God, I'm dying,' high-pitched and hoarse. Threatening to leave life too soon he stares at me. I look on slippery shaky hands dangling from nightshirt sleeves, frail face yellowish, hot, and fold back top sheet with gathering storms in my belly.

All Mister Sam's badness started years back from now. Reaching out fingertips him hand shakes horribly. Worry sharpens my thoughts but worry don't wash fear from my mind – I'm thinking of my daughter, Mary Ann. Up rise rank memories.

Dragging my old faded brown dress de shade of a rat-bat drawn to a flickering candle, hop-skipping, Mary Ann followed Mister Sam up Cinnamon Hill staircase. Though it was Mary Ann who danced, she was naked like a flame.

Charles I knew before that time always he was joking, always he was good to Mary Ann and me. All three together we'd sleep in attic room, until that dawn when conch-blow's uproar woke we to find Mary Ann no longer lay at we side. She said mattress was too hard and monsters walked in she head. Feet stealing down steep narrow attic ladder took she to sleeping below hall stairs. From then on Mary Ann had monsters in she head. Some days she skin went hot and strange smells lived in she hair. Charles said he'd flog Mary Ann if she didn't tell where she been almost all of every night. She took to hiding in daytime too. Mary Ann was like a snake, I never heard she coming; she'd slide around each room, sneaking up behind me. Then darting off. Hours later I'd find she – straw tangled into matted hair; dress skew-whiff; small body balled-up tight like she was cornered by life.

'Where yu bin?' I'd ask.

'Aint bin nowhere,' she'd answer. Pretending it was a game. Pretending she wasn't sure what I meant. Always she was pretending.

Charles' anger grew worse and worse. 'Sumting wrong,' he'd say, 'an if yu cyaan git she straight all we go fram ere.'

'No need to be rank, Charles,' I'd said. 'Yu dawta's only lazy, bin sleeping in stable, lying in hay.'

'No, Mary Ann's crazy,' he said.

Charles went to talk to church minister saying he worried something wicked going on. But Lord God couldn't lift big worryload about Mary Ann from we heads. And Charles' talk turned queer. All that church sermon stuff Charles began to believe. 'Let Satan have im way wid she,' he'd say.

'Is me fault she won't go to church? Me fault she's like she be?' I asked.

'God hurts dem dat hurt demself,' Charles said. So I started
going to Sunday church and encouraged Mary Ann to come, and
Pa felled trees by Barrett Hall lake, and he and others built church
school by church hothouse. Pa carved with Charles benches, altar,
and one table for minister's wife. But minister's wife got sick. She
never liked Mister Sam any more than anyone did. She wouldn't
set foot on Cinnamon Hill plantation land, though she got so sick
even Mister Sam offered to lend she a hothouse nurse. I started
working at night for minister in church school, sharing out corn
biscuits, teaching to pickney whatever I learned to read. Mister
Sam grew angry when he knew. He set me heavy daytime chores,
evening chores too, and I didn't mind much for church sermons
get so boring and minister always shouts, him face have hard woodgrain marks like white planks Pa planes. Minister's eyes look cold
and blue as deep freshwater pools. I know how England brings all
its coldness here, brings it with bleached white sheets or stony
faces; brings it as white stone ballast in ships English build great
houses with; brings it into cold air of each great chamber, savagely
cold at dawn; brings it with too much agony at de heart of each
slave's soul.

Then Charles asked me to marry him; he said minister said
marriage was good. But my own heart blew cold. I won't marry
Charles. Already I'm a slave to Mister Sam, don't want to be a
slave to anyone else ever again. And church spread like blister
rashes through Charles' life. Blisters Charles, it seemed, had to keep
picking at. More he picked, angry and red, bigger those bitter blisters grew. And Mary Ann grew lumps in she mouth, throat too,
and I took she to church hothouse. They said it's ulcers she'd got
and she must drink only seawater. Church felt even colder when I
found out what she'd done.

And she disappearing haunted me like all she other strange acts.
Why she cowered, cat-like, from everyone. Why she wouldn't do
any chores. Wouldn't shine Mister Sam's boots, scrub or polish
yacca floor in him blue bedchamber. Said she hated blue. Blue sky.
Blue sea. Blue light falling on blue-black floorboards. Blue dress
from England Mister Sam gave she. Only wanted to wear my ragged
brown dress. Kicking, fighting, snarling, wildly matted mane
muddled round she honey-brown neck, screaming like she felt to

tackle hell's fire when Mister Sam forced she into that blue dress. He forced my daughter into its bodice, stiff-shouldered and hunched as a soldier she strutted across great-house hall. Then spewed everywhere. Sick shot across yacca floor and all over she blue dress. That night she shredded that dress.

From then I watched Mary Ann much more closely. But it was Charles found out she truth.

Mister Sam now begs me to send for him cousin. *Mister Sam decide to make him will?* Worry tightens my belly. *Him will can make my sorrows go.* Sheets feel slimy with sweat and sick; him skin takes on a ghastly milky hue in dim moonlight.

Bracing myself as he rolls, I strip dirty sheets away and, easing him back into place, struggle to lay a bleached sheet beneath him, across bed mattress. Him body, twisting, breaks into sweat. *Soften rigid spine.*

Him voice strangle between lips taut like slave ship's rigging: 'My cousin, Kaydia, is he coming?'

'Soon come,' I say.

Whispering, 'Water, water,' he rests slanted awkwardly, a slab of flesh that's him shoulder cushioned by my knee, pain-creased face moonlight struck. I lever an arm from under him back, it dangles limp from a shoulder. I'm smoothing waves clean from wide sheet but its surface still crinkles like moon-white salt water. Him nightshirt's skewed; him collar, mattress cloth feels damp.

A yearning for my mama creeps out from floorboards up into bedchamber's dark air, seeping up like a yearning can. Haven't seen Rebecca Laslie for years. Waiting on Mister Sam, I long for she. Long to know if she dead or alive. How a mama can sever a daughter from she?

Something like Mama's face – if that's what she is – stares back from old stone rainwater jar when I go to fill Mister Sam's jug: my hair curls tied up in a ragged red scarf and, sharp as moon-shadows black on water, deep pits like Pa carved under Mama Laslie's eyes for crying and half drinking sheself to death. Rebecca Laslie lives. I swear she's not dead.

I have to take jug's weight, raise rim to Mister Sam's lips. Mister Sam tastes cool water, head jerking up down, up down, with each tiny sip. Eyes uplifting to mine, weakly he slides into pillows again.

Sounds I hardly know trickle into my ear, pulling my head round. Sounds like Mary Ann laughing, but how laughter can be mournful? Empty? Scared? Hall clock strikes eight, calling me for Doctor Demar's table laying. Why hall clock chimes so lonely sad?

Dancing, Mary Ann comes first into great-house dining-room. Stripes purple as lips still stand up vivid on she face. Worming a path from forehead to chin are bold lines of skin Charles' whip raised. But blue bruises faded long time past.

Cutlery in my hand, I pause from table laying. May, Jo, Friday, follow Mary Ann. Friday wears a nice green shirt, first time I seen him dress bright and crisp. But I feel badness in all this busha-house party mood.

'Pa treat Friday to it,' Mary Ann's singing, throwing she head round.

'Why yu tek so lang lang coming?' I ask Mary Ann. 'Yu tink me work fe yu?'

'It Friday's birthday,' she replies.

'Mary Ann, Mister Sam say don't ansa back,' May says mockingly.

Pa's cracked feet pad like leather on yacca floor. Same Pa. Same mama. *Sibyl and me both sister sameway. Why sameway Pa don't treat we? Shame! Me cyaan change me red skin colour. Cyaan kill it.*

Mary Ann's face aglow with wickedness. A thin brown hand stretches out, making for cutlery by Doctor Demar's plate. She all curiosity, Mary Ann. I wonder if she aware of Doctor Demar's gaze. But sparkling silver's within she reach. She dares to touch one fork, pretty plate.

Looking like Pa's about to attack, jaw hard-grinding roast coffee beans, him eyes sad, mean; Pa's lean shoulders set angrily. Lizards scuttle into hiding.

I cuss pickney, 'No, outta de weh.' Running around all with eyes of different colours – Friday's green, Jo's blue-brown, May's grey – pickney scatter onto dark verandah, bare backs half-black as my own daughter's.

Brooding, sucking him teeth, Pa gazes at Mary Ann. She head bobs beneath table-top, eyes peering up.

'Mary Ann, clear de hall table wen Doctor Demar rum finish,' I'm saying to she.

Pa, deciding something, teases dirt from under fingernails, flicks it towards sea. What's past's more real to him than what's present. Pa's arm skates Mary Ann. 'Cho! Cease an sekkle,' he yelling.

Ducking, Mary Ann squeals, 'Me aint done noting!'

Striding onto verandah Pa's foot scuffs a centipede, leaving a scaly smudge, oozing slightly.

Centipede's skewered on a splinter, scaly patterns delicate like lace. Mary Ann, in a trance, cages it between toes, hurting it for pleasure.

Turning, Pa says, 'De saltin fish yu mek dis mornin have a bad flavour.' He cut him eye at me. 'Wot mek yu not tek back yu baby fadda, Charles, huh?'

'Me bring Mary Ann into dis place,' I say. 'Me tek care of she.'

Mary Ann's mashing a withered claw between verandah planks, a twisting body. I know of all Pa's ways to bring Mary Ann pain.

'Git out, Mary Ann,' I shout. 'Git to kitchen block, do yu chores. Clear Doctor Demar's rum fram hall table.'

'Wa mek yu send me send fe Doctor Demar wen Doctor Demar ere?' Pa asks.

'Me didn't know dat, Pa.' Peering through open doorway moonlight moves darkly, sneaking across sea's endless blank face. I shout after Mary Ann into darkness, 'Yu skim de oil fe coconut meat? Yu do chores wid May, Jo an Friday? Fetch wata, bucket in dere fe yu.'

Looking like he could kill, Pa grinds him iron jaw. Like I making things worse, not better. 'Me didn't know,' he cuts.

Struck again by all badness that's happened I'm walking through great-house hall. Candle-light flickers along corridors. Strong smells seep from rum and coconut oil polish I rubbed into mahogany wall panels until they shone. Mary Ann — she misery stings cruelly, *If me stab meself pain'll go?* On hall table a rum tumbler, pitcher of water and strong rum punch jug set out earlier on silver tray for Doctor Demar, waits for Mary Ann to clear.

Shutting out sweeping ocean, both drawing-room doors I close. 'Mary Ann! Mary Ann!' I'm shouting. Mary Ann's where? Can't see or hear my daughter any more. Lantern don't shine from kitchen block. *God forgive all we here.* Mary Ann stood high as my shoulder, she was nine when she hiding began. Suddenly I can't stop crying and aching for she. I don't know how to wipe clean this stain that's Mister Sam's badness. Memories sicken me.

Mister Sam's door stands half open. Him eye plead helplessly. Blue in him eye's too dark to see. Arms lie like a cross on him chest.

Thrashing like him drowning, Mister Sam's hands crab sheets. Like a sudden raw energy throbs in him blood he vomits, full force, as I never seen man or woman vomit before. Kneeling, mopping up him vile mess, I'm thinking I'm no better than Mary Ann – Mister Sam's fancy thing – like all woman in this place, trampled by a man. Mister Sam's hands, hot as sun-scorched sand, reach for mine. Foul black bile streams from him mouth. Mister Sam's fever brings spasms all night.

Hot night passes. Mournfully conch-blow wails – monster's dawn-break sound. Punching pillows to make them light, my heart's pounding as surf crashes on pink coral reefs.

Sunlight spreads, glittering gold across blue sea. Mary Ann smiles wickedly from under Mister Sam's four-poster but she eye's glazed and crazed like Rebecca Laslie's.

'Gimme a cup a-chalklit, do,' Mary Ann says. Crawling lizard-like on she belly, she upsets Mister Sam's tray I hold.

'Yu dun yet? Wot a ting!' I'm saying to she.

Mary Ann searches for fruit, sugar grains, china chips. Scars don't show on Mary Ann's face when she's looking down. She mumbles, 'It brik,' trying to fit patterned china slices back together.

'Always yu brik crockeries. Go'way, Mary Ann,' I say, and haul sodden sheets from Mister Sam's mattress. 'Yu aint got betta sense?' I ask.

Moaning, 'It's breaking,' Mister Sam bends him spine until it bows and curves like machete blade.

Mary Ann stands up and says, turning, 'Me a-go now, Ma.' Gold sun rays thread between jalousie blinds. Silently Mary Ann slips out, she sun-gold back disappears.

In one sweeping movement Mister Sam swings him legs down from mattress, lunges for pineapple shape carved into mahogany-red bedhead. Sunlight splashes on shining wood. Him head thuds on yacca board flooring; face hidden by hair, a soft floppy mess of straw-coloured spikes. Breath comes so thin it's mysterious. I heave him up into bed, shake him shoulder, call him name.

Mister Sam's mouth opens and shuts like red snapper. *He does know? Him remembering?* My heart sounds like thudding drum beats, *walnut jewellery box on black dressing-table.* Blocking my thoughts. Sunlight strokes Mister Sam's sheets, him eyelids flicker into sleep.

Chapter Four

Elizabeth

My dearest Mary,

... Torquay is a beautiful place — but as to its human aspect, it is much more like a hospital than anything else, & so, none of the gayest — Respirators & stethoscopes 'go about the streets' — I have not made one acquaintance since I came, except my physician's — a privation for which you won't pity me ...

... I hear very often from Miss Mitford — who has been much distressed lately by the illness of her father. He is recovering almost miraculously. Ask for me whether there is an edition (in one work) of the Platonic philosophers — mind, not of Plato, but the Platonists in Greek ... My dearest Papa is with me just now. It is such a happiness! no room for a word more! ...

I am wondering, as I gaze across the monotonous sea, how to obey the conventions and etiquette of this world in which I exist and remain faithful to my heart and desires. For a falling-out has occurred. A falling-out within the family.

Bro *will* stay with me. He *must*. He *shall*. Or I shall be mad. Madness results from losing all one's loved ones. So I shall tell Papa I am going mad. My pleading for Bro to stay in Torquay so angered Papa he resorted to slamming the door minutes ago as he went out. Perhaps his temper will soften with the coming of spring. Though it doesn't usually. Chains heavy and cold enough to be iron would enter into my soul were Bro to leave. I don't understand why I must be separated from those whom I love, and who love me; nor do I understand why Papa tries to curb all that brings me joy.

5 February 1839

There has not been a reply to my last lengthy letter from anyone in London for ten days since. Sam docked in London weeks ago. Has he forgotten me altogether? He was never the most sagacious of writers. He must have been about sixteen when he wrote to Henrietta from Charterhouse whilst Mama was convalescing in Cheltenham: *I suppose the next thing I shall hear will be that Mama has been to one of the dashing Cheltenham balls and then I shall hear that you are gone off to Gretna Green with some dashing young man.* The next news Sam received of Mama was that she was dead.

All morning I have tolerated a humming buzzing noise inside my head which is equal, in annoyance, to one of Henrietta's tuning forks. Yet I am certain this noise comes from within, and is, perhaps, less of a noise and more a sensation. Am I tuning up for something? I rather fear I anticipate change. What the change actually is and how it will come about, I cannot say. Instinctively I feel it concerns matters I have never been able to discuss with Papa, matters weighing heavily upon my mind, such as Bro's need for direction.

Without warning the door blows open and the woman who watches me floats in. She seats herself before the window; her movements fluid, haunting. Might this creation have been formed by my morning medications? Surely my remedy – opium – hasn't soused reason with delusions. I fancy my mind has melted into pools of delirium. Shaken, and with a spiralling sense of dread, I am compelled to watch. Swiftly her head turns. She lifts her face, raises her wet eyes beneath a crêpe veil. But it is on the ocean that her look alights. She seems shut up in a world of her own. Shut up in her own darkness.

Whatever it is she's experienced is a particular kind of loss about which I understand nothing. I cannot read her thoughts yet sense she possesses an omniscient knowledge of mine. Now she weeps as I weep. Huge heart-wrenching sobs wrack her fragile frame. She resembles Mama when, when . . . this woman who comes to my bedside when others leave, why should *she* lose a baby? Life will never be the same for her, not after such grief, such intense pain. My sister, Mary, died at the age of four. I was eight, and Mama's sadness and suffering then was incomprehensible to me. I start thinking, what is it like to bury a baby? Is this the first she has lost?

Behind the woman I picture the slender shape of a gentleman, proud nose, noble head dark-haired, finely dressed in a tall hat, brown suit, lemon-coloured kid gloves and cravat. His eyes are filled with painful devotion. He is a lofty mountain peak clouded in silver mist. Brushing tears from my face, I experience a horrifying notion sprouting inside – a feeling of misappropriation, or a misreading of the world – the true nature of which I cannot imagine, nor the implications fathom.

'Sweet, sweet Miss Elizabeth,' Crow says comfortingly as she clears away my tray. I can barely hear her. I hear the other woman's sobs distinctly. She moans as though there's a hole in her heart. The man places his arms around the shoulders of her black satin dress. Tears stream down her cheeks. Bravely she turns to him. He exchanges for parchment and quill pen the sodden handkerchief scrumpled in the hard ball of her black-gloved hand. He murmurs reassurances in her ear. Warmth radiates from his face. Shell-pink as a tongue, sunlight sheers across the bay. She is pulling herself through years of anguish, shaking off the ache of loneliness – a path leading to hell – her lips melt into a smile for the first time. For a while the couple blend together completely against an auroral sky. Clasped hands cast in stone. Such trust, such intimacy, cannot be quantified. A pang of envy shoots through me. Were she to die in his arms could he breathe life into her again? Could I escape to the blessed land from whence they came?

7 March 1839

Ever dearest Miss Mitford,

. . . your last two delightful letters were received by me when I was quite confined to my bed, & in such a state of debility as rendered writing a thing impossible. Even at this time, altho' more than a month has passed since this laying up began, the extent of my strength is to bear being lifted to the sofa for three hours a day – & I have not left my bedroom for six weeks. The cold weather at the end of January irritated the chest a good deal – & then most unaccountably – I never suffered from such a thing my whole life before – I had for ten days a kind of bilious fever which necessitated the use of stronger

medicines than my state cd. very well bear — & then came on a terrible state of debility — the stomach out of sheer weakness, rejecting all sustenance except wine & water, & the chest, seeming to grudge the exercise of respiration. I felt oftener than once inclined to believe that the whole machine was giving away everywhere! But God has not willed it so! . . .

We are now stuck in the month of March. To my surprise, Crow's reading of the thermometer is sixty-five. Sharp winds weave their fingers beneath the sash windows, making me shiver. A good hour after Crow had lit the fire she returned to clear away a hamper-full of eagerly opened cards and presents. Another birthday has passed. Uneventfully.

Crow preens herself before my dressing-table. This maid and I share the same Christian name, thus the necessity of calling her by her surname. She may be a young creature but I can talk to Crow as if she were a friend. Whether it is good etiquette I care not. I like to be managed and she manages me well.

Outside, waves thrash and beat the rocks round the bay so frantically it is a wonder any creature survives.

10 March 1839

Flopping down on the company side of my bed, Bro says he does not feel alive any more. 'Is Bro in love?' I ask.

'No,' he replies.

'Is that true?' I say. Because, if he were, Papa would not approve.

Bro slopes over to the armchair and lights a cigarette. 'In some aspects of life we must be invisible to Papa,' he says. 'I am invisible. No, not to you, Ba. To you I am transparent. You see far more of me than others do.' We are at this moment looking into each other's eyes; vulnerable, like sea snails without shells; me curled in bed; Bro torpid in the armchair opposite.

'I would have loved a water-colour from you on my birthday,' I say. Bro replies by calling his water-colours sundry and ungainly.

Bro says he is bored. Interminably. Never have I seen his spirits so low. He misses Sam sorely. I suspect it is Sam's good company at the parties Bro frequents here that he desires most — but funny Sam amused us all with his odd pranks.

'Where are you going today?' I ask.

'I don't know,' Bro replies mournfully. 'I was up after eleven again last night writing to Sam.'

'He has suffered all winter long from shivering fits, feeling hot and cold and with fever. I suggested to Arabel he take arsenic.'

Bro yawns. 'I know. I have asked him to bring from London boots from Judd's, and for Henrietta a pair of yellow satin kid gloves.' He trudges downstairs from my room to lie in his.

I shout after Bro, 'Please take my letters to catch today's post,' and there is a dormant pause on the stairs. This post will carry a long despatch from Henrietta and a note from me to Sam, requesting he visit Torquay as soon as Papa and his health will allow.

11 March 1839

My dearest Miss Mitford,

Thank you for all your encouraging kindnesses (how they multiply) about my poetry. But dearest Miss Mitford, if it were really the fashion to like it, wdnt it be a little so to buy it! And Messrs. Saunders & Otley gave bad accounts in the early part of the winter. Do you think there shd. be more advertisements? . . .

27 March 1839

'Is it not true that one man's greed is another man's hunger?' I ask Bro after he has read from *The Times* an article accusing West Indian plantation owners of a continuing excessive desire to possess more than they need.

'There are probably exceptions,' he replies.

Poor Bro looks strained, puffing on that cigarette – his hair remains as long and lanky as ever. I would prefer it if he would refrain from smoking in my chamber; smoke does affect my chest so. I wish indeed, as does Henrietta, that Bro was independent. I have advised him to pursue his interest in painting water-colours. He says he will, when the weather improves, but I don't see what the weather has to do with it. He can paint just as well inside as out!

28 March 1839

I have asked Henrietta to tell Sam that a black elastic band for my waist – one of the ones worn over the gown – would be very acceptable, and to bring a bottle or two of eau de cologne; my stock has dwindled. She suggests we write to Sam now but I am exhausted, having undergone the fatigue of being brought down stairs, carried up again, undressed, and put to bed.

'Ba, I can tell when you're awake,' Henrietta says, and giggles.

I peer from one eye, 'How?' searching for an angle from which to broach discussions on my recent preoccupations.

'Because I just saw you lay your book down.'

During our exchange, which, on account of my hoarseness, is brief, I tell Henrietta to use her head just this once. Is she too thick-skinned to feel the swords of truth? Henrietta's nice – I'm not thinking she isn't – I am making my best effort to explain to her the conclusions I have reached: that we must see poetry, suffering, as the way to truth. Is not the Bible poetry? Are not hymns poetic expression of the love of God, however unworthy? I ask. All things were created by the poet, God. Christ is poetry. The accumulated benefits of the wealthy have been derived from others' suffering, and our sinful debt to Christ is best represented in poetic utterance.

'Have you never wondered about this?'

Scratching her neatly arranged hair as though trawling for a thought in there, Henrietta replies, 'Do you *always* have to be serious?'

I look away from her face, wishing Arabel would hurry up and arrive, for she is graced with much more sense. I should love Arabel even if she were not my sister; and even if she did not love me.

The skirts of Henrietta's new violet dress swish across the red Persian rugs as she sails from my bedside to fetch my tray of wine and oysters from the drawing-room.

Bro excused himself from coming to wish me good-night, having disappeared to I know not where. Another party I suspect.

Bro said this afternoon he heard that Tennyson, who I understand to be handsome despite having an unduly large head and fathoming eye, has separated from his family because they distracted him. He is settled in a cottage not far from here, in Devonshire, where he composes poems and smokes all day.

I miss London. I miss busy shops. The jostle of London's streets. I long for my doves and my little slip of a sitting-room, my shelves of books. My window-panes ivy-trailed and draped like curtains drawn. The heads from Brucciani's – busts of poets and philosophers, Chaucer and Homer in particular – which kind Papa, how I know not, found time to purchase, and to remember such light a thing as my pleasure in all the bustle and vexations of his life.

1 April 1839

My ever dearest Arabel,

I meant to have written to my own beloved Papa – but altho' beginning days ago this series of replies to letters sent to me so long since, I am tired today, & Henrietta, scolding like a virago! Tell him how he is missed every night, & all day too – but most *at night! & tell him he shall have a long letter from me very soon in reply to your blank corner – dearest dearest Papa! . . .*

. . . I meant to have written too to dearest Sam. Tell him so.

10 April 1839

My beloved friend,

. . . They carried me downstairs into the drawing-room for two weary hours about ten days ago – but the weather has since kept me upstairs. For weeks before I was reduced to all but the harmlessness of babyhood – lifting a spoon to my own lips being the only point on which I cd. claim precedence. Even now I am sure I cd. not stand a moment alone – but here is summer, coming *tho' not in sight, & she sends a sort of mental sunshine* before . . .

Give my kind & grateful regards to dear Dr. Mitford! How kind of him to drink my health – & to think of me at any time. He shall have more fish when they will be caught. Did you send the basket? We have not heard of it! . . .

14 April 1839

Though I suffer enormous embarrassment for my eating habit I will not, and *can not*, devour and digest that stringy yellow substance identified by Bro as chicken. I would rather starve to death than eat chicken, or, worse, red meat. When dinner – a dish of transparent greenish gravy-like soup, broccoli florets, chicken in some viscid sauce whitish-yellow as custard and grainy as tapioca (a sort of bread sauce with saffron), tasteless rice pellets that resemble white mouse droppings – was set before me on a tray just now, I so very nearly cried. Bro saw my disgust and ordered the cook bring oysters and macaroni, then Crow gave me an additional opium dose and the world came back to me again. Or I to it. But now I am bloated I cannot sleep. Or write. Or anything!

19 April 1839

My dear Sam,

... Tell Arabel that I can't wait any longer for Miss Bordman's note ... She must have quite forgotten me to have such an idea of my patience. Tell her she had far better put everything into a bandbox &, with them, a packet of letters & my satin bonnet. Dr. Barry told me two or three days ago that he hoped to get me into the air in a month's time!! & I can't go out without a bonnet. That's certain! & I have not any here except a black one. So tell Arabel to pack up the bandbox, & send it – not in a month but NOW!

27 April 1839

What a dreadful year is this? The sudden death of Cousin Richard, Custos of St. James, Jamaica; Speaker of the House of Assembly. Richard, dear Papa's illegitimate cousin, had blood from we know not where, and now rumour has reached us that Richard was murdered – may the Lord God rest his soul.

Handsome, after a fashion, though not as dark and handsome as Papa, Richard's was a face that I, as a child, did not care to look upon. His short upper lip was full of expression. His laughter rang harshly through Hope End. All too well he described his daily path as leading from cane fields – a world of vindictive torture, where the standard punishment for any act considered a misdeed was thirty-nine lashes of a thick cattle whip – to Barrett Hall great house, a residence to him of exquisite comfort and bliss.

Contrary to Papa's belief, I was neither sleeping nor in bed when Cousin Richard related fateful tales of runaway slaves. Straining to hear from my seat on the stairs, I glimpsed the Negroes' untold misery and the savagery of white Jamaicans. Heartily Richard described punishments impossible to forget, yet ones I wish I could not remember; described wrong following greater wrong. Described how he galloped from Falmouth along Jamaica's north coast to Greenwood then Barrett Hall and Cinnamon Hill. Clouting the door, 'Open up! Open up!' he had shouted to summon each militia member. He described the militia, all with horses and in their best finery, mustering around one hundred slaves to track down the runaways; one a man, one a woman. 'Cousin,' I said with tears in my eyes, 'speak no more of this.' Yet his voice has never left my ears – such a frightfully terrible tale he did bestow upon them that I now cannot help my thoughts dwelling on that black woman slave they cornered.

I am an abolitionist. I belong to a family who have long been West Indian slave-holders, and if I believed in curses, I should be afraid. Richard said of the slave in question – Quasheba – was that her name? – 'We trapped her, but it occurs to me that she did not die from that or a flogging.' Richard then had the audacity to say that slave women should be treated more kindly when about to give birth. That night with us at Hope End he drank heartily. Five bottles of the best Bordeaux claret; rum; whisky.

I saw Cousin Richard last five years ago. Still a man of violence, and some malice. A man too of ill repute – the house of which he was Speaker was known as the House of Forty Thieves. A man of talent, I have to say, who at one time did all he could to trample down poor Papa. His speech in the House of Commons was not well received, in particular his views on flogging women. It was around that time, or possibly a little before, that Bro read to me of a large West Indian proprietor examined by a committee of the House of Lords who could not name any overseer, driver, or other man in authority who did not keep an African mistress.

Did my own father's cousin commit murder? Was the victim a child or *with* child? Might the child have been his? God forgive us and help us. The moon's silver mantle shines boldly. And although Bro sleeps nearby on the sofa I cannot, gripped at night by such thoughts.

30 April 1839

Ever dearest Miss Mitford,
*   . . . It seems so long since I heard last, & there are so many disagreeable*
& painful things in the world notwithstanding all these spring flowers, & I

have such a knack of imagining them, that I wd. gladly be sure of none of them having touched you. Don't fancy me forgetful of the fish basket. But our servant seems to be a very nervous person as to the qualifications of travelling fish – and I told you before that fish in this market, when worth anything, is not very often fish directly from the sea . . .

. . . Did you look into Blackwood *this month – & (apropos to fish) perceive how Christopher's 'Oystereater' congenially with Tait's Opium Eater, apostrophizes the 'charming & adorable Mary Russell Mitford'? – You see, no sort of diet will expel the admirations due to you – & the imaginative with their opium, & the literal with their oysters come to the same point at last. Nay – the oysters are infected, if it be true that 'the WORLD'S mine oyster'.*

. . . Again disappointed about the fish! But there is hope for tomorrow . . .

Dear Hugh Stuart Boyd,

. . . I have a confusion of poems running about in my head – a chaos of beginnings & endings & little pieces of middles, which are not likely to end in an Iliad *& so help Atheism to an argument. I shd. be glad to be allowed to get them (not in the character of an Iliad) into some little nutshell of my own, but Dr. Barry insists upon my not writing, and as you taught me passive obedience a long time ago, I have been practising it like St Aylmer – not that I mean to do this all summer, if it pleases God to spare me through it. I ought to say with a deep-felt thanksgiving, how much better I am . . . The weakness was excessive – & indeed, I have not even tried to stand up since January – but everything is in 'good time' Dr. Barry says, & it is planned for me to go upon the sea before the present week closes, which would be a 'vision of delight' for me if it were not for the fatigue . . .*

I do so hope Hugh Stuart Boyd can read my handwriting – as I look back over my pen-strokes I see they are rather irregular and cramped from my writing this horizontally in bed. Why has he left my last three letters unanswered? Has he not managed to read them? Why, when we spent so much time together at Hope End, precious happy literary hours over cups of strong black West Indian coffee, can he not reply?

15 May 1839
This continuing aching sense of weakness I suffer is intolerable. I have told Dr. Barry that Dr. Chambers tried every other kind of

narcotic in vain. Opium does me no harm. Despite taking twenty-five drops daily, I have mastered seven languages – French, Italian, Latin and German, Spanish, Hebrew and Byzantine Greek.

Yet today Crow forgot an afternoon dose.

I now experience restlessness till it makes me quite mad, like an imprisoned bird, impotently beating and fluttering at all the doors and windows to escape. My elixir should be served throughout the day, first as a breakfast when wafting up to my room is a disturbing odour of kippers, the crunch of toast, the clatter of knives and forks and cups against saucers and plates.

Imprisoned on the sofa close to the window, close to a cold and violent sea, I lie listening to the dry wind as it leans eastwards, whipping up surf. My face, reflected in the glass of the bookcase opposite, is yellowed with jaundice. I am glad setons are not used as a method of curing my ailments, for I cannot bear the sensation caused when tape is passed by means of a needle through folds of one's skin – I have no folds of skin to pass through.

Old books are stacked at my bedside, each holds the fragrance of the past, like the scent of lavender – remote, fragmented – pressed into sheets. The woman drifts through my thoughts and into the room. Standing at my bedside, she is in girlhood and seems to be suffering a general feeling of malaise, aches and pains and convulsive twitches of the muscles. Her skin is blotched red as if affected by measles. Natural ill health impedes her movements with paroxysms, until she enters a hell of writhing agitation, into which most would feel loath to look. Vainly does she struggle. She's been buried for thousands of years in a coffin of the thickest wood, the conflicts and horrors and evil nightmares are over-powering. Already the gates to her freedom are locked, draped with black garments and funeral cloths, the key thrown away.

Everywhere are memories. Everywhere I am unfolding. Pains stretch right round my back; my spine feels swollen; and, from straining a muscle whilst saddling Moses, I suffer recurring agony. Dear Papa, and finally Mama, visit intermittently. I am treated for disease of the spine. This entails the horror of regular cuppings, which I only just survive; and being strung up four feet from the ground in a spine crib, and – with the fear of being driven, quite literally, batty, by boredom and inactivity – told to lie and *wait*. Never have I been without that dusky-brown drug since. Many women now take it from babyhood. Were I to completely cease the consumption of it, I would die.

The woman stares across the room. Whey-faced, she rises, a sombre figure in a black satin dress; stumbles, falls. She tries to scoop herself up and then from exhaustion, collapses again, wilting into the smog of despair. For once our eyes truly meet, that she might reach me; a mysterious brown look with a mischievous glint. Closing my eyes I tell myself I will not look at her any more, that I have been dreaming. When I open my eyes she is staring at me. Have I been hypnotized? Can such a thing be achieved in the murky depths of sleep?

Dimly I see the woman now as a whisper not of the past or present but of the future. Vast clouds of the agony of disappointment loom over her body. As long as she takes opium, that path journeying to hell remains open to me.

16 May 1839

I shall demand Bro stay on the sofa in my room after the sun has set. Is this selfish of me? This afternoon Henrietta and I had another scrape.

All about me is red. Red as poppies' yearning open succulent mouths. Mist breathes across the bloodshot sky, over cerise sheets of deep water. Mist circles the masts of the *Hopeful Adventure* as she slips sedately from the bay, sliding into that wondrous sea – forgetfulness.

My dearest Miss Mitford,

. . . what makes me write to you so very soon as this morning, is to beg you not to take the slightest trouble about the baskets which are worth none, & also to beg for Mr. Naylor's book . . . Don't send it in the basket, because that would be the overthrowing of the return-basket principle. I mentioned the returning of the baskets only because I had fancied you would have no more trouble in accomplishing it than was involved in writing my name on the other side of the direction card (by the way – the first came back safely), but I do assure you that the race of basket-makers is not extinct here, barbarous as we are, & that Dr. Mitford may & shall have his fish without any return-basket

to put it in. In the meantime, try to forgive me. *I am sure it must need an effort — for if it had not been for this fussy & most unpoetical thrift of mine, you might not have known a word of the neighbourhood of the omnibus — not for another year at least! . . .*

. . . No plan fixed about my removal to London! I LONG to be at home — but am none the nearer for that . . .

I must train my thoughts away from the trivia of fish baskets. But does my dear friend Miss Mitford know *what it is to be shut up in a room by oneself, to multiply one's thoughts by one's thoughts — how hard it is to know what 'one's thought is like' — how it grows and grows, and spreads and spreads, and ends in taking some supernatural colour — just like mustard and cress on a (wet) flannel in a dark closet?*

4 June 1839

Ever dearest Arabel,

Bummy has just interrupted me by bringing in a 'water-colour drawing left as a gift by Mr. Weale to me'. But no, no, Bummy! You can't take me in so adroitly. It is a copy of a drawing of Mr. Weale's, & very well executed by Brozie — excellently well considering that he never tried water-colours before, & I shall praise him for it up to the tops of the hills. In the meantime I am to tell you about our late visitors . . .

Seeing Mr. Weale gave to me tremendous pleasure. He entered my bedroom. My heart leapt up. Could he not have stood nearer? Or, better still, sat upon the bed itself instead of the armchair opposite? There are two sides to my bed: the company side and the private side. This I will not explain to Mr. Weale should he return to Torquay, but instead beg that he take the private side, for it never shall be tainted with the memory of anyone else's presence. Mr. Weale is a noble and handsome naval doctor from Plymouth. His strong Irish accent is potent music to my ears. His sepia paintings fill me with fire. My desire to touch him was overwhelming, to reach out and . . . If our lips should meet I would not faint but would draw him closer by warm tides of hope.

Mr. Weale's visit also brought certain discomforts — I longed so much for him *not* to leave my bedside.

When Bro said, 'Mr. Weale is half mad,' I could have thrown my arms around Bro. I adore the wild spontaneity in Mr. Weale's nature. I did implore him to examine me. And this he did twice for an hour and a half at a time. I felt then, as I do now, that *I was purring*. It was *extraordinary*. '*The cough is spinal*,' he finally said. When we were next alone Mr. Weale said it was a '*nervous cough*'. He then made me talk of poetry, and gave me Coleridge's works – though I was nervous, I did not cough. I remember one sentence he said when last examining me word for word: '*There may be disease upon the lungs, but it is* not *beyond the reach of remedies, or you could scarcely have that countenance which buoys me up with hope every time I look at you.*' He asked, '*Has the stethoscope been used?*' I replied, 'Yes,' thinking he would examine me with his. He did not. Yet I know he took a great fancy to me, and I to him. More of his exact words come to me; not words he said to me but to others *of me*: '*As long as Miss Barrett is in the drawing-room I certainly will not think of going out of the house. She is a sensitive person, and whilst I was conversing with Miss Barrett, it was only by the strongest effort that I could keep myself from bursting into tears.*' How I would have wept too! Wept to share such deep emotion with him as he with me. Bro says Mr. Weale has confided to him his tendencies to fall in love, and his predilection to wanting to commit suicide, which still constantly recurs. He confided to Bro that, like me, he sometimes hates to be alive.

And yet all joy turns to sadness – there is his wife, Mrs. Weale, to consider. I despise creatures such as she for their *unwomanliness*. Is despise too strong a word? I think not. I had to force my hand to shake hers. Simply touching her skin caused my insides to shiver. But she is of little – no – no importance to me. Mrs. Weale shed many tears and Bro tells me she said she was '*very sure she was insane*'. I could hardly keep from going downstairs to Mr. Weale and would have stayed there until dawn had Bro not carried me, bodily, protesting and gesticulating otherwise, from the drawing-room.

I blame my frailness on this weather, and on gathering dust in bed for so long. *I Believe I Am Better*. Everyone was on the beach today but Bro laid me down and shut the door. He threatened to lock me into my room. I have persuaded Dr. Barry to let me go out. But 'in the chair'! Staying 'in the chair' he insists upon. I shall show him I can do more. Papa has allowed Bro to purchase for me a small yacht, *Bella Donna*. I wish my yacht to be brought to the front door because the chairs are liable to irregular outbreaks of tremors and convulsions and give me palpitations.

Dr. Barry has lent me *Wanderings in Search of Health* by Dr. Cummings, another of his patients. My discovery from having studied this is that my sudden improvement results from a healing of the soul and spirit effected by Mr. Weale, to whom, if he would but allow me, I would give all mine own inheritance in order for him to work no longer as a doctor but to give his days to artistry. He is to commence a series of graphic illustrations of English poetry and I am to let him have some references to passages susceptible of such illustration. Already I know what I will send – extracts from Prior, Chaucer, Browne and Fletcher. For me, Mr. Weale will do some illustrations to my poems in *The Seraphim*.

. . . There now! You are more than obeyed. I have told you everything. Oh! but I shdnt. forget a parting party on Friday night. Dr. & Mrs. Barry stopped once or twice to beg Mr. Weale to moderate his ardour a little, as really nobody cd. hear them for him! Certainly he does 'roar like a nightingale'. But I kept my gravity admirably upstairs – having got over the first shock. Really, that first night there did seem no prospect for me but to laugh on till dawn! And Crow's imperative, 'Now indeed, ma'am, you MUST read your Psalms', didn't do much good – as you may suppose! . . .

11 June 1839

Dear Mr. Weale,

The water-colour drawing is extremely beautiful and suggestive. The moonlight in it cannot be said to have 'no business there' – for it comes like a spirit upon the ruin – the place for spirits – and reconciles us to desolation. You have done what is said to be impossible, 'painted a thought'. And I am satisfied to hear in the silence of your picture, Spenser's very own voice . . .

. . . Thank you again and again! I have written out some suggestions for paintings – as you asked me to do. Should you like any of them and wish for more, I shall be very glad to purvey for you again . . .

My dear friend Mr. Hugh Stuart Boyd,

I take the liberty, which I know you will not be angry about, of enclosing to you a letter of private gossip for my dear Arabel. Will you be so very kind as to enclose it to her as soon as you conveniently can. Perhaps you would allow a servant to take it to her in the course of the day . . .

Dr. Barry says today is the day I am to go out on the sea.

I experience a rush of energy – oh, to be out on the sea with no walls, simply breezes; no ceiling but the blue imposing sky; no hard floors.

'Am *I* to sail the yacht?' I ask Bro.

'We'll see,' Bro replies.

Bella Donna is at the end of a short jetty, the sails wrapped about the mast. Beside her, an aged barefoot sailor. His trousers, patched with sail cloth, emit the strong odour of sun-dried seaweed and stale salt-fish. The skin on his face resembles old wet leather. He speaks a language unknown to me. No doubt he is at home on the bare and empty water's reach.

'You must be the boatswain. Payment, in lieu of your mackerel catch, comes when the ladies are safely back. Understand?' Bro says to him. The old boatswain doesn't look like he understood.

'Poor old beast,' Bummy murmurs. 'Won't you join us?' she asks Bro.

'No'. He hesitates, glances along the jetty. 'Tomorrow?'

Crow unburdens herself of the blankets, pillows and feather eiderdowns, and they tumble onto thick sodden ropes coiled, hideously, in the bottom of the boat. She reaches a hand up to mine. I can only nod thanks. I am near to fainting on the cushioning when Bro says I must stand up to let Bummy in then sit down. This rocking sensation is abysmal. I find this place abhorrent and sourly dislike the low unharmonious lap of water against the blue clinker sides. I wish I was back on dry land, and as far from the sea as Hope End was. *Places are ideas that can madden or kill.*

'Can you move?'

'No,' I say.

'No, can *you* move?' Bro asks the boatswain. The old man is searching the stern for the baler which, it transpires, I am seated upon; he then glares at Bro.

My past seems to rise from the seabed, to the pitching tossing surface. Memories of girlhood: I am looking out across the Hope End gardens at rain melting snow; a hollowness inside me stares out too. I am searching through books for life's answers, a feeling fizzes up like bubbles from an ocean bed; I miss the sensual pleasure of movement. Of feeling free. Aching with dispiritedness. It is that piercing pain of being worthless. I am searching through books for life's answers . . .

Leaning over the side of the boat, my face is broken into a thousand pieces; and, as the reflections floating on the gloomy surface diverge and diffuse into fragments that stare up at me, my life seems to be drifting far and rapidly.

First we row out, then, before I know it, the boom is lowered. We women struggle ineffectually with the sheets and cloth. A fresh wind plays with my ringlets. The patched sails are hoisted. We are a jolly party of three in the boat: Bummy, Crow and me.

The boatswain has shipped the oars. His hands are gnarled and scarred from rope cuts and sunburn. A cormorant circles the hull. Afternoon sunlight glints across the waves. Slanting its wings the bird dives – a black arrow driving at full speed after the flight of fish. It surfaces unexpectedly far from the boat, flapping wildly, gulping a large bulge down a thin throat set, impossibly, at right angles.

The hull skims through waves. The sea seems flattened. Torquay is a thin line. Storms roll in from the sea.

Sailing into the wind is reminiscent of galloping Moses on gusty days across the Malvern Hills. Wind gusts buffeted so strongly one could barely breathe. Moses angled into squalls, the wind blowing itself into a fury. I see a mistress in early girlhood who enjoyed riding best of all . . . *galloping 'til the trees raced past her and clouds were shot over her head like horizontal arrows from a giant's bow . . . leaping over ditches – feeling the live creature beneath her swerve and bound with its own force.* And, with her hair splaying, she lets the reins fall slack. Moses gains speed in a sudden spurt, launching over a brook. Sky and hills, a boundless sea.

Watching the hull rising and falling, I feel flushed and warm

inside. I am almost venturesome for a long sea-voyage. With the
boatswain holding the main sheet taut and steadying my hand on
the tiller – I am sailing! As the boat leans more heavily the water
lures me. Quite unexpectedly I fall in love. I do love the sea. Waves
are liquid passion. The sea is *visible poetry*.

The boatswain says, 'Rain comin.' Unmoved, he stares ahead.
The sky is wild. Above the chop of waves an elevated dark jagged
dome appears, thrashed by spuming foaming breakers. I watch black
wings of clouds unfold against the sky. The boatswain swoops
down on me, the tiller shudders under my grip; the rudder resists
shoving weighty water around.

'Good steering, by Jove!' Bummy shouts. 'That rock, I see it
clearly now.'

And, as the sky grows darker, for the swarthy bank of cloud
rolls nearer, I turn my head quickly. This makes me giddy. The
boatswain says not a word.

From the water Torquay is a long green line backed by deep
blue hills. It is like viewing the bay through a telescope; houses
reside snugly folded into dales. I can make out people on the
steep rises up cliffs, between buildings and on winding paths;
paths which look the same as those I thought nothing of scrambling up six years ago when scaling the slopes to Ruby
Cottage . . . *the view is grand, extensive, and beautiful beyond description.* But the five-mile journey to the Boyds' was problematic,
with the toll to pay to pass through two turnpikes. Oh, but the
scenery was glorious. *Such a sea of land; the sunshine throwing its
light; & the clouds, their shadows, upon it! Sublime sight . . . I looked
on each side of the elevated place where I sat. Herefordshire all hill
& wood – undulating & broken ground! – Worcestershire throwing
out a grand, unbroken extent . . . One prospect attracting the eye, by
picturesqueness: the other the mind, by sublimity. My mind seemed
spread north, south, east & west over the surface of those extended
lands: and, to gather it up again into its usual compass, was an effort.*
But I was full of energy then. *Dashing up hills; rolling presto,
prestissimo down.*

Mr. Boyd and I had corresponded for nearly a year before our
first meeting. Papa would not permit me to visit Mr. Boyd before
he had visited me, because that 'wouldn't do'. But I was lucky

enough to pass him one morning on my way to the Trants' and a
meeting was arranged. As luck would have it though, when the
day arrived, the pony pulling the wheelbarrow, our three-wheeled
carriage, bolted downhill, throwing Arabel and me from our vehicle,
which promptly overturned. So I was badly shocked when intro-
duced to this pleasantly attractive man, tallish and yet like a boy,
with a slight figure. I remember his fair features; his skin almost
bleached of colour; his expression, placid. He is completely blind.
His eyes lack even the slightest hint of life, and any promise of
ever having sight! Hugh Stuart Boyd. I am not as cold as he, & if
our friendship seemed strained it was because of this: *I am not of
a cold nature, & cannot bear to be treated coldly. When cold water is
thrown upon a hot iron, the iron hisses.* So I would boil over for hours
in near hysterics after my long visits amounted, at most, to my
reading Greek aloud to him. How often did I wail *O God, if there
is a God, save my soul, if I have a soul.*

Bummy leans over the yacht's side, suddenly horribly sick.
Fluctuating with now gentle breezes are waves of a nauseous stench,
as the long white trail sinks. Bummy questioned my visits, she
could see through a post.

She decided Boyd ungentlemanly and disgusting – because I was
goose enough to say I'd spent an evening alone with him. She had
an evident aversion to my friendship and everything and anybody
connected with him, which lighted me up into a passion. I must
have been twenty-five when I wrote of him excessively in my
diary . . . *the mention of Mr. Boyd's name at a dinner party amongst a
crowd of people whom I cared nothing about was like Robinson Crusoe's
detection of a man's footprint in the sand.* But my diary was not to be
shown to anyone. How many entries Mr. Boyd has I dare not think.
I remember once writing . . . *I wish I had half the regard which I
retain for him impressed on this paper that I might erase it thus* ****.
But I could not! In truth I longed for love, exceeding love; a love
which after dear Mama died I would never find again. Poor health,
as many a Shakespearean character demonstrates, comes from unre-
quited love.

Did Mr. Boyd ever feel *anything* for me? My feelings for him
now are tarnished.

On land the boatswain moves awkwardly, like a wounded animal.

'Poor beast,' I echo Bummy in a muffled voice. Bro says he was worried we had been caught in the throes of a storm and would never again be seen. He scolds the boatswain. For a weird moment the breath of life deserts me. Resting in the bottom of the boat, I am shattered, broken. I fear it is Bro who will leave, never to return. This madness – a deep, deep woe, the crippling agony of sorrow; of grief – departs as quickly as it came as Bro helps me from the boat. He carries me to the chair and wheels me back to Beacon Terrace, and I see the fear for what it was. Absolute madness.

Chapter Five

Sheba

CINNAMON HILL ESTATE
August 1838

'Run! Run!' Lickle Phoebe's yelling. 'Run! Run!' she keeps up yelling. Smooth as palm oil she's running over hillside sloping down to shack village. *Fuuuuffuu-ffuu* abeng sounds. Dusk glow's a-coming.

'Roof! De roof!' Phoebe bawls.

Sun's dying on a string of sweat-glistening backs stumbling all over cane-piece track, passing distant mountain ridges, bush, wild creeper-strung forests, blue far-reaching sea. We cane-workers walk tired, too tired to even raise we heads to familiar smells moving on evening breeze – pigs, chickens, shit, sugar, sweat, drifting and mixing and swelling with fire-smoke from somewhere, and a strong sickly scent of flowers rising up in falling rain.

But sour smoke stings me nostril, and me get a funny feeling, hearing Phoebe's bawl grow louder though she runs further away.

'Fiah-smoke!' Phoebe's bawling. Past trash-house she body flits, thin, shadow-like, fast-moving where oil-lamps light sand in yellow-brown strips, screaming, 'Guinea grass gawn fram de roof!'

Smoke turns sky a dusky mule grey. Steamy jets snort from boiler-house and suddenly we all running, cutting narrow lanes twisting between shacks, hearts thumping, dreading galloping hollering militiamen, bounding, baying dogs.

Eleanor shrieks, 'Me shack! Me shack!' at fleeing shadows.

Reaching Eleanor's yard me stop. Old Simeon's mule starts up braying. Smoky fog curls from Eleanor's open-mouthed shack – me sleeping place since Isaac's gone.

Streaming sweat, breathing hard, 'Oo yu did see?' Windsor ask him little sister, Phoebe.

'No,' say Lickle Phoebe. 'Me cyaan say oo me did see.'

Windsor's eyes roll back in him head. 'W'appen den? Duppy set shack on fiah?'

Lickle Phoebe's turned mute. She stares at she brother with dulled eyes. Rain patters keenly – a sad answer – falling into we stunned silence of shock.

Dashing forward, Eleanor flings a skin bottle of drinking water at shack roof. A small sheet of water opens up, singed wattle walls sizzle and seethe. Another bottle of water catches shack with a wet slap, rushing down shack's wattle body.

Panting, Big Robert plods up all floppy-bellied from drinking first cane juice. Caught in shock, 'Where yu hab to sleep?' he say. 'W'appen? Where Eleanor, Phoebe, Sheba sleep now?'

Windsor shouts at Robert, 'Best ting yu cun do's shut yu mouth.'

Big Robert stands by Eleanor's doorway, nodding, taking stock. Then he grabs Eleanor's bottle and hastily thrusts it on dusty yard dirt. Making off he runs to milking shack, picks biggest skin buckets in shack doorway, takes off running again, heading fe millstream. Kneeling at stream bank he ducks, dunking buckets once, twice. Soon he's running back, shooting great bucketfuls of water into dusk-darkened sky. Journey after journey Big Robert makes, running like some wild thing until Eleanor's shack's soaked.

'E'll empty millstream,' Windsor say, and all we laugh guilty, shifting into a huddled body. Water crashes against once bunch-grass thatched beams, water beads mix with rain spraying from dark red-hot sky, giving shack a dripping skin.

Me close into a ring with Sylvia, Windsor and Lickle Phoebe; heads jerked forward, hunched shoulder rubbing hunched shoulder; voices, a low rumble in night's gathering darkness.

'Where Mister Sam?' me ask.

Lickle Phoebe's words dash out, 'Yu tink e to blame?'

'Some say e ride to Spanish Town,' Sylvia say.

'No,' say Uncle Ned gruffly, 'e stay at Greenwood.' Sylvia, Uncle Ned and me try to wrap we arms round Eleanor but Eleanor breaks free and turns towards village edge, a grey shape melting into tall grass heads. Sickness settles deep in me belly as dusk settles on tall grasses Eleanor's become part of.

'Only lesson we learn's cheat, steal, punish wid violent deed,' Sylvia say.

'We swear,' Big Robert pleads. 'We swear to minister nebber again we show anger. Whip's bin we teacher, true, but whatebber buckra do we cyaan go back on we werd.'

Windsor's eyes roll back in him head. 'Robert, dem a-cheat. Dem a-cheat we.'

'If it wasn't fe de rain all we shacks'd be in flames,' me say. 'Buckra mek dis into war village. Betta we live dan die. Break away to Maroon Town. Break away to Mountain People.'

'Amen. Amen,' Sylvia say. 'But sometime Maroons betray we people.'

'Shsh!' say Windsor.

Silence rings in me ear, broken by a deep growling coming from village edge leading to cane piece.

'Yu sleep wid we tonite,' Sylvia whispers to me. 'Don't go back to Isaac's empty shack.' Sharply Sylvia's voice turns on Eleanor's dawta, 'Phoebe, fetch wood fram yard stack, feed up cook-fiah.'

'Shsh!' say Windsor. 'Wot's dat?'

We listen. Harsh gasps stab smoke-flooded air.

Lickle Phoebe unties she old ash-dusted head rag, scratches flattened hair. Then she just stands, stone-like, eye-searching fe she mama, Eleanor. 'Me cyaan see far,' she say, 'me eye not good. Most ting far away turn soft an blur.'

Sylvia's raising a fist to clout Lickle Phoebe. 'Chile, yu cyaan ear? Phoebe, fetch wood fram yard stack, feed up cook-fiah!'

'No. No,' me say to Sylvia. 'Mek Lickle Phoebe run to rum shop, fetch white rum fe Eleanor, tell Uncle Ned me pay im.'

Eleanor's yard backs onto Sylvia's. Burnt-out windows of Eleanor's still smoking shack watch Sylvia plod heavily round shack back and towards she yard.

Me eye, then feet, follow de path Lickle Phoebe's stare made. It leads me into grasses rooted on shack-village edge. Palms stand high above, huge fern-like fronds shuffling and swaying in warm winds, black against a blue-black sky. Grasses feel up all around tickling me legs. From grasses rises a sound, a humming, not 'Hi!

de buckra, hi!' but a new lonelier song, a song me think me don't know before now, like rasping sound of sand on metal or stone. Me eye and ear keep hunting fe danger making this growling tune. Grassy patches twitch-shiver. Darkly a shape moves. Tough to me ears this tune torments me, fe deep inside me can tell it's one me do know.

'Eleanor,' me call softly. 'Eleanor.' Snarling growl steadily comes louder, clearer, but just as strange. Like a mill grinding corn on a silent afternoon it cuts, torments, this rasping scrunch scrunch scrunch grating sound filling me with fear. Me keep trying to find where this coarse singing comes from. Behind, gnarling de tune, me hear a rhythmic murmur.

Crouched down, Eleanor's body me find in a quivering nest of hip-high grasses. Reaching onto hands, knees, Eleanor's blind to me; shaking she head, fingers digging sharp into cracked earth. Me shiver, knowing what this music must be. Lying on she belly, Eleanor presses she wide nose and proud face flat in dirt.

'Where's we God?' she wails.

Me only have one answer, 'Dere's no God ere,' me say.

Softly Eleanor moans, 'So fear of God don't touch me.' Squatting down by Eleanor me hand reaches out to feel she ash-sprinkled hair. 'Don't touch!' Eleanor shouts, and at last she head twists to me, tears streaming down cheeks, into mouth corners. Panic grips me. She looks at me but doesn't seem to know who me is.

Kneeling at she side, 'Wot yu say?' me ask, and wipe tears with skirt cloth from she cheeks, nose. But she weary face won't come settled. Cyaan wipe we past away cyaan wipe we past away.

Through rustling grass walks Lickle Phoebe. 'Phoebe! Over ere,' me shout. Lickle Phoebe hands me rum bottle she's carried from Uncle Ned's. Eleanor puts rum bottle to she lips and, supping and swallowing, shudders, fe Ned's white rum must bite she throat fe it strong like buckra's paint stripper.

'All dat's left me sack, Eleanor's sack de blaze caught,' me say to Lickle Phoebe.

Lickle Phoebe looks at me blankly. Then she head swings round fe grasses rustle again as gentle-slow Big Robert strolls up.

Peeling rum bottle from Eleanor's grasp, 'Dis won't elp,' Big Robert say bluntly, thrusting bottle back into Lickle Phoebe's hands.

He prises Eleanor up off folded knees. She don't resist. Lifting Eleanor bodily, he locks she into forceful arms and, going limp – legs flopping like a sleepy pickney's – she looks smaller than she did. With thoughtful movements Big Robert short-steps, careful as chicken searching fe grain in tall grasses, past palms, past Eleanor's ash-stained shack and cook-fiah Sylvia's laid in she yard. Tenderly, so she don't hit wood planks hard, he releases Eleanor onto Sylvia's verandah.

Curling before fiah me just want to sink down into roots of mountains, into land, dirt, be part earth again. All we shack village fallen quiet. Sameway as hate, something strong have risen up, hot like flames. But Eleanor cyaan take no more uprisings since losing Isaac, she younger son, and all we drenched in a dreadful knowledge that whatever we do – even though we have freedom – we cyaan gain, cyaan win. All we numbed into a new silence fe though no one can say it, Eleanor's teeth crunched dirt, eating dirt that one day soon will wrap all we so we disappear forever in its warm clutch. And all she want – all we want's that day to hurry up and come.

Windsor's shack faces Sylvia's. Windsor shuffles from him doorway, across front yard to Sylvia's verandah, hunched over with weight of a prize kid goat he carries slung across shoulders by its hooves. Folding himself down beside Eleanor, Windsor say, 'Big feed tonite, Mama.' Neatly Windsor's cane-scarred hands slide pigknife from creeper-rope belt. Skilfully he plunges knife blade into goat flesh, screwing up him eyes, face. He peels back tough lithe goatskin.

'Phoebe, fetch wood fram yard stack, feed up cook-fiah,' Sylvia say.

Peering out from Sylvia's doorway, Lickle Phoebe beckons me to follow. Over yard sand and into burnt-out shack she heads.

Eleanor's yard's just that. One yard square. She shack – a one-chamber shed – holds little room to move. No chair. No table. No window. No bed. Just remains of one ragged charred sleeping sack. Air inside's sliced and tainted by strong smoke strands. Wattle walls Isaac and me clay-plastered and whitewashed with lime we dug from riverbanks where soft limestone rises, all scorched black, branded with charcoal-chip burns. Bunch-grass clumps have fallen on sodden breadnut-tree board flooring. Stars glint between shack's roof-beam shell.

Tiny love marks Isaac and me scratched into clay walls first night Isaac kissed me, gone.

'Phoebe! Sheba!' Sylvia shouts. 'Come out-a dere!' Sylvia's still shaking she head when we peer round Eleanor's doorway.

Cook-fires leap in each yard, sparks jump from whining flames into softly falling rain. Yard-dogs draw in on firesides. Fat moon now lights yards blue. Squatting beside Sylvia, rocking on heels, Windsor fondles a tobacco pipe silently, and a picture of what yard was comes back to me. Yard's a place on fine nights fe gossip, story-telling; a place we group around gambling fe buttons, tobacco, rum. When flames burst me see you. Me see you tall. Standing proud. Me miss you arm round me shoulder. Dappled with dancing light you features flow into each other – a beautiful shimmer of black skin – as you face fattens with laughter. Isaac, me watch till me cyaan watch no more.

'Phoebe!' Sylvia's shouting. 'Fetch sack fulla peas fe shelling.'

Up Lickle Phoebe gets and disappears behind fruit sacks slung over hardwood beams of Sylvia's room.

Smoke sighs long, threading its grey curls between pimento leaves arrayed over cook-fire. Slowly yard returns to a place of warmth. Humping pea sack up on verandah rail, Lickle Phoebe sings out to Windsor, 'Goat dun yet?'

Wiping hands on trousers, Windsor strolls around goat pelt pegged out to dry and cure before it's tanned fe jerkin. Crouching, he prods ribs, goat flank, shin, roasting over flames. Rising, he levers fat steaks out with poking sticks. Squatting back on heels, fanning heat, Windsor drives smoke from him face like swatting flies away. He hands best bits – goat liver, heart – to Eleanor, him mama, first. Shuffling, curving aside snake-like, Eleanor coils back from she son's hand offering goat meat.

Me move over to Windsor, whisper what me have to tell. Brow crinkling, Windsor's head shakes, nods. He passes Trouble-Too-Much and Lickle Phoebe best goat meat wrapped in palm fronds, then forces a fatty slab into him own mouth, bulging jaw muscles working. Eleanor takes on pea sack and shelling. Lickle Phoebe's teeth tear goat flesh.

'Phoebe, yu so hungry yu eat goat raw?' Trouble-Too-Much jokes. Phoebe looks at him blankly, munches meat chunks, swallows hard. Waiting fe meat to cool, Trouble sucks on him pipe, watching me through curling tobacco smoke. 'Elp me,' Trouble say to me, 'carry drinking water fram Charles' well by boiler-house.'

Deep gazing into firelight me answer Trouble-Too-Much, 'Also me tek back rum bottle an give money to Uncle Ned.'

So, after we finish feeding, me go beside Trouble down moonlit paths, passing below great house, by overseer's house, by sugar works, to fetch boiler-house water, then me head off, pay fe rum and wander back alone through grasses and along beaten track towards shack village. Footfalls reach me ear, padding soft like a stray dog following scent trails. *Is yu, Isaac, come back? No, sounds too solid fe yu tread.* And then me think me hear many feet tramping paths leading to shacks. Like hurricane rips leaves from a trembling tree till it's blown flat, me feel fear strip me, rush up me back, fe me cyaan suffer no more, me crave calm, peace, me hunger fe you, Isaac – soft soft curve of you lips.

Thundering from nowhere and everywhere buckra boots make de stiff sound of men running. Scorching fast through tall grass like a horse-team suddenly let loose, stampeding behind me. Veering off trash-house path, leaping into waist-deep grass, me head fe provision grounds, darting through pools of moonlight, arms, legs branch-scratched. Tearing along cane-piece track, what flashes through me mind's how did me reach cane rows so quickly? Sprinting faster than spirit winds me feet dash into ratoon rows, bound through rippling knee-high cane.

But they're ahead of me – cane swirling water-like round legs – and behind, herding me towards cane-piece heart, bringing me stumbling onto knees, tumbling down on hard night-cooled earth.

Men shouting across me fallen crumpled body: 'Richard!'

'Over here! I'm here!'

'Where's Richard Barrett?' another shout ask.

Cyaan heave meself up. Night sky opens, heavily dropping its insides till me crushed crushed crushed.

Sea of sugar killed me? Pure darkness comes. How to move, get up, get out, escape from a sea of hurt inside?

Yanking me arm's Lickle Phoebe. *Buckra's face lives in me head. Me clawed de pit of him back; skin, flesh. Flattened into earth, forced down by raw shafts of pain; in me blood buckra's runs, slippery red between me legs, me belly-guts ripped savagely.*

Sky spits on me face. Woken again by Lickle Phoebe me wanting to ask, *Me drowned and buried already?* but words don't surface. Inside me swells like a large sea face – unthinking, unfeeling but moving.

'W'appen?' Phoebe asks, as heavily more rains come.

Me told Phoebe? No, me cyaan, fe this happened too many times fe me to talk. Words and arms drag me up, hold me, crutch-like. Clinging to Lickle Phoebe, blundering past spirits whirling round trees, me feet search fe a path to wattle-shack village and Sylvia's yard.

'Tek off she clothes,' Sylvia's voice say. *Rasp of cloth tearing. Peeled petticoat over me head.*

'She don't have no clothes left,' Phoebe say. 'Skin's caked in mud.'

'Well, wrap she in someting.'

All me feel's one endless ache as Sylvia and Phoebe lay me down.

'Eleanor an Sheba cun say w'appen to dem at Mo'bay court-room,' me see Trouble's lips say to me.

Violently me laugh. Trouble-Too-Much's lantern-lit face charges towards me, him flashing eyes hold loathing. No cure come fe me laughter, and loss of clear thought.

Towering above like a dark tree in shack doorway, Trouble shifts from foot to foot. Shoulders rolling, he leans against rotten wood.

But Windsor have kind eyes, gentle voice fe him stand further back. 'It don't matter oo does go. Yu know buckra don't know one nigger fram anodder.'

'True,' say Sylvia.

Memories fade when me think of revenge. *Smashup everyting? Fight buckra laws? Cyaan fight fe justice in dis lawless place.* Me head's thudding, heart's hammering, sickness's a blister spreading out from me belly, out from between legs. Hurt's beyond me now, so is rage.

Chapter Six

Kaydia

CINNAMON HILL ESTATE
15 February 1840

Raising him head low from soft pillows, 'Is it Sunday yet?' asks
Mister Sam.

'Sunday come tomorrow,' I say, and turn to open jalousie blinds.
How I find it within me to speak gently, I don't know.

Hens cackle below bedchamber, rooting around clutches of eggs.
Friday lies in Mister Sam's hammock, slung between two cottonwood trees. Stretching arms skyward, he yawns sleepily. Dawn
glows golden orange. Blue hills. Blue sea.

'Yu must mek yu will, Mister Sam,' I say.

He flinches horribly. 'Kaydie, Kaydie, help me,' he moans. 'Is it
heaven awaits me?'

'Church minister e can ansa yu dat.'

'Are they coming, my cousin, Demar and Carey?'

Hall clock strikes six. Cold blue eyes stare straight through me.
How to slip from what's past, from what is, from what will be?
Can't nurse you night and day, I'm thinking. Can't do this heavy
job. Mister Sam's eyes close to escape my accusing face. Feeling
bruised and beaten I'm searching for quill pen, inkwell, nibs, fighting
back strong emotions. Can't fight memories. Can't ever be rid of
Sunday. Sunday crashes through bedchamber, smashing in Sunday
comes. Sunday storms into my head, that Sunday when I first wished
Mister Sam dead.

Charles was bashing Cinnamon Hill front door, bellowing, 'Kaydia!
Kaydia! Mary Ann hide where?'

'Wot yu waan she for?' I asked. 'Yu don't go to church no more?'

'Mister Sam! Mister Sam! Me come fe Mister Sam! Let me in, Kaydia, e bin wid we Mary Ann.'

'Me cyaan let yu in,' I whispered, my hands behind my back clutching door-frame.

Clouting solid front door, 'Open! Open!' Charles screamed. 'Old Simeon might be half blind but e aint deaf, e tell me Mister Sam have him way wid we dawta. Me kill im!' Charles screamed.

Cold. I went cold, though it was hot like every other day. Dreading what I might see I was walking up stairs, along corridors, my belly a churning sea, heart beating fast, painfully – I felt I shouldn't be there. Noises leaked from blue bedchamber, odd muffled grunts, one long deep wheeze. Struck by a bolt of fear I stood unable to walk on in. But I did, being tied to Mary Ann by my heartstrings which came from inside out by then. What was I to do but turn brass handle slowly, silently, opening door enough for my eyes to move across bedchamber? Mister Sam was astride Mary Ann doing what they do. I closed door shut stealthily, noiselessly. Swallowing vile bile in my saliva what I felt I'm too sick to explain.

Down stairs I ran and through great hall to dining-room. I saw Charles' head outside sink below a window until it almost disappeared and all I could see was a brown brow topped with a curly crop of black hair.

'Me cyaan let yu in,' I whispered. 'Yu voice threaten murder.'

Window glass rattled; one pane was unlatched. Charles shoved frame up, glass shuddering, and slid a thickset arm inside. 'Ow yu can call yuself she mama? See,' he cried. 'See dese tings?' Charles' hand unfolded. Earrings flashed and glinted, guilty rocking on him palm. 'Old Simeon say e did yesterday find dem under flagstones in stable-block. Mary Ann hide dere.' Charles' cheek muscles twisted tight as rope, he slipped him thin slanted bearded face through window opening. 'Now, tell me it isn't true!' he screamed. Crouched on wide window-sill this new sharp-faced Charles glared wide. I knew every muscle in that trembling body. He slid down onto yacca floor. We stared at each other, eyes making four – shouting *Who destroyed we dawta? Mister Sam? Yu? Me? Yu love she, don't yu? We both do* – we thoughts echoing from one mind to another.

Full of badness Charles pushed past me, hurled himself up stairs, shouting over top banister, 'Yu cyaan work fe im no more, Mister Sam. Yu ear? Me kill im!'

I dashed after Charles. He bashed blue chamber door, I remember brass lock hanging loose then dropping clang on yacca floor. At first I thought Mister Sam was still in blue bedchamber too.

'Rass ooman out! Gwan!' Charles bawled at me. I fled to upper verandah, huddled in a corner, clinging onto rails.

'No! No!' Mary Ann was bawling. 'Me won't leave!' Charles dragged she shrieking body round blue bedchamber, I heard each horrible bumping sound. Loud thuds too. Like she tortured in hell's fire Mary Ann bawled and shrieked.

'Leave she alone!' I yelled, coming out from my cowering place. 'For God's sake leave she alone!'

Throwing Mary Ann at my feet, 'Filth!' Charles shouted. Him face had turned iron grey.

'Afore Mister Sam mek militia assemble yu must be away!' I screamed. 'Gwane! Militiamen'll shoot if dem find yu ere like dis.'

'Mary Ann tek no more presents fram Mister Sam,' Charles said to me. 'E teach we pickney to be bad. Yu know Minister Waddell offering me church eldership? No! Me say no! Fe me watch over me lickle girl! Yu cyaan care fe she!'

Hot blood rushed up my face. Shaking, I drew Mary Ann up, clasping she head to my chest. Pressed like geckos against verandah wall, mama against flattened daughter – if I could have made she and me disappear then I would have – she head nestling into my dress, my fingertips taming, sinking into wild matted hair.

Clinging so tight they burned, Mary Ann's little hands riveted onto my arms; nails scraping, tearing skin.

'Me tek care of she best way me can,' I finally said. Charles threw himself at me. Dashed against stone wall I couldn't breathe, or see. My body burned prickly red, spicy rage filled my head. Suddenly Mary Ann broke free.

Bawling over him shoulder, 'Wotever yu do, God, E'll know,' Charles scurried, rat-like, down stairs, dragging Mary Ann. She quick eyes searched mine. Then she vanished with him.

Peeping from shoe closet now Charles gone, Mister Sam's face wore a silly meek grin, hungry for forgiveness. I couldn't find any words, Mary Ann torn from me.

Always I'll be hunted down by this. Though I too hungered – hungered for peace – sickness rose in my belly. Disgust. Guilt. Shame. Hating myself, I moved away from him.

Charles kept Mary Ann in old shacks near sugar boiling house. Weeks passed before I saw she again. Months passed before Mary Ann came back to work at great house.

Door handle creaks, breaking into my thoughts. Opening blue bedchamber door, in steals Doctor Demar, muddy-eyed face still swollen with drink. He looks hard at Mister Sam's sleeping body. Behind Demar, stealthily quiet, creeps Mister Sam's cousin from Greenwood and Mister Carey. Mister Carey have hairy hands, too large for him lanky arms and lean body; stringy hair curls straggle round him doleful face.

Rooting through all trouble that's been I step back from bedside. Mister Carey whispers in Doctor Demar's ear, 'You put it perfectly. You're right, Sam's father could have done more, yet granting Sam attorneyship of this particular estate was his only option for keeping the boy here. And what with the apprenticeship system over and done with I will have less to do, that's for sure.'

Mister Sam's cousin says, 'It's not the fact the debts –'

'Shsh,' Mister Carey warns him. 'Better remove your hat.'

'Right then,' says Doctor Demar, 'let's get down to work. Carey, Sam's will? You've got the testament, haven't you? You brought it here from Greenwood?'

Mister Carey says, 'I did. What should I do? Read it back to Sam?'

'Well, we're here as witnesses. Yes,' Doctor Demar says.

Grouped around bedside, three men try to wake Mister Sam. Listening, watching, a sea stretches wide between me and them. Reddened by webs of broken lines Mister Sam's eyes open, then dim, like agony runs through him back and head.

What's past don't go. Don't grow thin. But I feel small stone of hope snug in my belly. Lightness streams into my head while heart-searing sadness swells in my chest. If joy and fear can live together they do, now, within me.

Mister Sam dips nib in inkwell cradled in my palm. *If he tie me into him will Mary Ann should come back closer to me. Pa might change, might treat me better.* Quill quivers, scrape-scratching ink tracks swirl. *That sprawling pattern sign him will?* Stretching out to Doctor Demar, holding up parchment, quill pen, Mister Sam's hand's shaking – I'm sinking into a basin of blue sea. Silence cuts. Lips murmur, a deeper level than him. My floating feeling vanishes. My name wasn't spoken. *Mister Sam would leave me with him pickney, without money fram him will? Can hope be ended this easily?* I'm thrown, twisting turning without warning into sea's drowning grasp. Tears won't stop coming. Can't swim from painful memories. If Mister Sam could live longer he might mention me.

Mister Sam's cousin sighs. First time I've seen him sober. Mister Carey's eyebrows crinkle together, he steps around dirty sheets and bedclothes. I try to hold Mister Sam in my sight but sameway as me to him, Mister Sam's just shadow. Can't see for pain of swelling anger. Can't hardly breathe for loathing him.

Taking up parchment, Doctor Demar says, 'The maid will make things more orderly in here after we've finished. You'd better hang onto Sam's will, Carey, for safe keeping.' Slowly he crosses blue bedchamber, turns, retraces each step.

Waves draw back, crash forward. Mister Sam's chest rises, falls. Him head flops sideways, words leak from him throat, 'Sacra . . . Hope . . . Kaydie. Sacra . . . Sacram . . . Sacra . . . Hope.' Hope giving me courage. 'Kaydie. Hope.'

Flipping through stiff note books, Doctor Demar asks, 'Carey, can you decipher any of this?' Doctor Demar glances at me, 'Kaydia, can you interpret what Sam says?'

Melting out from chamber wall, 'Me cyaan mek sense out-a nonsense,' I'm saying, hunting for answers before they come. I feel twinges as a dull ache darts like little stitches deep inside my belly. *Mister Sam's pickney stirs. Already?*

'Kaydie . . . Kaydie,' Mister Sam moans.

I'm wanting to punch him up, but I can only stand thinking I'm losing everything; thinking, Pa takes happiness from me. All them do, Charles, Sibyl, Friday, Rebecca Laslie, Mister Sam, Mary Ann. What happens to Mary Ann if I go like Rebecca Laslie, a lunatic way? How Mary Ann'll find love with she face like it is? Scars she have outside. Scars she have within. Ruin and chaos he move into she life.

Straining to raise him head, 'Kaydie,' Mister Sam sighs, 'Hope.

Hope . . .' Four-poster bed's spinning, chamber's spinning. *Him mind changing? Him remembering?* I'm trying to say what's knocking loudly in my head.

Doctor Demar looks round, 'What?' and unplugs stethoscope from one ear.

Me care fe Mary Ann, me dawta. Mister Sam, yu can do what?

'Get Hope, Kaydie. Get Hope,' Mister Sam croaks; lines twitch across him face.

'E waan Ope. Mister Sam ast fe Ope,' I say.

Sitting down on mattress edge, wiping glasses with Mister Sam's clean bed sheet, 'Sam,' Doctor Demar bellows. 'Sam, can you hear me?'

Leaning forward, I listen to Mister Sam's mutterings. 'Me tink e say e waan tek bread an wine,' I tell Doctor Demar. 'Cornwall minister called Hope.'

Doctor Demar quickly stands up rigid. 'Sam wants to partake of the Sacrament?'

'Impossible!' exclaims Mister Sam's cousin.

Carey's mouth twists in surprise. 'After all that's happened, is that wise?'

Doctor Demar prods Mister Sam's chest. 'He hasn't eaten for two whole days.'

Spinning don't stop, trembling beginning. Sweat of cold loss beads my forehead. 'Me cyaan do noting wid im, Mister Demar,' I say, feeling if more tears come I'll never surface again.

'What?' says Doctor Demar. 'What's the matter with the maid?'

Morning shadows slide from Mister Sam's face, turning it yellow-white as planks Pa planes. Sun strikes Christ's body hanging in pure wretchedness above Mister Sam's head, wearing creased crucifix cloth Pa carved for Friday. My eyes turn to floorboards and make out patterns in woodgrain. I have no body to bury but enough loss to drown slow slow slow in raw pain. I hear sea's queer moan rushing out from a shell's open mouth, rushing in. Lost in a blur of arms, legs, floor hits my face.

Pressing on my forehead's a hand, a strong force clamps down my legs. 'Quick, Demar!' Carey shouts. 'Help me restrain the girl. She's liable to attack someone.'

Voices drift overhead. Cool air breathes across my eyelids; jalousie blinds whisper, *Mister Sam, yu a sin. Yu remember wot yu did?* If life could be called back I'd call what happened from that night, change it with a flood of rage: *Yu a man of lies. Pity on you. Shame. Shame. Shame.*

Tugging me by an elbow up onto my feet, Doctor Demar says, 'It's just a mild fainting fit.'

'Are you sure?' asks Carey.

Doctor Demar says, 'See?' fixing my head between firm hands. 'She's acting worse than she feels.'

'God, whatever next?' says Mister Carey in one breath.

'Send for someone to deliver this.' Mister Sam's cousin hurriedly writes a note, blots ink dry, seals parchment with red wax stamp, and gives it to Doctor Demar. 'To Hope Masterton Waddell at Cornwall great house.'

My legs rush away. Stumbling onto knees again, sea-washed shells I hear, hot pink lips pressed to my ear singing, swirling, hissing wave upon wave of sadness reaches from my childhood. From chamber door I see Doctor Demar cross great hall, plunge deep into pressing heat. I wish Rebecca Laslie never left me here at Cinnamon Hill. I wish Mister Sam dead.

'I'm not mistaken,' says Mister Sam's cousin, peering over open desk. 'That *is* Maria's handwriting. You know my wife, Maria. Well, she wrote to Sam last Christmas about a missing jewellery box. She believes Old Simeon stole it while we were staying here about twelve months past. It was a while before Maria realized the box was gone. The box was her mother's – a family heirloom. We never had a reply from Sam to our letter.'

Fear inside me mixes with pure hatred. *Jewellery box on dressing-table. They can tell? Mama Laslie say it not thieving. What we take's still theirs.*

'Sam's been busy in England and with extra responsibilities,' Carey says.

'I know, but once when we stayed at Cinnamon Hill, Old Simeon was caught red-handed with Maria's silver crucifix.'

'Yes, I remember,' Carey says. 'Old Simeon said he'd found the crucifix under a table and was going to return it to Maria.'

'Believe that and you'll believe anything,' Mister Sam's cousin replies. 'I can't understand why Sam kept the monkey on.'

'Give the matter to Junius to resolve. He's the store-key keeper. He's trustworthy enough,' says Mister Carey.

I care not who jewellery box belonged to but am scared for Old Simeon. *Is me do it*, my head-tongue says.

Mister Sam's violently sick again. Waves crest over. Mister Sam's face rolls on pillow lace, skin sameway pale as porcelain jug I bring.

Doctor Demar says, walking in from landing, 'Girl, clear your master's chamber.'

Gathering scrumpled bed shirts, trousers, I can't stand straight to suffer all this shock. I shake trouser pockets out. 'Wantin laundry, Mister Doctor,' I say, and slip Mister Sam's loose coins into my hand as I scoop up a spotted neck-cloth.

I hardly notice other buckra men go while stacking nibs, quills in blue-black desk wood.

Mister Sam's chin's grown stubble. Sweat jewels him back. Him body – a powerful snake – squirms with sudden strength, tightly wrapped in swirling white linen. Letters on Mister Sam's desk catch my eye. Musty memories move, unfolding stiff parchment, of Mister Sam scrumpling up bills. He never paid them.

Lizard-like, Mister Sam's heavily hooded eyes slide shut. He lies still and dumb again. Writing's scrawled across both sides of parchment in my hand, aloud I read but strain to make any meaning of such fancy words: *31st July 1838. Sir Joshua Rowe, Kingston.* I remember Sir Joshua Rowe, Chief Justice of Jamaica, staying at Cinnamon Hill. Memories pour into my head. Disasters long past appear clearly now. Even Chief Justice of Jamaica knew of Mister Sam's wicked ways.

Standing behind Mister Sam in Cinnamon Hill study, wondering how to protect Mary Ann from him, I watched packet ship's sails tighten, white blades slicing a blue skyline.

'When Sir Joshua Rowe arrives I shall enlist his assistance for my swift departure for America,' Mister Sam said. He broke red wax letter seal.

'Packet come?' I asked, watching him read.

Lolling back, he tipped chair up on its legs, rested boots on study-desk edge. He cared little for what I said. Him eye flickered, 'News of the brats at last.' He laughed. 'My sister, Henrietta, would find me a wife. Shall I tell her I already have one?' He glanced through an open window at glistening sea. 'William Weld, damn him. Thank heaven *that* lawsuit's over.' Raising a glass, saying, 'Freedom! At last!' Mister Sam sipped rum then turned straight to me. Back then he had a straw-coloured moustache, it went up and down whenever him lips moved. 'My cousin says we should expect trouble with the slaves tonight. A minor uprising again. Is that true?'

'Me cyaan say, sir.'

Knocking at hardwood study door Old Simeon, munching tobacco, shuffled in. 'Me announcin Minister Ope. E walk in by back door, says e wait in great all fe yu.'

'You can take your leave for now, Kaydie,' Mister Sam said. 'Yes, and before you disappear, remember to leave a full bottle of rum out there for me in the drawing-room.'

But I stayed in study-room after he left. I spied though open door crack and heard all Mister Sam and Minister Hope Waddell said.

They argued. Argued. Argued all afternoon in drawing-room over no more Sunday worship, wages for freed apprentices.

Minister Hope suddenly bawled, 'Sam, you will cease your wicked ways.'

Mister Sam tore through great hall, darted up stairs, shouting, 'What right have you to tell me how to run my own plantation?'

Hope Waddell was shouting, 'The plantation is your father's. Carey's still the attorney!'

Upstairs doors opened and slammed shut. From outside came distant cheering; shouts; it was hard to tell what made such a noise. Looking out from study-room side window, I saw Mary Ann soaking up late-afternoon sunlight beside stove-wood bundles. I saw she in my head – wildly she bolted back and forth in a blue blur. Between me, Charles, Mister Sam, she was caught – a doctor-bird trapped in a glass case. Reason and order vanished in a haze of beating wings flying like my own rage. Mary Ann had not long been back with me working in great house after first time I found she with Mister Sam and Charles had hid she in old shacks. Charles told me minister said he would speak with Mister Sam, put an end to Mister Sam's wicked ways. I went from study-room, ran to minister.

He had fallen silent and was gazing through jalousie blinds across Cinnamon Hill garden. A powerful anger came upon me.

Into drawing-room Mary Ann came running. 'Wot's dat noise, Mama? Wot de cane-cutters waan?' Pulling my apron she said, 'Cane-cutters going down plantation hill.' I glanced through front window and saw a crowd streaming past great-house driveway.

Minister's bawl carried up staircase: 'Sam, the Lord is your Master. Let His spirit guide you.' Shaking with anger minister made to climb staircase. Him soft hand went hard like it'd throttle wood banister.

Afraid to leave Mary Ann near Mister Sam I told she, 'Go. Do yu chores.' I looked down into she twisted and burning with love face.

Yanking my apron, Mary Ann was chanting 'Freedom! Freedom! Freedom! Dat wot cane-cutters say.'

'Trouble reach ere,' I said. 'Mek yuself go, Minister Waddell. Slip troo back door, ride out by cut wind.' Minister's cheeks drained white like bleached starched linen. 'Me lock door behind yu wid Mister Sam key fram under doormat, ere.'

Glancing at we as he left, 'I pity you,' minister said. 'May the good Lord fill you with His strength, for I'll not return to Cinnamon Hill.' He couldn't look at Mary Ann. He knew he had betrayed she. Quickly he was gone. Cinnamon Hill air felt much colder after that.

I don't care if you don't return, I was thinking. You too weak, minister, to change Mister Sam from doing what he do to Mary Ann, for all you promised Charles, for all you ranting too.

Mary Ann led me to upper verandah. Overlooking sugar works we eyes clearly drank in what trouble was about. Slaves bobbed out from bushes and along goat tracks. Mounting saddle as horse flung up its tail, minister galloped down plantation path.

Ragged and crude drumbeat pulsed through evening air. Mary Ann scraped sharp fingernails up and down she arms, like she skin was crawling alive with biting bugs.

'Papa say me turn yu crazy,' Mary Ann said with honest voice and face. 'Papa say yu a lunatic like yu ma.'

Wanting to say I'm not mad, don't fret, don't be vexed, Mary Ann – *Lord, lift me dawta up to Yu,* I was praying. 'Look,' I said, 'Mary Ann, flowers.' Wanting to distract she from scratching I pointed at flowers of half-bud half-blossom nosing between orange-tree leaves in front garden below. But she paid me no heed.

'Oo sleep on de ocean bed, Mama?' she small voice asked. 'Monsters?'

'Only fish.' I was gazing between side-window shutters as Jancra's black wings slipped from a branch into soft blue sky.

'Me tink it monsters, or bad men dere. Me head full of monsters,' she said. Peering down between verandah rails, Mary Ann cowered, shrinking from Jancra's path. 'Mama, ow yu do know wen yu ded?'

I moved behind Mary Ann, lifted up she chin and looked hard into she small, more than sad face. 'Jancra cyaan hurt yu,' I said. She didn't want to look at me. Not then. Not ever since, it seems. She stood up straight, each pointed step she took leading to Mister Sam's ottoman.

Lying down, Mary Ann stretched, tiny feet feeling for a silk-covered footstool. She voice, faint as harp strings, sang, 'Me mama not fraid fe Jancra.'

My eyes followed a cloud of darkness unravelling from east to west. 'Look! We can see round de world fram dis verandah. Dere's de moon, see, on dat side. See sun setting on de odder.'

'Kaydia! Kaydie!' Mister Sam called.

Turning for stairwell bottom I said to Mary Ann, 'Wait ere fe me.'

Mister Sam called me back into him study. 'Fetch my uniform.' He folded a key into my hand. 'And musket. I'm going to keep watch from here. Mary Ann, polish my boots. Mary Ann!' he called. 'Mary Ann! Where in hell is she?'

I ran to upper verandah, chasing my hope that Mary Ann would still be there. Every room I ran through stared starkly. 'Mary Ann! Mary Ann!' I bawled. Fearing Mister Sam, Mary Ann will have run to stable-block, crept to strong raw-leather smell behind saddle rack. Always my daughter hide in some dark corner. Perhaps where pimento trees' shadows play in warm fragrant shade of crumbling stable walls. Peering over stable-door tops nibbled jagged by horses' teeth, darkness answered me.

From chamber closet I brought Mister Sam's red militia jacket and hard cured cowhide belt.

I sat alone against whitewashed upper verandah wall, gazing out over sugar works and thickly wooded slopes stretching through swampy saltwater morass to open sea. Cane-cutters from hill villages poured down valleys by now to flat land at foothill's base, round swampy morass, dancing onto coast road in a mess of colour. And noise. Whistles, cowbells, horns, reeds. Goatskin drums. My head throbbed with strange yet familiar sounds. Women with rattles strapped to wrists, ankles, came dancing from slave quarters around great house.

Hundreds of people, young and old, who'd been forced into slavery at Cinnamon Hill, Greenwood and Barrett Hall, celebrated, rushing from shacks to join this parade. But I cared little. Everything I reached for turned into dirt.

Leaning on verandah rail I strained to see if Mary Ann's head bobbed out at sea. That ever deepening blue was broken only by grey patches of reefs close to shore. Inland, patches of sunlight spilled gold across treetops, light flared from candle-wood torches. Under beds; behind curtains I made a search.

'Me look fe Mary Ann everywhere an me cyaan find she,' I said when Mister Sam returned in red militia uniform.

Mister Sam's deadly pale face watched hillside coming to life. 'Where do they go?'

'William Knibb in Falmouth church.'

'But the church can't hold this many.'

'Den dey fill school-house, court-house.'

'Surely Demar will order the militia to assemble.'

But Doctor Demar didn't come. Mister Richard Barrett gone to Spanish Town in Kingston. Militia messenger didn't appear. All Cinnamon Hill cane piece deserted.

'Yu treat cane-cutters strong, too strong,' I said. Mister Sam wrung him hands. Dusk hovered. Birds chattered. My ears throbbed and burned with straining to hear Mary Ann's voice sweeten evening air. 'Me dawta, where she? Me have to know. Yu must ansa me.'

Mister Sam was silent. On upper verandah he stood, where earlier that day me and Mary Ann had watched minister gallop away, struck by a screaming sun, a flashing, glittering sea. Sea was now a rippling cool turquoise blue. Hurrying from filthy quarters others still joined slaves' wild dance, lit by orange torch flames now.

'Lock the doors,' Mister Sam's voice trembled. All he saw he still believed he had a right to. We watched carts cross flat swamp at foothill's base to Falmouth – that distant, strange land – yet all paths led there, and red-yellow flames on black night sky blazed with one lifelong desire. 'God only knows how we'll get the crop in with this ... this ... farrago.' Slaves, as Mister Sam's mouth moved, still crossed Salt Marsh for Falmouth, creeping night heavy with thunder of pounding drums. Light from candle-wood torches licked empty stomachs, backs. It was a mass of black skin, animal masks, feathered headdresses. Heathen practices – as Pa calls them. Rebecca Laslie ... What would she have said?

Night, a dark smear, drew across pink sky. A manic chant of mockery grew louder. Below me swirled an ocean of defeat. One man, with grey flowing beard and stringy mop of hair – him too a slave, ragged, lewd, cut from Africa – joined slaves' wild dance on stilts.

'Your daughter,' Mister Sam said, 'is probably running with those lawless lunatics.' He then looked away from me, and said in a quiet tone, 'I have been recalled.'

'Recalled?' I said.

'Papa's letter in today's packet said I have been recalled to England for readjustment. I must sail very soon.'

Struck off short in wonder that Mister Sam could leave for ever, I stood in quiet wonderment. No more injury? Me, Charles and Mary Ann will have freedom to live again? That happy moment lasted long. So very long. Peace, it hit my body so strong my legs quaked.

'Hope Masterton Waddell is behind this. The decision smells of him,' Mister Sam said. 'Without Carey's attorneyship I'm a bloody impotent manager. Waddell's forcing me to leave Jamaica. Mend my wicked ways. Bastard! The bastard!' he hissed between clenched teeth.

I knew what was coming. And I knew it wouldn't be quick. Mister Sam can turn feisty bad. Each shout shook stonework and echoed in my head sameway as rocks rumble down mountainsides. Hurling books from shelves, ripping down curtains, bashing jalousie blinds. Then he shrieked like a parakeet. A staring-glass crashed. Smashed. Splinters spun over polished floors. Sweeping chaos across silk rugs Mister Sam's rage rushed like hurricane. Anger weaving through my body, I was running over parchments strewn about cool dark chambers, calling, 'Mary Ann! Mary Ann!'

Fixing my eyes on Mister Sam's dressing-table I seized a walnut jewellery box with no sense of how to open it, how hard to throw. Until. It smashed. Gathering gold chains, brooches, dagger-sharp split wood, moving quick on worry, up narrow ladder I scrambled and into attic room. Except for Mary Ann I wasn't afraid there. Perfectly silent I became, lying on my back, listening, breathing darkness in.

Knots of stars in dusk-dark sky shone between roof shingles. Deeper, deeper I fell, drifting in attic's crib of darkness, sinking into a lumpy mattress Charles and I once used as we bed. Lifeless. But for breath stroking top lip. Even clatter coming up from down-stairs, wrapped up in greater dark, became swallowed by black. Something like strong wind I need, that I can feel. That can hold me, cradle me, so there's more sense to life. Wood floor's dis-appeared, and I'm groping for something to hold on to. Someone. But there isn't anything until I see Mama again, and find Mary Ann.

Dawn light slid across dusty floorboards when I climbed down attic ladder. Cinnamon Hill great house huge rooms felt odd when Mister Sam's fury had passed. One shattered bedchamber mirror had kept its glass. Mister Sam's face stared from it. Veins rose on each side of him head; cheeks sprung red, mouth forming a soft O, marooned in a sea of papers, books, still like Barrett portraits, locked still; he was staring staring staring at cobweb-like cracks in glass.

Under staring mirror stood Mister Sam's desk. He unlocked it, slid out rests. 'What did you do with my musket?'

'Musket me lock up,' I said.

Mister Sam's hands outstretched. Sad hands for me to drop closet key into.

Beneath tiny hidden drawers at desk back lay low boxes split for parchment, goose quills, nibs, keys, maps. Mister Sam's fingers brushed an estate map and, sliding up, stroked neck of empty white-rum bottle living in desk belly. Shaking rum bottle, straw-yellow hair flopping over him brow, he wrung bottle's neck until drops dotted Barrett estates.

What happened then I couldn't have foreseen. Mister Sam stood nearer to me. A weird feeling of hatred and passion ran through my body. I couldn't swallow, a lump blocked my throat. Him look was searching; pink lips waited. I felt each breath he took flow across my skin. I swallowed painfully, I wanted to coil away. My cheeks were burning. I'd never kissed a white man. It seemed a dirty thing to do. It felt worse than betrayal. It felt evil. I felt contempt for him. He'd destroyed Mary Ann as a pickney breaks a plaything. Then I felt a hollow chill, a darkening in my soul. I've even prayed to Him in heaven for mercy for what I did. White crest of Mister Sam's neck was in my hand, blue-grey mistiness of him eye closed as him mouth closed on mine. He held me tight then shaking him head, turned away. And something else strange was in Mister Sam's chamber. Something even more threatening. Beneath four-poster bedspread a sugar-sack-sized bundle stirred.

'How would you like to live in England, Kaydie? Visit America?' Mister Sam said.

'Wot, yu mean yu tek me?' I asked, wanting to hear him say it again. Anything I'd do, I thought, to protect Mary Ann for ever from him.

Mister Sam hastily said, 'Yes. You can go now,' as shape beneath bedspread uncurled, drew sheets from head, shoulders, legs. 'Go! Leave this room, Kaydia! Immediately!' But Mister Sam's order came too late.

Covers were cast over griffin crests carved in mahogany-smooth bedhead. Dark curls streamed across she face. Beautiful she looked. Painfully open.

'Why? How Mary Ann in ere? Walk on silent feet?' I said. Why Mary Ann in Mister Sam's bed? Why she's undressed?

Using arms to cover bumps where breasts soon would grow, Mary Ann struggled to tie long-faded brown petticoat of mine, gathering it into bunches round she waist with string. Looking older now than Mary Ann, shattered like my own reflection – trapped – in Mister Sam's staring-glass, soundlessly she tiptoed through chamber doorway, and scuttled towards main stairs.

Pulling me from wreckage of memory, 'When will my cousin be here, Kaydia?' Mister Sam says drowsily. 'He's coming to see us at Wimpole Street, is he not?'

'Cousin already come,' I say. I move to close jalousie blinds. From below a soft clucking rises up to bedchamber from scrawny chickens of part fluff, part feather, scraping earth bare.

Mister Sam mumbles again, 'When will my cousin be here, Kaydia?' But I can't turn round. Can't look no more on Mister Sam. 'When will my cousin be here? I have to write to William Carey . . . Papa and Elizabeth told me . . .'

Outside, Mister Carey emerge with Mister Sam's cousin from behind stable-block, each leading a handsome horse. Before mounting both men pause, squinting, shading eyes from morning sun, most likely looking for Old Simeon, then tighten horses' girth. Mister Carey seemed no worse to me than other Cinnamon Hill buckra men until he brought a too terrible story and gave me bigger fever and anger than Mister Sam's. Mister Sam was back in England; then memories swirl painfully. I am sick to my bones.

I was sitting on whistling walk when Mister Carey had come, sun bouncing off him white skin and flashing from banana leaves by back verandah. 'News has come,' Mister Carey's voice sounded flat, dead, 'of your master Sam's imminent return. He'll be docking in Kingston any day.'

Sadness filled mid-day air like rank smells can. Only this sadness was stronger than any stench. Inside I was crumbling.

Me, Charles and Mary Ann had gone back to sleeping together in attic room, until that day we heard Mister Sam would soon come. Me and Charles can cope with anything buckra do. Anything. Everything. But we can't cope with these things time after time after time Mister Sam does to Mary Ann.

Hair splayed about golden shoulders like black flame, Mary Ann began wandering again — always she'll be my pickney, I thought, though she sparkling brown eyes have died out like stars can. Before dawn glow she would sneak across creak creak creaking floorboards. Glide along upper verandah, down over wide chilly drawing-room. I remember thinking she don't belong to me any more. Who can help she? often flashed through my mind. Obeah woman, Leah? I wondered.

What happened in England I'll never know but Mister Sam

sailed back here to Cinnamon Hill with him brother, Stormie, almost as soon as he'd gone. Like he couldn't keep away.

'The niggers' children carried yellow umbrellas strapped to bamboo sticks high up over the Blue Mountains to shield me from the sun,' exclaimed Mister Sam when he strode into great-house hall with a trunk fleet of boxes, baskets, bundles, bags, packages all shapes, sizes, carried on heads, sumpter-horses, mules.

At first when Mister Sam returned he buried him badness better, and I began to believe he might have changed. But he never hid what he did to my daughter from me or Charles for long. That isn't all Mister Sam does, preying on Mary Ann again and again and again, but those other faults I could bear and so could Charles. Though I hardly ever saw Charles now.

I fought Mister Sam when he pestered Mary Ann, I fought him with my mind. I lost my battle last Christmas, just weeks back, when Sir Joshua Rowe told Mister Sam he must hold parties less.

But Mister Sam told me, 'This year Christmas will be celebrated at Greenwood great house.' After militia body assembled and troops mounted, I watched their dead white England faces; they missed chainings and whippings of slaves. I looked from cold face to cold face. All drunk. I can still remember Mister Sam's bottle list, remember it like I remember songs. Mister Sam said he liked to 'indulge' at Christmas time. Good ale; cheese. Roast beef legs. 'Women,' Mister Sam had said, 'are like laudanum; you have to double the dose as the senses decline.' And then he said I must find and round up young girls on coast road, take them to Greenwood big party, big busha-house dance. Each night he drank himself into daylight, rum tumbler draining empty only as red sun rose.

Early one dawn I went with Mary Ann gathering wild cashew nuts. Straying from forest path Mary Ann danced a dream-like dance. My eyes strained to fix on she sliding into shadow, darting round trees, through brushwood scrub she moved by scratching branches, gossiping leaves. Following lightly crunching footsteps past giant hand-shaped ferns, high over moss-covered rocks, through silver webs of streams seeping into deep blue pools, I was calling anxiously. Then I ran fast, dragging heavy pain, yelling, 'Mary Ann! Mary Ann! Mary Ann!' She led me to a place I felt was not good. Slowly tramping on, I reached a tall stone wall, a ruin blocking my path, draped in old ivy rugs. I gave up calling for Mary Ann for she never climbed stone walls so high; turning back I saw a hut I knew must be Leah's. Would Mary Ann run-hide in Leah's obeah hut? What had I to lose?

Fountains of tree ferns I remember, every shade of green; bushes creeping across sandy floor of Leah's pimento-grove clearing, and them red flowers cascading over she shingle-roof. Soft, wispy bamboo. Mauve mountains. Blue behind blue. Wattle hut was quiet. Secluded. Small stacks of shrivelled lizards lay on Leah's doorstep before black darkness surrounding she. Sleepily a black dog stirred, sighed. Dried herb bunches hung from leather pouches hooked on wattle walls, or tied to rafters; leather buckets overflowed decaying flowers, roots.

Leah never heard from me what Mister Sam did to Mary Ann. But I believe she knew what went on between them because, 'Me understand,' Leah said, 'Mister Sam e'll want yu in im bed, yu'll see.'

'If me can mek money me might,' I had said.

Leah said, 'Kaydia, mek Mister Sam eye fix on yu an not on yu dawta.'

'Wot if it don't work?'

Leah said she no care, making me nervous of following obeah word.

Back through lonely dark woods I walked. When I came out on a path by sugar works, sunlight was too thick to see more than Mary Ann's blurred shrinking shape running up plantation path, heading for great house. I reached Cinnamon Hill gardens and found Mister Sam not sleeping as most often he was when sun had risen high and hot. He was spread in osnaburg cloth hammock slung between cotton trees. I dreaded walking past.

'Over here!' he shouted at me, swinging an arm above him head. Cautiously I went into cotton-tree shade. 'Is it true a group of field-hands attending Waddell's church services are refusing to take the Christmas rum ration?' he asked. 'I believe this stupidity was encouraged by my carpenter. When did he give up drinking?'

Fear slapped my face. 'Yu cyaan fix de blame on Pa,' I said. 'Pa's yu carpenter but Pa don't drink for long time past.'

'Kaydia,' Mister Sam said, as he eased both legs over hammock edge, 'do you know what's in this bottle?' I nodded. 'Take it to your father. You'll find him in the lock-up.'

'Pa don't drink, don't tek no more rum.'

'A seasonal present. He must take it from his master, as any good Christian would.'

A sickly rum smell leaked up white stone steps from lock-up in basement beneath great house. I hid rum bottle in my apron, hearing Pa curse Mister Sam. Bending down to lock-up keyhole I saw Old Simeon shake and shake him skinny arm. Face cut, lower lip swollen up, that's what I'd seen.

'Wayah! Wa mek yu both down ere?' I was shouting at lock-up door.

Through thick door wood Old Simeon sounded far away. 'Me n Pa won't tek rum so Mister Sam give we no Christmas sugar.'

'Me won't dance at busha-house!' Pa shouted. 'Mister Sam too wicked, too bad, too rough.'

'Tek dis, Pa, fore Mister Sam mek yu,' I said, and forced rum bottle down stone wall gun slot softly coated with yellow moss.

'Yu cyaan gwan tell me wot to do. Yu full-a foolishness,' Pa shouted.

'Mister Sam and him cousin treat we sameway lek Old Mister Richard,' Old Simeon said. From keyhole I saw Old Simeon's sad heavy form lurch across lock-up, grab at a sugar barrel, stumble against oak door. Open welts on Old Simeon's back wriggled with maggots, flies.

Days later Mister Sam told me he was inviting Doctor Demar, Mister Carey and other court-house friends to stay at Greenwood for Christmas.

Greenwood great house, a long low building of finely cut ballast stones, like all them large outhouses standing round its pretty grounds, was built only for parties, Mister Sam said, and he was to be head buckra for him cousin, who often stayed at Greenwood but was travelling to Kingston for Christmas to join with pickneys and wife.

Rats rummaged in rubbish and yam cuttings Mary Ann put out for field-slaves. Mister Sam rounded a corner and, head held high, came gaily strutting by in showy fashioned clothes.

'Hey. What's going on?' he asked me. I was in Greenwood kitchen plucking chickens. 'It's a holiday,' Mister Sam said.

A stronger than strong thirst rose from my belly to shelter Mary Ann from him come hell's fire. *Keep yu eye fixed on yu dawta betta*, my head-voice said. But Mister Sam and me we sameway too much – both binding nearer to Mary Ann. A closeness between we from this filled each day before Christmas. Him eye would turn greedily on Mary Ann's body curves, bare arms, muscular calves, smooth slim ankles.

Air tasted rich from black crab pepper-pot bubbling over cook-fire on Christmas Eve. Mister Sam had brought to Greenwood a ship's French cook, a woman he called Chef who could cook any dish.

He dropped a mottled blue jade-orchid flower on kitchen flag-stones carefully at Mary Ann's feet. She smiled at him, uncertainly, bent down to petals speckled blue-purple, soft like Mister Sam's neck-cloth he call silk cravat. Carrying blue jade flower Mary Ann went through doorway, disappeared into jade vine tunnels leading to rose gardens.

Fat gobs oozed from wild-boar flesh on roasting spit, making cook-fire throw out loud hisses. I looked up again from chicken plucking, feeling Mister Sam watching me. He gave me a sharp stare; sheer blue-green eyes so clear I could see through to a more crafty stormy sea-blue. My stomach started shrivelling – he had seen fire in mine? – but him gone, disappearing behind huge carved great-house mahogany doors.

Carriage wheels crunched on dusty stony drive winding from coast road to Greenwood. Red faces roared with laughter. Some had two chins, some three or four. Dressed as English pages, freed slaves with stony-black faces stared out like statues across Greenwood lawn.

Ladies fluttered in dresses bright as butterflies. Candles lit tables, mirrored yellow in chinking glasses, silver cutlery. Greenwood dining-room air came alive, tasting of warm red hot spices. Mister Sam's family portraits hung on walls; cheeks pale, slightly flushed; small slits for lips; sharp curved English noses like Mister Sam's Cousin Richard's – new paintings from England met my eyes – Mister Sam. Another showed a woman's face buttermilk-white framed with black ringlets *Elizabeth Barrett Moulton Barrett* inscribed on brass lettering plaque.

Mister Sam slumped down at black oak dining-table cluttered for grand feast and drink. Sangaree tumblers. Spiced wine. Jerked pork. Hot and cold pickled barracuda. Sweetmeats. Madeira. Lime juice water. Claret. Cassava. Beer tankards. Hock-negus. Rum punch. Turtle soup.

Even seated Mister Sam swayed. 'Kaydia!' he called. 'You've fed Henrietta, my new African pet?'

'Saltwater nigger dirty,' I said. 'Ugly, mek too much nize.'

Saltwater Henrietta's chubby black face, scarred with Congo slashes, peeped from under Mister Sam's elbow.

'I can't believe she understands a word I say, my new little girl, Henrietta, but I do believe she may be hungry,' Mister Sam replied.

Sniggering, Mary Ann held up a taper, flame flickering, wax melting easily as promises can. Mary Ann lit Mister Sam's fat brown cigar; tobacco-leaf end flared up, crackled. Resting blue eyes on me, Mister Sam quietly puffed. An odour spiced with doom seeped up my nose like strange plunking English slow waltz running through my ears. Smoke clouds now masked Mister Sam's face. This smokey smell was like false jangling music, strange to me. Nodding, Mister Sam grunted, a sleepy smile curving lips; missing him glass he sloshed white rum across oak table-top.

Walking up behind Mister Sam Doctor Demar said, 'For goodness sakes man, watch yourself.'

Suddenly Mister Sam flicked bottle upright. Doctor Demar shook him head. Mary Ann giggled. Henrietta's sticking to Mister Sam like a leech. Rubbing neck base, Mister Sam caught sight of Mary Ann's gleeful face. Him mouth clamp onto anyone's, by him eye-look I could tell. Never will I forget him lips closing onto mine before he sailed for England, and how Mary Ann was in him chamber. I'm going to help you, Mary Ann, a tongue inside me said. I'm going to win this battle. Going to keep Mister Sam from you. And now I know how. I'm going to do to him what he did to you. I'm going to follow Leah's words. Not only that – by having Mister Sam's pickney he'll leave money to care for we when him dead.

'Yu waan elp Mister Sam, eh?' I asked Doctor Demar. I pointed to my daughter and Henrietta. 'Tek she way. An she.'

Dragging Henrietta and Mary Ann by their braids, Doctor Demar marched through grand dining-room, vanishing into swirling ballroom colours, waltzing satin, silks.

Winding my waist, making him think I'm loose and begging for it, I rolled my eyes at Mister Sam. Thin straight lips curled up into a familiar smirk. Slipping one hand up my skirt, 'I like pretty girls,' he said. My eyes stung, making me turn away, almost making me weep as him other hand reached for a rum tumbler on drinks tray I held. Quickly I passed him a full tumbler, letting a little rum slop from its rim. A dark patch spread across trouser-cloth like it was soaking through to skin.

'Good heavens!' he yelled. 'Kaydia's trying to drown me!' But no one cared to save Mister Sam. He straightened him high cravat.

'It was by accident, Mister.' Sliding serving napkins between him legs, I pressed and rubbed him tool until it hard like wood.

'Black magic,' he mumbled into him chest. He didn't take him eyes from me yet him face showed no emotion.

Up broad mahogany stairs Mister Sam staggered. I followed him into a spare chamber, as Leah had said he would want. He swung against four-poster bedstead. Collapsed. Rum stench – steamy, sticky scent of sweat, tobacco, sadness, sugar, shouts of overseers plump from drinking sugar juice soured Mister Sam's breath. I looked away – this wasn't happening but I stayed – blood pumping through my veins quicker. On a chest of drawers I found a black glass perfume bottle, a red silk tassel tied about its neck. Over my arms, into air, I sprayed to drive away Mister Sam's stink. Perfume made in Paris, he said. Deceitful smell – too sour, too bitter sameway as over-ripe mango fruit. Mister Sam's hands grabbed my clothes; skin. Him shoulders tasted slippery, salty. I kissed swirling fair hairs on him chest, my eyes downcast.

Climbing free of him heavily sleeping, gathering up my skirts, I went up narrow sharp rise of wood ladder to long attic where rat-bat now rest.

Mary Ann slept in attic doorway. I carried she inside. Sadly my thoughts moved back reaching way into shadows where what's past fades into darkness fast as a falling star. Deep down I was shamed, for I knew Mary Ann felt Charles and me battle long before she was born. And when she was a warm bundle tied to my back she would cry whenever I laid she to rest or left she for work. I want to unsay all I said back then. Undo all I did.

Laying she on coconut-hair mattress, moon rays touched she pinched-up skin, smiles turned on she lips. Memories of a newly-born pickney fluttered in my heart, my head, though all childish looks had long fled from she face. Through tiny attic window I watched night sky. Clouds, carved like cook-fire smoke breathed across old moon's face. Wave crests flickered white in sea bay below. Mister Sam stole innocence from Mary Ann. Mister Sam I can blame. But Charles? Me? I kissed she branded forehead skin, curled my body round she, and I felt myself falling.

No yacca board flooring, no walls. Nothing. But me own secret in Mister Sam's life. Darkness within darkness. Safety inside unsafeness. A needle of sunlight pricked my cheek. Light suddenly streamed through windows. I was laughing, my head back. I ran towards Mama and she lifted me up. I was in she arms. But I wanted to be free.

When my eye opened to moonlight-filled attic I looked for Mama for a long time. I wished I could remember she.

Taking me from that time, Mister Sam mumbles, 'I fear I have done wrong since sailing from England.' Reaching my hand onto him, I feel burning skin yellow with fever. Eyes, bloodshot yellow, turn looking up and back inside him head.

I stand hot with anger. A well of pain and wanting opens inside with a rush. Quick as a trigger my thoughts click back to Rebecca Laslie. Wherever you are I need you, to make suffering mean something. Show me where's a path.

'Why yu don't make me into yu will,' I'm saying to Mister Sam through clenched teeth. 'Leave lickle ting fe we pickney. Leave money fe Mary Ann.'

Mister Sam don't flinch at all. I look on him with pure bare hatred. Already he sleeps like him dead.

Black gown flapping like mainsail in harsh Montego Bay wind, minister now strides from dazzling white wall of light into blue bedchamber, leaving yellow-green prints from tiny fluffy wild-sage flowers squashed on my polished yacca floor. Minister have clean-shaved cheek. Wispy goat beard fringes him chin and runs from ear to ear like church picture-book devil. Small square hands shaped as little cloven hooves flick back smooth leather Bible clasps. Batting lids of wide-set eyes he gasps; falls onto knees at four-poster bedside, places Bible on Mister Sam's fancy table. 'What is the burden that troubles you?' he asks.

A strange look crosses Mister Sam's face. It open. Him eyes go past me to minister, beyond minister to blue.

'Maskitta bit hard,' I say.

Minister's thickly brown-haired head bows, turns to me, frowning; him voice pointed, accusing, says, 'Bring only water,' and when I do he says, 'Go.' But him shouting stops me in hallway. 'Kaydia, what's the date? Have you any idea of the date?' Tall brass hall clock's ticking, striking, shrieking, howling up to eleven o'clock. 'Can't you read the date hand? Can't you read a clock?'

Swaying through great-hall darkness, I can't see for tears make time impossible to read. Before I lay with Mister Sam inside I was crumbling, now I've lost too much of myself to hold on to days. Live. Freedom don't come to anyone here. Ocean rim creeps dark blue from behind white stone wall. Wind rolls up fiercely, its breath too hot, too sweet, too sugar-cane sickly. Choked up inside, crossing back verandah, roaring air rushes round legs, over feet; I'm trying to smother what's in my mind but everywhere memories sprout like weeds round ruins, growing up into this island's foul air.

Swinging in Mister Sam's hammock, Mary Ann and Friday chew sugar-cane sticks and pass between them an English china mug brimming with honey and buttermilk.

'Pa tink me'll be a-carpenter,' Friday sings. 'Me have no work on Sataday. No pay. No work on Sataday. No pay, no pay.'

'Why yu cry?' Mary Ann asks me.

Wiping my eyes I turn to answer with all my love I can muster. 'Dey'll sort out wot to pay now we free.'

Friday asks, 'Yu ove any peas? We a-hungry.'

'Yu eat too much. Friday, yu big nuff fe workin wid Pa.'

'Where Pa?'

'Ow me know dat, bwoy? Come now, we must mek money an go. We a-go to provision ground to keep belly full, see. Come, Mary Ann,' I say. 'Fetch cassava fe selling at Sunday market. We ration not match field-slave. Salt. Pickled fish. Sugar. Rum.'

'Gimme a-rum,' Friday giggles, swinging, singing carelessly in Mister Sam's cloth cot. 'Rum an wata ple-e-e-se.' Rum spikes Friday's hot breath gushing across my face. Still plump from drinking first cane juice, Friday spits out chewed cane-wood chunks, sips honey and buttermilk.

'Mek up yu mind,' I say.

But Friday keeps up singing rowdily, 'Rum an wata ple-e-e-se.'

'Mek we galang now. Friday! Mary Ann! Why yu tek so lang?'

Mary Ann flops down beside me saying, 'Me a-come.'

Friday slides from hammock perch. Him dirt-stained green shirt dances ahead along great-house drive, past tethered donkeys' lowered snorting heads, over plantation path, in and out of slave shacks' tiny yards. Friday's singing voice stays close and loud, 'Me a-go Barrett Town Sunday market.'

Crushing cordia flowers Mary Ann and me walk on grass. Mary Ann's forehead skin's drawn bumpy, sameway as finger-like ridges of cotton tree's spreading roots. Light sings yellow between cotton-tree leaves, golden-orange notes scream.

'Kaydia! Kaydia!' minister's shout comes faintly along driveway.

Brow scars wrinkling and fattening, Mary Ann's looking up to me. Taking she hand, I say in a strained half-whisper, 'Minister want me to run back an nurse Mister Sam.' Slow turning, we follow minister's call back across plantation path to Cinnamon Hill drive. Over lawn slow slow. Cotton-tree roots, too overgrown to see, prod bare feet soles.

'Coming, Mister Waddell,' I'm shouting. To Mary Ann I say, 'Keep close in hall till me a-come.'

'Me go see me Pa in rum store in still-house.'

'No, Mary Ann, keep close wid Friday. Soon me a-come.' I look for Friday. But all I'd seen of Friday's gone. He fall asleep, I think, under mango trees. Already drunk on rum.

Mouth gaping, eyes open wide, Junius, storekeeper man, comes up against me like he about to crash into Mister Sam's chamber. He takes my wrist. 'Look. Ere. Read!'

I read letter Junius have. Many words I can't make out but kernel's clear to me – letter accuses Old Simeon of theft of Barrett jewellery box. Signature I see belongs to Mister Sam's cousin. 'Ol Simeon bin an stole sumting?'

'Yeh,' Junius says.

I pass back letter. 'Im tief! Old Simeon, im tief!' *Is me do it,* I want to say.

'Yu see Ol Simeon,' says Junius, 'yu ax im to see me.'

Walking from Mister Sam's chamber with short jerky halting steps, 'Pray,' Minister Waddell asks, 'what is the matter, Kaydia? Can you not come when called?' Wearily dropping my head I follow minister to Mister Sam's bedside. 'Should I tell you of Sam's condition first as I think I see it now?' Minister asks me. 'Can you then explain this to Doctor Demar when he arrives?' Firmly he shuts Mister Sam's door. 'On but Monday Sam was well enough yet to me he has admitted to his wish to partake of the Sacrament of the Lord's supper, as he has never partaken of it and had been, he was sorry to say, very inattentive to the importance of the crucifixion – too much of the deadly opiate hardened in sin, I dare say. Nevertheless, to follow Sam's desire through might give rise to a fatal delusion. I begged of him not to fix his mind so intently on that particular thing – a popish superstition – as it is but a sign of the death of Our Lord Jesus Christ, but to give all his thoughts to the Saviour himself who died the just one for the unjust that he might bring us to God. The Sacrament, I have reminded Sam, is not essential, but faith in Christ and repentance for our sins are absolutely necessary, for without them we must perish. Let this not alarm you, Kaydia, for as you well know the Lord is always with us. But Sam said,' and minister whispers, '"I do not expect to recover and I fear that I am not prepared for another world."' Nodding knowingly minister raises him eyebrows. 'I then offered to make use of your master's own church prayers, if he preferred them, but he requested I should not, but pray as I always do. Whilst thus engaged he joined in the most earnest manner with many tears. I pressed particularly on his attention that he should fully confess his sins to God as a necessary part of repentance and essential to his peace of mind and procuring of pardon; quoting to him, "He that covereth his sins shall not prosper, but he that confesseth and forsaketh them shall find mercy." As ever, I spoke to him as a faithful Christian friend. Having quoted a number of passages of Scriptures on these points, I inquired if Sam believed them, he eagerly answered, "I believe them, Mr Waddell, every one." Being unable to hear more,' minister goes on, 'your master has requested that I return as soon as I may on the morrow.'

'Mister Waddell?'

'If Sam changes time for eternity and I haven't arrived, arrange for him to be interred the same evening in the Barrett family burial ground.' Minister pauses, chewing on him bottom lip. 'There's something else. Kindly remember to tell the good Doctor Demar that one of the reasons I am unable to administer the Sacrament to your master is because I am deeply sorry to say that I know Sam hasn't changed in the ways one might have hoped. Tell the doctor the minister knows this to be true, Kaydia, because Charles has informed him, and I know Charles and Charles is truthful. The other reason being that I do not approve of administering the Sacrament as a preparation for death, as I have already said. I am not myself a clergyman in the Established Church so should not be called upon to administer sacred rites. What I mean, Kaydia, is . . .' Minister's eye makes four with mine. 'No need to explain too much, Kaydia,' minister says almost to himself, 'Demar will, I believe, understand. Yes, you will communicate my words to Doctor Demar?' I nod. 'And what of the African Negroes from the *Ulysses*? Near on eighty are here attending Barrett Town church regularly. All must be baptised, given Christian names.'

'Me teach em to read word of good God Lard Jesus Christ,' I say. Leaving blue chamber I curtsey.

I step out onto front verandah. My nails pierce closed palm of my hand. Palms bristle. Old Simeon's shadow drags across front lawn. Jancra's slanted shadow glances across wooded slopes glowing orange-gold. Clouds grow red faintly, pouring pink light over blue sea. Clouds I've known since I was a little pickney. Nothing's changed. Each day's clouded by misery.

Quietly shutting Mister Sam's door behind him, Minister Waddell yells, 'Ensure Friday, that house-boy, Kaydia, has lit the cook-fires.' *Loneliness is walking into fire, or sinking to sea's bed, swallowed; drowned. Alone.*

Chapter Seven

Elizabeth

TORQUAY
12 June 1839

Sam moves across the window before a golden sun. I am on the sofa immediately before the open window which is, I dare say, much the same as being outdoors. Shadows lie beneath Sam's eyes. He looks at me quickly. Where is the white skin, the smooth neatly combed hair? The contours of his gaunt dark body seem ungainly; his face tanned to a tawny yellow; his expression, spiritless.

He places a purple vine on the arm of the sofa near my head-rest, a host of magenta flowers entwine with a scent – a passionate poison – too powerful, too intoxicating.

'Sam!' I exclaim, overjoyed to see him. I stretch up open arms to draw his bowed form against my breast.

He leans over to kiss me, eyes tightly screwed. 'I'm sorry,' he says, pulling back from my embrace. 'If I could . . .'

I say, 'Could what?'

Cigar smoke has left its acrid trace on his new damask jacket. His skin becomes mottled, purple and red sneaking up his neck. He slowly shakes his head. I tell him I will be unable to sleep if he refuses to explain.

'I don't believe you.' He hesitates. 'You're sick, aren't you?' The ends of his lips curl up as he turns his eyes from mine. It is *extremely* peculiar. 'I've not been well myself.' He coughs. 'I can't sleep either.'

Wanting to hold him close again I reach out. Lo! he steps back and away. Marooned, estranged, on my bed, I long to hug him now. Sam seats himself before the window fidgeting with his jacket lapel, though the view of sea before him lies beautiful and uninterrupted.

A figure rises from a time when clouds reflected in the lake and I, clad as Byron's page, was convinced I would succeed as a poet if I could but live in the world of men. Sam, the little angel, stood no higher than the door-knob then. But it was impossible for my fanciful speculations to persist when Sam, laughing at my attire, gambolled across the garden to be at my side. Happiness, lit by his wit, would leap into my heart. I try to throw a lifeline through these thoughts. Does he feel the first thought's touch? Does my well-loved brother remember his clowning, his jokes, and my face ablaze with laughter? His face gleamed with inquisitive joy, open and fresh like the yellow-hearted buttercups and daisies spotting the lawns in summer months. Small posies I would pick, thread, loop about his neck; this enchanting child, the subject of many of my early poems, decked in bright blue breeches and jacket, his head crowned with laurel wreaths.

Sam's eyes narrow. They speak a different language. Why, I know not. Does he remember all Papa's preaching before a captive audience – the family warmth; and my own sermons when we played church in the nursery; did he not kneel before our home-made altar? No, hiding himself in the rich velvety folds of curtains he swathed himself in soft blushing red; has that colour drained from those ruddy cheeks, never to return?

He avoided Holy Communion – why? What heavy cross does he bear? Sam, a grinning infant with four milk teeth missing, once clung to my skirts. He was always the dandy, even back then. Who tore sweet little Sam from me?

It seems he can do naught but stare me out. I pray for God to restore my faith in his humanity.

Does he hear my sighs? Although he is seated not a yard away we have never been this far apart. When I speak in my small whisper, he looks up with stark blue eyes completely impoverished and destitute. I ask him how he is. Was he happy in Jamaica? Has he missed me? Will he stay the whole summer with us in Torquay? His demeanour of condemnation does not lighten. His answers are brief and none are in the definitive.

Dressing up with Henrietta for the plays I wrote, grandly Sam paraded about the drawing-room. Inside the cape in which he was wrapped he had concealed the much-adored doll, with its pretty fur cap and a cloth coat night-gown Grandmother Moulton had sent me. Little judge Georgie reprimanded Sam sharply. I now can't help smiling inside, yet with eleven of us, dear Mama couldn't control Sam. Another memory comes to mind, though only vaguely, of a poem Sam wrote many years ago for Papa's birthday . . . *the happiest day of the year, I'll swig to pass the time away*. Surely Sam hasn't behaved unreasonably under the influence of Jamaican rum?

Having barely said hello he heads for the drawing-room. Yet my room is twice as pleasant. My windows seem to hang over the bay, the balcony cuts the sea into a myriad of sparkling stars. And, as strong pillars of dust-laden light brighten and dim across my coverlet, the smells, the many discordant and strident summer sounds, muffled and softened by the distance of this floor from the ground, all fall with a certain difference now: laughter; screaming babies; the sharp shriek of children dashing in and out of waves; the resonant rattle of fashionable four-wheeled cabs on cobbled streets; the sonorous bellow of a donkey. Indeed, Sam says with a faint-hearted smile before turning from the landing, that should I be here during the Torquay August regatta, I could let out sittings upstairs.

Salt on the window-panes filters out the sun's harsh rays.

My dear Lady Margaret,

. . . since October I have never walked without support, & since January never in any way. Indeed at that time & afterwards the state of debility, induced not merely by the complaint on the chest but by the incidental & unaccountable attack of jaundice, was excessive. No baby could be more helpless – only – my voice having quite sunk away to a whisper – I had not the baby's privilege of screaming . . .

. . . I have been dumb with my pen almost all the winter – & even now am under an awful medical ban in regard to any sort of composition. Books too have been ordered away, but they, being faithful friends, wouldn't go *– so that now Dr. Barry restricts his disapprobation to a shaking of the head when he happens to see one larger than usual. I am about to, in spite of the ban, to contribute again to* Finden's Tableaux *– a vow having been vowed to that effect months ago, to my dear friend Miss Mitford, in the case of her retaining the editorship. There will be three other poets – I mean besides me – and Miss*

Mitford will write the whole of the prose. What my subject is, I have no imag-ination of yet – & am only today beginning to expect a suggestive sketch . . .

15 June 1839
Sealed off and shut up as I am, how could Papa have withheld this engraving portraying a sleeping child surrounded by nuns and monks? To prevent me writing poetry? Dear Miss Mitford sent the engraving to illustrate my next ballad, with a request for it to be forwarded to Torquay. I have waited for too long. What else does he keep from me? I fear I must let Miss Mitford know that my ballad for *Finden's Tableaux* will be delayed for this reason only. And I shall send Papa a savage letter explaining how hurried and frustrated I shall be in my writing of the ballad and that he should have, if for that reason alone, sent the illustration immediately it was delivered to Wimpole Street. I am in two minds as to the title: 'Lenora,' or 'The Legend of the Brown Rosary'?

19 June 1839
I am not one for gossip yet I do find the suspense of lying on this bed, waiting for mail, almost kills me.

Sam, Bro and Sette vanished after luncheon to I know not where, for it is neither the season for hunting, nor shooting, and they can't walk on the beach in this rain – Sam's and Sette's London coif-fures are almost too fashionable for *any* outdoors.

Seated at my bedside before luncheon was served, with sounds of summer laughter washing over everything, and his face flushed with the now familiar blush from too much pink champagne, Sam advised me that he, Papa and Sette may shortly depart for London. He assured me he will return to Torquay within one month.

I suspect that were Bro to journey with them he would be returned, coercively, to Jamaica to manage the family interests. Bro is safe as long as he remains within my sight. There is no sepa-rating Brozie from me. He so dreads returning to plantation life. Papa has not the audacity to tear him from my bedside; I have pleaded and begged until too weak to speak. 'We have a tyrant for a father,' Bro said when I consulted him.

I long to bring back the sweet Sam I once knew, and am wondering, as I twiddle the crucifix on a chain Bro earlier fastened round my neck, how I might appeal to him. I often feel shattered, and fear some dreadful disaster is about to befall us all.

The total abolition of slavery in the West Indies passed over all Papa did like a sombre cloud – this threat became a reality, and one which cost beloved Papa dearly – I grew into girlhood against this turbulent backdrop. Nevertheless, it did not strike me as strange that dark-skinned people lived and ate with us under the same Hope End roof.

There is a racket of window sashes rattling from the approaching tempest. Thunder booms, splitting the air with rumbling crashes, taking me back to a clear virtually cloudless day when lightning shot from blue sky. Hope End's cast-iron domelets and spires attracted thunderstorms. During one such summer storm an exceptionally loud thunderclap caused Mama's black manservant, Junius, to drop a tray of white-and-blue willow-patterned teacups, and one of our finest Barrett-crested crockery jugs, decorated with the griffin in deep red. Remarkably *that* didn't smash, but many cup handles broke clean off. Startled by another appalling crash, I ran up to my bedroom and from the window witnessed lightning strike a tree. The bark torn from the top to bottom . . . *rent and ripped into long ribbons by dreadful fiery hands, and dashed about into the air, leaving twisted branches shredded, as a flower picked by a child might be.* But worse, I later discovered four people were killed. Two of them, girls, picnicking on Pinnacle Hill, had tried to shelter in an iron-roofed shack. Their breasts were sliced by lightning; killed in an instant no doubt. Terror sweeps through me whenever a thunderstorm strikes.

Trippy, a Creole orphan, grew up with Papa at Cinnamon Hill great house and later came to work with Mama. She is now a motherly figure in my life and the lives of my siblings. Little Sam would crawl in and out of her legs whilst she crocheted the yellow shawl I wear. Her pudgy, pasty-brown face was to me, as a small child, an unobliging sight – quick eyes and thick West Indian accent. I hid from her chiding tones by slipping away to my menagerie of pets where clove-scented gillyflowers tumbled fragrant white and pink down bricks of the walled garden. Yet she covered the expense of my first publication, *An Essay on Mind* with fourteen shorter poems.

Trippy was not opposed to slavery. In fact, she sketched a pretty scene of how happily the Negroes lived when the sugar estates were in their prime. Like Papa, she described an idyllic Jamaican childhood. Thinking further on this, how she loved my great-grandfather, Edward of Cinnamon Hill, is easily understood, for although he *flogged his slaves like a divinity* – that was the standard phrase the family used to describe Grandpapa – he adopted Trippy, and afforded her great luxuries.

I saw the open slave markets of Montego Bay Trippy painted with words when I was a girl, as many as fifty men, women and children were purchased at any one time and branded as cattle. The most beautiful mulatto girls wore brightly patterned turbans; their skin was bleached with chalk and lemon juice to increase the price. These children of African and European mix commanded some of the highest bids. Auctioned as part of a lot were goats, chickens, pigs, whilst scents spicy and exotic – cinnamon, cloves, a faint hint of oranges – wafted from the many busy stalls. The English traders had a multitude of categories for variations in the shade of skin within the 'brown-skinned' group – mulatto being the most sought after, true black and pure albino the least; but between these were mustees, mustaphinos, quarteroons or quadroons, octoroons, and Sambos (children of mulatto and African mix). These names have a strange poetry in their sounds. There are Barretts who are mulattos, mustees, mustaphinos, octoroons. Mountains of problems have resulted from these illegitimate offspring.

Thomas Peters, one of my great-grandfather's illegitimate grand sons, was a quadroon, a brown-skinned man, tall as a palm tree and living in a district near the Thames; Walworth I think it was. He was appointed executor and trustee of one of the Jamaican estates and had wished, in his youth, to buy a commission in a British Army regiment. I discovered a truth which casts a shadow over Papa, and put us in grave financial danger. It was a truth I could barely face, and one which when reflected upon keeps me lying perfectly still. The legal case with Richard Barrett, Papa's illegitimate white Jamaican cousin, and Thomas Peters. A large sum – over six thousands pounds – was due to Thomas as a legacy. The case contested Papa's grandfather's will and was partly responsible for bringing about our huge financial downfall: this interminable family lawsuit, which cost Papa our Hope End home and continues to draw from him much strength. I was shocked to discover all this.

I went straight to my room at the top of the house. Many tearful hours passed. It was unusually cold in my room. I didn't care. Overwrought with confusion and distress, conflicts between my commitment to justice and my loyalty to Papa wrangled and festered within my heart. I am deeply divided to this day. I never talked of this to Bro, and for some days, because Papa was in such trouble, avoided speaking to anyone.

Divisions within me reigned to such an extent I finished crocheting a shawl. I wished for a while that I were dead. How much I loved and cherished Papa! I must help, I thought. I couldn't tell him face to face because when I tried to voice what I felt it sounded foolish. I lay on the bed and even practised cross stitch, hoping Papa loved me as I loved him.

A lively *pop-thwack!* of a flying cork hits the ceiling below, followed in quick pursuit by the gushing fizz of champagne. Peals of Sam's reckless laughter lance up through the floorboards.

Sam, the hard-drinking fool – it is seldom now that he mentions the estates. Must I live with the monster little Sam has become? As the eldest brother, Bro should rightly set sail for Jamaica. It would be preferable if *Sam* sailed back in place of him. The extent of the discomfort I feel is not measurable – the tension between us is mounting – I sense Sam hides deviant folly and erroneous deeds.

20 June 1839
June has kept Sam safely in Torquay for eight days.

After yesterday's party to celebrate Stormie's arrival, Sam said that whilst in London he prevailed on Trippy to present him with my picture, 'with a few alterations for which Arabella sat'; he added, 'Trippy succeeded in obtaining a likeness', and I glimpsed the sweet Sam of yesteryear. He told me he will value my portrait as much as a companion if he returns to Jamaica.

This morning he was in fine spirits, and after breakfasting told me a dreadful tale which I think he had considered would gladden my heart.

It seems that before Uncle Samuel died in Jamaica over a year ago he altered his will three times to benefit a black female servant attendant, one Rebecca Laslie, declaring finally that a legacy should be payable to the servant upon his death only if his executors considered her conduct and attention during his illness to have merited such a mark of his approval. Whether Rebecca Laslie *should* or *should not* be bequeathed the grand sum of one hundred Jamaican pounds, Uncle Samuel could not himself decide. Sam, the executor, cannot decide either. He claims that to allow the duties of a devoted servant to go unrewarded in the West Indies will never do. Sam's situation is delicate, he said. He asked me what he should do. If I could assist him in some even small way, I would. He swore rumours of improprieties between this servant and Uncle Samuel will spread like fire across Jamaica if she *does* receive the legacy. Well!

The sky is almost dark. Sam has brought two letters with him from our cousin, Samuel Goodin Barrett in Jamaica, which he now takes the trouble to read. Our cousin is quite recovered from an attack of fever caught, he says, by his own impudence for not changing wet shoes for dry after descending the Blue Mountain peak. With regard to Papa's properties, little or no labour has been obtained. Cane-cutters at Cinnamon Hill have staged a strike for higher pay and the overseer obliged to stop work – this news duly brings unease to Sam's voice as he reads on.

'Sam! Sam!' Bro calls from the dining-room. 'We need you here for dinner. Hurry up, by Jove!'

Before I know it, and with the strangest smile, Sam is gone.

A shadow slopes across the landing threatening my doorway. 'Now Papa has reconsidered Uncle's will,' it says in a thick drunken brawl, chin dropping to chest, the neck too weak to hold up the head, 'I'm more than certain I'll be granted attorneyship of our Jamaican estates when I return.' I cannot understand the meaning of the words sliding from thin lips into dusky air.

A mask has slipped. The Sam-who-is-no-longer-Sam stands aloof on the threshold of my chamber. Dubiously his head shakes; he appears to be speaking to the chair adjacent to my bed. 'One Sunday morning, shortly after arriving in Jamaica two years ago, and whilst still becoming acquainted with Papa's estates, I was riding.' Stoop-shouldered, he props his torso against the door-frame, his hand muzzles a yawn. 'I was riding down Cinnamon Hill plantation path, when I knocked heavily filled market baskets from slaves' heads, thus forcing, *forcing* Negro women to dash about, grovelling on the ground, chasing rolling mangoes all over the place.' Glancing at me he sniggers and, from a small silver twin case, singles out a cigar, lights it, eyes flickering, and exhales a tube of blue smoke into the room. In him I see a selfish, brutal, indulged man.

'Yes, continue,' I say.

'Then, showering the slaves with handfuls of silver coins –'

'As some crude compensation?'

'– I galloped away!'

Despite the confusion it has brought at a tender time of change on the West Indian estates, Sam now admits Papa *ordered* his return – because of this and other tales, and the latest controversy involving him which he and Papa still refuse to reveal.

Well! Although pity is poor charity I *do* pity poor Papa for Sam's jests, and I am frequently visited by the disquieting notion that West Indian influences may – contrary to Papa's readjustment plan – have corrupted Sam, morally, all the more. Were I to attempt to raise this matter with Papa I am certain he would treat me very cruelly indeed, *but I never was acquainted with a* young *man of any mind or imagination,* except, of course, dear Brozie, and Brozie believes I inhabit such high moral ground that he'll never climb to where I stand.

I am turning over in my mind a question which has haunted me for many a long month: what are the implications of my family's fast-diminishing wealth having been derived from others' suffering? God chose not to grace me with Voltaire's genius, but a likeness to one situation Voltaire and I do share, for 'It is a dreadful bore to be here, but it is very advantageous' for weighing up such concerns of the mind.

'Sam,' I inquire, 'if one man's greed is another man's hunger, who paid the price for our luxuries?'

This time he grins shiftily. Crossing the room with cigar in hand he bows then kisses my forehead good-night.

No amount of denial will erase the painful truth confirmed by Sam's silence.

I let my eyelids fall shut. Hope End rises immense, palatial, from the bosom of the Malvern Hills. Shockingly exotic with its neo-Turkish minarets, domelets and metal spires. Oriental pagoda-like architecture, flamboyant and bizarre, and as eccentric as Papa could design, it attracts much attention; the young Princess Victoria is even surveying the grounds. I can see through the dining-room, with its crimson flock wallpaper, to peacocks strutting on the terrace; the circular-ended drawing-room decorated in the Italian style; the Moorish views hanging in the billiard room; the handsomely stuccoed library; and the views across the parkland which was well stocked with doe and stags until they threatened the Spanish chestnuts, Portuguese laurels and other rarer trees.

All the splendour by which I am surrounded, all Papa has gained, comes from that bitter-sweet substance, sugar.

I have pushed this away, fought it, but like the sinister silk-black salt water stirring beneath the waxing moon, which can seep through the tiniest crack in the underbelly of a boat, or lashing rain that bleeds through a chink in a rotten window-frame, forming a pool on the sill, this fear has leaked into my thoughts.

Guilt pierces like lightning, like a truth; but unlike truth it fills me with shame. No consolations exist. How to be rid of what's past?

How to escape a polluted family? A family of thieves who stole not only money, but lives. Who took from children what wasn't theirs to take; who perpetuated great injustices that sanctioned rebellions. My thoughts become a garden. Too overgrown with no clear path. Prickly, riddled with tunnels leading nowhere. My faith, my belief, is nailed to emptiness. Empty thoughts. Empty words. Empty deeds.

I care little for material possessions and clothes but that last glimpse of Hope End's domes disappearing behind trees was like being cast out of paradise. Our Hope End home in the Malvern Hills *was* paradise. And yet not for the all the earthly wonders would I sit in the sunlight and shade of those hills any more. It would be a travesty to live in such false glory, like the stitching back together of the torn petals of a rose. I would as soon exhume a corpse as do it. Did hope for ever end there?

What strikes me now is that not only my brother Sam, Uncle

Samuel and Cousin Richard in Jamaica, but Papa, Mama – all those whom I most dearly love – each brother and sister of mine are implicated in this crime, as well as myself. Our decadence makes me sick. I lie stunned as if by a blow to the head. Why has it taken so long for this realization to form, and for me to confront the facts? Can so thin a body carry such a thick mind?

I have long known that the human race is cruel and unscrupulous. I was only thirteen when I wrote *The Battle of Marathon*. Papa had fifteen copies printed, distributed and circulated. Aware, all those years ago, of the powers of the ruling classes and the way that what is past and present can be manipulated as a political tool, I was a tethered bird, striving to fly beyond a narrow perspective in order to see a greater picture, a more sympathetic view of the world.

This narrow strip on which I have balanced, this journey of a woman's soul, one whose privileges depend upon the suffering of others, seems yet more desolate, yet more bleak.

Freed from a girlhood crisis in faith – I am gladdened for *that* being behind me – I now cannot trust to joy. To me, wisdom lies in recognizing that all the kindness and excellences of this earth must be paid for by grief. I shall always be wary of happiness. Everything has its price.

'You were crying out loud,' Bro says. Looking down anxiously, he stands over my bed. 'Was it another bad dream?' He has brought a lighted candle; behind his shadowy head glimmers a pearl-white moon.

'It was,' I reply. 'My heart is so full I can barely breathe.' Bro smiles patiently. He comes nearer. His cheeks, though creamy-smooth, are flushed from salt-winds with a rouge which suggests roses bloom beneath the skin. His eyes hold an iridescent yellow, the pupils shine as if tiny stars sparkle within. 'It was as if I had closed a door on the world and had shut myself up in a room of my own, shut up in darkness. The door was shut and it would not open.'

Sam, the creature I do not know, seats himself on the end of my bed.

Henrietta drifts about in the gloom. 'Ba's distress,' she murmurs in Sam's ear, 'is due to an over-stimulated mind. Too many books.'

To Bro I turn a tear-stained face, searching his eyes for an answer. Bro's look is increasingly troubled. I say to him, 'In God my faith has strengthened. *He* is the saver of souls. *He* is the Supreme Being above, who delivers to man all that is true, all that is good. *He* is the divine grace, the powerful, beautiful, almighty one who teaches the holy principle of love.'

'Dear Ba,' Bro replies, kneeling at my bedside for evening prayers.

One of my favourite passages from the Holy Scriptures creeps into my mind: '*The Lord of peace Himself give you peace always and by all means*' − *it strikes upon this disquieted earth with such a* foreignness *of heavenly music* − *surely the 'variety', the* change, *is to find a silence and a calm.*

25 June 1839

'Papa has not granted Sam attorneyship of Cinnamon Hill,' Henrietta says. She is seated on the window-sill. 'And Papa has told me that *we* are going *downhill* so fast we shall soon reach the bottom, "the Negroes *won't* work and there is no crop".'

'Should he have to return,' I say, 'Sam had better send Papa better accounts, or he will have us all in Jamaica before long.'

Henrietta's lugubrious eyes avoid mine. I notice her face is swollen from crying. 'Sam says the heat in Jamaica alone is enough to drive him mad.' She turns to finish her crochet work.

'He is not the brother I once knew,' I add. 'He has changed, well . . . dramatically. He was always closer to you, Henrietta, than anyone else in the family.' Feeling Henrietta's pain, tentatively I inquire, 'Before leaving for London did he spend much time with you, dear?'

'He is a man of much business,' she replies.

Part of me longs to see Papa's true home, for I know he thinks of Jamaica in that way. To see those majestic stone walls soaked with the sunlit shafts that stream through a lattice of lime-green leaves and drench the flagstones of the back verandah. Cinnamon Hill great house − I wonder why I should feel nostalgia for a world I never knew. I picture a long, low, rambling grey stone building looking out across the face of the ocean. Palms, in silhouette, a burst of dark green. Banana leaves glisten on densely forested slopes hung thickly with creeper ropes. The arching sky is heavy, blue; the heat leaden with the scent of sugar. Bro said the panoramic view from the sundial opposite the steps to the piazza shows the ocean's various shades of indigo through to turquoise, lightening to pale sapphire, blending into the hollow dome of sky. I see plantations of coconut trees, acres of guinea grasses; sugar canes; gardens ornate and exotic; plantain walks; lofty mountains; wells, pastures, ponds, lime kilns; Negro cottages, kitchens, hospitals, stillhouses, mills, roads, paths and tracks, all leading to the Caribbean sea. But in regard to slavery – No. No. No. That system was monstrous for those wretched souls. Mahogany-faced Junius objected to accompanying Sam on his first journey to the West Indies because he greatly feared entering even the apprenticeship system. According to Junius it is not yet true that slavery is abolished (and Papa says he wishes to start it up again). Sam says the Jamaican lowlands are infested with biting insects. Papa's cousin, Richard, although he did have one guide, the Lord Our Saviour, had many tales of undesirable practices, as do Sam and Brozie.

Instinctively I feel we must be open to a new age, not turn our backs on this grimness that we as a family have sustained. Walls of silence have been erected and these must be knocked down. I shall either write against the tide, or drown. I have a loyalty to liberty, to justice, to my own self. Yet to act in conformity with my moral values will outrage my beloved Papa. He is the embodiment of religious principle, a truer more devout believer could not walk this earth. To him I am a blessed one, a handmaid of the Lord's. No one could love me better.

I am to remain confined but it is a jail of my own making for I am *not* a slave, and my pain *cannot* be compared to that of the poor Negroes. It is not through life's privileges that I can reach the poor and deprived but through pain – and the high art of poetry. Poetry brings self and life into judgment. I have a vision of a poet. *A poet's vision.*

8 July 1839

In my fingertips I take the letter Henrietta passes from the silver server. The handwriting looks familiar. Suddenly I experience a terrible sensation, and know the letter is the portent of another awful happening.

Because I cannot see for tears Henrietta proceeds. '*Twenty-second of June, 1839.*' Pausing to wipe her own tears from the parchment, her speech stifled by whimpering, Henrietta commences again. '*Twenty-second of June, 1839 . . . I have deeply felt my absence from you all at Torquay; but when I know how painful a parting scene would be to us all and how injurious it might be to dear Ba, I rather rejoice we have escaped it.*'

Henrietta stifles a moan. She searches her pocket for a handkerchief with which to blow her congested nose. '*My most affectionate love to dear Ba who I am sure will bear this temporary separation with patience for our sakes . . . Write to me regularly about Ba once a fortnight and commence on the first of July, you well know my anxiety and will, I am sure, not disappoint me . . . Twenty-sixth of June. Once more my own dearest Henrietta and Ba, God bless you both, we sail in two hours from this: That God in His mercy may protect and return our dear Ba is the earnest prayer of your fondly attached Sam.*'

Although Henrietta has done her best to scold me out of them, I suffer horrible forebodings that Sam and Stormie's sudden and secretive departure will serve to bring us more bad news. Sam is to reside again at Cinnamon Hill, Stormie at Cambridge Estate. Matthew Farquharson will relinquish charge of Cinnamon Hill on Sam's return.

I feel furious for a time that Henrietta had not left my bedside to say farewell to them, but she assures me she did not know of our brothers' departure until this woeful letter emerged. How am I to accept that it is better for me this way? I shall always be angry. Will I ever see them again? Henrietta says she is angry too.

Could their departure not have been delayed? I ask Henrietta. Well, she says, she doesn't know. My beloved brothers, Sam and Stormie, my dear, dear Stormie who shrinks from public examination on account of the hesitation of his speech. Gone. Without farewells!

Bro says this evening that, like Henrietta and me, he received no warning of Sam and Stormie's departure from London. 'Preparing to partake of the Holy Sacrament might have sent Sam in quieter service into the world,' Bro says. 'I advised him to make the preparations.'

'I could not agree more,' Henrietta replies.

To Henrietta I say, 'But the hour for that is now passed. The only consolation we all share is that Papa did not force Bro to set sail for Jamaica.'

Because I am too weakened by grief to write, I have asked Henrietta to tell Sam how we feel; that it is hard upon us indeed that during all the time he was in England he should only have spent a few short days with us in Torquay; that we wish his visit to England had been postponed until next year; that his and Stormie's coming here was just to wish us good-bye – a very painful pleasure to be sure.

9 July 1839

Dr. Barry is suggesting I reside in Hastings or Southampton for the remainder of the summer. Unbelievable! Southampton is a fearful place, I have told Papa so.

They considered me too fatigued to wish my brothers farewell yet are prepared to drag me about the country like some sort of package when all I desire, now Sam and Stormie are gone, is my removal from this dizzying view of sea.

Uncle Hedley is still packing up books and furniture which will be removed directly to Southampton; he will then follow with the boys. Jane Hedley, Arabel – even their lovely little daughter Ibbit – are gone there. It is on account of the dampness occasioned by the wet mud of the river that I am afraid to travel to that part of coastal country. Papa has written to Bro requesting he advise Dr. Barry that my chair outings do not run on two consecutive days, on account of how tired I am becoming since Sam and Stormie left. I will write to assure Papa that at present in Torquay I am taken care of as if I were made of Venetian glass.

Bro looks decidedly more shaggy with his long veil of hair. He has spent the best part of the summer painting water-colours, fishing, smoking.

10 July 1839

An arch of light hangs yellow over the horizon. The chilled fingers of a summer sea breeze reach through cracked window-frames.

Henrietta sits and sews. A fine silver needle threads memories.

Memories of Sam and Stormie etched on my mind stipple my skin with pin-pricks. Sharp pains spread through my abdomen. I slide beneath the covers. Drugged by weariness, I struggle to keep my eyes open, and feel myself falling into a pit, clawing at collapsing walls. Through the sheets I pick out a faint figure. She signals to me. A scream stabs inside my head, frightening me back to the bleak reality of being closed in, irrevocably, and of the suffocating loneliness living inside whether Henrietta, Bro, Papa, or the weird creature beside the window are with me, or after they are gone.

And feelings from memories swell in waves through my body down to my legs. Memories held in mist like the sea is early each morning in summer.

A deathly stillness encases the room. Silence pierces my ears. A great booming silence. The woman appears in the armchair, unearthly, not inhuman. A man moves towards me; he is the gentleman I saw once before. His touch ghosts across my hand. And when I sit up and lean back, thumping my head on the bedstead, causing a taste steely and bloody to seep into my mouth, they both withdraw.

To the east a medley of clouds play. I cannot see them now and yet feel them all around. The man holds me, his legs entwined with mine, his arms tangled about me.

A dazzle of sunlight breaks through the mottled marbled sea of grey-blue. The rays light up neglected anger within.

This morning Bro said he has written to Papa for my move to Southampton to be cancelled. *That* settles *that.* He also said a Presbyterian minister on the island of Jamaica definitely wrote to Papa shortly before Sam's removal to England. Not only was Sam paying his ex-slaves a miserable pittance of a wage, but, worse, Sam had a Creole mistress and was himself in grave moral danger.

For a while words were strangled in my throat. 'If Sam *was* recalled to England by Papa,' I eventually said, 'why did Papa only allow him to stay here but once, paying us such a brief visit? Barely a full ten days. Given more time, we might have offered Sam the guidance and advice I now so deeply feel he needs.'

Bro covered his face with his hands, a prayer stumbled from his lips; Amens. A pause. He disappeared downstairs.

Why has Crow not brought my evening opium dose? Baleful pools of light from the burnished glass of a flickering bedside lamp float across my hands. Has Crow slipped in to turn up the flame? I am staring into its deep yellow heart. Crow should have drawn the curtains by now.

It is late. Outside the darkness scares me so. My fear is sealed in a black satin sky; the ever-changing black or blue of sea, to the grey-white shimmer of dawn. A dawn of discontent; of wandering through ruins. What will rise from them?

Look how the fire has died. I must ring for Crow.

11 July 1839

Ever dearest Miss Mitford,

... When the sea is calm again, I am to repeat my visits to it, not the dear sea itself, that being too sublime not to be gentle & harmless to the weak; and the intervening distance is not of many yards – not fifty, I shd. think – only the chairs have earthquakes in them ...

... Oh, Miss Mitford, I am in such a 'fuss' (to use an expressive word, which means here however something sadder than itself) about 'my people' in Wimpole Street – about their coming here to spend the summer with me. George is at any rate coming next week – & my dearest Papa will, I know, do what he can about packing up the others – but nobody deals in positives & universals, & says 'we are coming'. The end of it is, naturally, that I am in a fuss. Do you really think I can stay here until next spring – here, comparatively alone? That is proposed to me. I am told that I can't go back to London this winter without performing a suicide! If they wd. but come, I might think temperately of these things – but indeed it is necessary to gather strength of heart from the sight of everybody, to be able to look forwards to another year of exile ...

... The worst grief of all (a very heavy grief at first – until I learned to be wise & submissive about it) has been the departure for the West Indies of two of my dear brothers, who went from London without a last word or look from me. It was all kindly done – and I am reconciled – but I can't write of it now ...

12 July 1839

'Delightful!' Bro exclaimed after reading my final draft of 'The Legend of the Brown Rosary', though he finds it melancholy and fears, as I do, that the ballad may be too long for *Finden*. It is soon to be despatched, accompanied by an apology on account of the length.

Again I have written to Papa and demanded that Bro stay. Am I being selfish? Am I trying to feather-line my life and cushion myself from past griefs at my brother's expense? The days spent together in our Hope End drawing-room were heavenly. Sam enchanted us all with his gadding tongue, black silk stocks and *couleur de rose* garters. Such wit! Such a dandy! So amiable in every way. Sam's is one of the faces, one most loved face, that never ceases to be present with me in this room. It was he who first told me that Hope End was advertised, and with a full description, in *The Sun*. The sound of prospective buyers' footsteps brought terror to our hearts. Bro, Sam, Henrietta and I clung for comfort to the legs of chairs like silent cold clingy bats unable to flutter our black wings. All those horrible sounds . . . *the noise of hammering and men walking up and down stairs, from morning to night.* Five cart-loads of packing-cases went to the warehouse – the timber for the packing-cases alone cost one hundred pounds. It was clear we were leaving. Papa found it more difficult to accept than the rest of us. On a practical level all the arrangements had been made but mentally Papa seemed to be dodging the move. He spent our final evening playing cricket on the lawn with Bro and Sam. Smiling externally but his eyes couldn't mask the blinding pain held within.

13 July 1839

My ever very dearest Arabel

   . . . My difficulty in regard to sleep, ordinarily, is from a want of calmness in the nervous system & circulation – therefore it stands to reason that whatever is of a disturbing character to body or mind, must increase the difficulty a little. But use *will remove the obstacle (i.e. the irritation from moving) and in the process of doing this, my dearest papa's wishes shall be attended to. There has been a week's rest in consequence of the weather, for me, so that I ought to be fit for sailing round the world by today; and I expect Dr. Barry every moment to come & say so. He does not* coerce, *as it used to be his gracious pleasure to do once – and indeed Crow observed to me yesterday, 'I am sure, ma'am, you are a much greater favourite of Dr. Barry's than you used to be.'*

'How do you mean, Crow?' 'Why, I observe that he does not seem to like to press you to do anything disagreeable to you. He gives up in a minute when he sees that you don't like what he proposes – he seems so much more good-natured altogether.' He is very kind, & I have nothing to complain of – & certainly if he does (as he does) treat me like a child, it is now like a very good child indeed – 'it shall have its sugar plum! that it shall!' – and not like a naughty perverse child that looks best with its face in the corner . . .

. . . The ballad went away this morning. Brozie encourages me about it very much, but my impression is still that Miss Mitford won't like it nearly as much as the last – without reference to the length, which is past all reason. Above three hundred & fifty lines, for the most part of fourteen syllables! A ballad in four parts. I have told her that as she can't see me blush through England she must take my word for it! When you once begin a story you can't bring it to an end all in a moment – & what with nuns & devils & angels & marriages & deaths & little boys, I couldn't get out of the mud without a great deal of splashing, which Brozie liked extremely but which may cause less gentle critics to take up their doublets. The title is 'The Legend of the Brown Rosary', & the little heroine's name is Lenora.

> 'Lenora, Lenora!' her mother is calling! –
> She sits at the lattice & hears the dew falling –

There are the first two lines – & the only ones you shall see until I show them to you myself either HERE or in LONDON. I have vowed upon my rosary that you shall not!

Since Sam's departure Papa looks years, not weeks, older. And I feel a grating, gnawing, rising tension in my chest.

An atmosphere of disquiet hangs about this room in which I lie for half the day and more. The tall masts of a vessel pierce the blueness where sea and sky meet. I pray the white sails billowing so magnificently in the bay are not those of the *Hopeful Adventure*, the packet bringing mail and yet more dreadful tales from the West Indies. Hours will pass before I can tell for sure.

Most days now Dr. Barry allows me peace until almost two in the afternoon but this morning he suggested I went straight to the boat without touching down in the drawing-room. Brozie was excited by my *broncher* and later brought me two extraordinarily slim and high blue glass vases. I think only one flower will fit into each for their necks taper severely. *How pretty they look upon the chimney-piece opposite the bed, & on either side of a blue flower-pot from which grow some most splendid geraniums;* their luminous red faces so filled with the rage of loneliness as quite to flare through the room.

14 July 1839

My ever dearest Arabel,
*   . . . My best love to dearest Trippy. She is a very naughty person to think of sending me or Henrietta either these mantillas. Why won't she pack up herself to our direction, in a fit of generosity which we cd. appreciate? . . .*

I am exhausted and must rest a while longer to reflect upon the gladness filling my heart. I am joyful. It was an article in *The Times* Bro read at breakfast that brought the glad tidings. Corporal punishment of the freed Negroes is to be ended in Jamaica and, due to extreme hardships and inhuman conditions, the management of Jamaican prisons is to be transferred from local authorities to the Governor. So glad was I when I heard last August that the apprenticeship system, which brought only sadness, bitterness and greed, had officially ended and set *all* the Negroes *completely free!* Although the Negro apprentices received low wages, I do not doubt dear Uncle Samuel was always more than generous; I still possess a pretty locket he gave me as a child. Uncle Samuel not only left me shares in his ship, the *David Lyon,* but also a legacy of several thousand pounds: that, combined with the four thousand I received from dear Grandmama – profits from the enormous holding of *her* father, Edward of Cinnamon Hill – allows me this past year eight thousand for investment.

The legacies give great independence: Bro has pointed this out to me.

3 August 1839

Dearest Miss Mitford,
*   . . . Between my physician & my maid I did what is called* walking *(by courtesy) a few days ago . . .*

15 August 1839

Papa's lips breeze across mine as he stands from prayer. 'It's nearly eleven o'clock, I must write to George.' But Papa is given to a sudden change of mind and turns back from the doorway. His voice covers the room: 'Ba, you cause me much displeasure. Not only do you refrain from living by the Scriptures daily, Henrietta tells me you fail to read them, that it is your preference to write poetry.' His expression frightens me, so often is his face drawn with fury, with fear. It is one of those suffocating family moments when there's too little space, and what little there is closes in. I hear my own footsteps in flight. I know how dearly Papa loves me. He loves me too well.

Sometimes at Hope End the walls would shake with his wrath. I pray he won't go into a passion, as I fear I would if I thought someone had betrayed my love. Papa's hand smothers mine. His touch speaks, each veined ridge of his skin yearning for all I cannot give, for he wants everything.

Henrietta looks away, despairingly. I cannot live up to either of their expectations. Emotions, like drawstrings tightening, pull on Papa's jaw.

'Believe me,' Papa says. 'Trust in God for your swift recovery. You must do as is His will. We each are one of His children.' He drops to his knees. I wish he had Mama to talk to.

'A year ago, my dear,' he says earnestly, 'I received from Jamaica a letter which illustrated the interment of a coffin containing chains and with the inscription upon it: *The monster is dead.* You may recall the occasion, the first of August, 1838. I am now in receipt of more correspondence upon matters connected with the management of my estates, from an informant of William Knibb. There is sufficient condemnation of Mr Knibb as an interferer in other men's affairs. Had it not been for Wilberforce, and now Knibb, the situation on my estates would have remained stable. Of the abolitionist missionaries continually stirring up unrest – and the House of Assembly is in concordance with me on this – Knibb is the most despicable.'

I give to him a questioning glance. 'The West Indian magistrates began burning Baptist chapels; surely you did not agree with that.'

'Religion should not be mixed with politics. The Baptist preachers' testimonies poisoned the slaves' minds, causing rebellions and violent destructive crimes and, in turn, the deaths of many great British planters. King Knibb indeed! He made peace impossible.'

'Papa . . .'

'What was and what is his object in remaining in Jamaica? If he wants to preach glad tidings unto all men, to advance the house of God Our Saviour unto all with a meek and quiet spirit, to direct the people to the mountain which, we are told, is the will of God, and to know nothing amongst men but Jesus Christ; to exchange ill for good, to spread the word of the Gospel of Christ, to show faith in all ways and by all actions in word and conduct that Jesus Christ, who was crucified for us, was unlike other men – as your dear brother Sam has done, for he strives to be like the Prince of Peace – I say, if these are his objects, then I hesitate not to say that he has woefully blundered. But on the contrary; if to attack secular affairs, if to decide worldly bargains for the people, if to get up political union, if to set man against man, truly William Knibb has fulfilled his vocation.'

As though blind and treading a rocky path Papa moves to leave my chamber.

I daren't mention Mama. Nor Sam. Nor dare I ever mention Hope End to Papa. *He loved the place so . . . And I cannot bear to think that the rooms and walls in which we have not been for so long will be inhabited and trodden and laughed in by strangers.*

'Papa, I don't wish you to feel deceived by me,' I say after him. 'Let's read the Scriptures together tomorrow.'

Staring as though afflicted by a violent memory, his expression is the want of indescribable desires. 'Don't you recall? Tomorrow I must journey to London.' He closes the door.

It is clear I cannot obey him as Sam has attempted to do. Papa is obsessed with his own beliefs. His acute sternness and harshness – something beyond eccentricity – leaves one feeling cold and dead, and I feel unable to remain part of a family financially supported by a vulgar industry. Can I carry this weight with which I am burdened?

Tentatively, Crow enters my room to make Henrietta's bed on

the sofa. Caught on the edge of my mind is an episode which now becomes central to my reverie. In my twenty-sixth year I showed Papa a poem on the development of genius, his biting reply comes clearly: *'You see, the subject is beyond your grasp — and you must be content with what you can reach . . . I advise you to burn the wretched thing.'*

Thus I was dismissed after months of anxious solitary thought, after months of apprehension mingled with rejoicing expectation. I did not say a word: it was harder to prevent myself from shedding a tear . . . I have hardly ever been mortified as I was last night . . . For all my futile scribblings and study Papa's expression that *'my subject was beyond my grasp'*, lets me see . . . *how limited he considers my talents. I believe I did not consider my talents so limited, and I certainly did not know he thought so . . . I could not give up completing the poem I was advised to burn.*

I lie back on soft pillows, Papa's fingerprints ingrained on my skin.

17 August 1839

My dear Lady Margaret,

. . . I must *stay, I suppose, here until next spring again — and indeed it is grievous to think of such an absence — grievous not merely to my own account but on my poor dearest Papa's whose comforts it breaks up in many ways. His tender affection for me has expressed itself so touchingly & disinterestedly that I am deeply moved into adverting to it — and now he has made* presents *to me of my brother George who is here for his law vacation (he is to be called to the Bar in November) & my sister Arabel who is coming to me immediately by some element or other — which, I cannot guess at. And Papa too is coming — and I am as happy as I can be under the circumstance of feeling that they must, one after another, before the winter, go away again & leave me to the consciousness of exile & winds. But it is ingratitude to God's mercy (is it not, dear Lady Margaret?) to be sad now . . . to begin to shiver before the time comes for lighting fires? . . .*

21 August 1839

Arabel sits at my bedside. She arrived from London this afternoon bursting with news. George, it transpires, had sent Papa my latest ballad. Papa says in doing so George has committed a breach of morality. Papa refuses to read the ballad until I know, and have given him permission to do so. Thankfully Arabel is not so strict. She read the ballad immediately it arrived and thinks it *'most superior'* to the 'Romaunt of the Page' and *'very beautiful'*. But dearest Arabel did admit that her hair tended to curl upward as she read it for she found the events *so* horrible.

I have told Arabel to send the ballad to Sam and Stormie and to warn them that no one should read it by candle-light and far less by rush-light. I have said she must tell them that though still weak I am better, that I will write to them once I have regained more strength, that I am praying God will keep them always in His sight, and that they must not worry on account of my health. *For I am better!* Much better than I was in London last summer, at least.

I shall not think on verses I have recently published in *The Seraphim, and Other Poems* – all of which were pervaded by a deathly odour – I shall meditate on future works.

But I taste my own tears again. I live as a blind poet, only inwardly. Although I wish my imagination to soar it refuses to do so. My helpless knowledge of books has built cumbersome walls around my creative mind, my ideas are caged by want of experience. There is an exquisite pain and silence to this lack of life, a profound and painful silence within. Reaching into the dungeon of myself, penetrating walls of darkness, I *will* strive to breathe life through words. Past hills and hollows I will soar and into the landscape of mind, through to the understanding and wisdom that brings with it freedom and liberation to experience – with intensity, with vitality – an *otherness*. If I can sweeten this strange music called life, add light to dismal, sombre, unharmonious tones, I shall be pleased yet.

31 August 1839

Papa, Bro, Henrietta and Georgie all come up to my bedside this evening to pray. Papa says, after reading the reviews, that much of the British public agree with *The Metropolitan Magazine* reviewer's opinion that *'the awful mysteries of the Christian faith are not suited to mortal verse'*. That is the core of Papa's argument against *The*

Seraphim, and so it remains. Expressing my own opinions on this matter I am unable to agree less with Papa and the reviews. I *will not* be pinned down on politics! As a child, I was in danger of becoming the founder of a religion based upon my own imaginings. Though unfit to attend prayer meetings, and may I suffer all the more for it, I am henceforth a tolerant Congregationalist – a kind of heretic believer – I was always of an Eveish constitution, and always shall be. I am certain that if the goodness of Christianity could be suffocated by evils in society and die, tragedy would persist. Tragedy *is* the highest form of poetry. I tell Papa this. I tell Papa I believe that in almost every religious controversy there are two wrong sides – and one bad spirit, which is common to both; this angers Papa dreadfully. He is fanatical. He *sees* the law and gospel on his side.

'Now, Henrietta, listen to me,' I say as Papa, Bro and Georgie descend to the drawing-room for their dinner aperitif, 'the review of *The Seraphim* in *The Examiner* commented that "*sacred objects*" are not fit for poetry except on very rare and brief occasions. What do *you* think of *that,* and of *The Metropolitan Magazine's* response?' Henrietta lies on the sofa, eyes tightly shut. The silence is wintry. Is my sister ignoring me? 'To me, God's love is the true mystery,' I continue, 'whether we are, or are not, at home speculating on the minds of angels.' Perhaps Henrietta is sleeping already. She said earlier she was too exhausted to eat.

Sleep escapes me tonight. I wrestle with too many thoughts, and am at odds with my world in general, and no matter how many times I say to myself I won't see Papa's furious face in my mind any more, there it constantly remains. I can't forget his expression. It grows more clearly defined whenever I close my eyes.

Papa is impossible to understand. Impossible. He seems unable to express feelings to anyone except me. His violent temper is equal in strength to a hurricane. His will, inflexible.

1 September 1839
Tonight Dr. Barry was late and his consultation brief to say the least. He came in from a torrential shower, trouser bottoms dripping, and had barely finished unbuckling his brown leather bag than he was rushing downstairs.

I have taken Dr. Barry under my protection and will not have him chastised, yet I find annoyance grips me. Henrietta believes one hundred and twenty-five pounds to be a moderate charge. Though I may be unreasonable, I think otherwise, because of the number of months Dr. Barry has taken to send the pecuniary part of my obligations to him. I also have the druggist's bill to pay — fifty pounds. With all these expenses my finances will hardly bear the rent at this house.

Surprisingly good news has come in light of this — and when I least expected it — although the income isn't reliable — the last sheets from my publisher showed a significant increase in my poetry sales.

> *My dear Lady Margaret,*
>
> *. . . I had expected most of the copies to be sent to me for the waste paper by this time — & had put off all my notable sewing, as well as curling my hair, from last year, that I might peradventure come into an inheritance of thread papers & curling papers — You know Milton's idea of fame is 'to think to burst out in sudden blaze'. But in this utilitarian age (& I wd. not be behind my age for the world!) I cd. not think of putting my books into the fire! — No! not for a 'sudden blaze' in our east wind! . . .*

2 September 1839

Autumn is close at hand. Corn heads have been cut, the wind wails terribly by the crumbling casement, and despite my protestations, visits from my able and most kind physician, Dr. Barry, have become still briefer and less frequent.

Dr. Barry, who has attended to me almost every day for above a year, attended at my best estate and never left me longer than a day, was taken dreadfully ill and is confined to his bed with rheumatic and nervous fever.

3 September 1839

Dr. Barry is again too sick to visit.

Yet my medical examinations are necessary. *I* am particularly unwell tonight as a consequence of the moist, heavy and changeable state of the atmosphere and, for some days recently, have suffered from old symptoms — oppression on the chest and expectoration. It now seems my condition is bronchial.

My yearning to return to London only increases as September progresses. September – the one month in which I tend, nay *intended*, to flee the peculiar position in which I find myself. I continue to confute the view held by my old friend, Mr. Boyd, *'that women never improve'* – a most dreadful theory – although I conversely belong to that pitiful order of weak women who cannot command their bodies with their souls at every moment, and who sink down in hysterical disorder when they ought to act and resist. *Heart and will are great things, but after all I, like everyone else, carry a barrowful of clay about me, and I must carry it a little carefully if I mean to keep to the path.*

I was always of a determined and, if thwarted, violent disposition. Come storms or sunshine I *must* have Dr. Barry visit me, and *only* Dr. Barry.

10 September 1839

I have decided we are to up and move from this house to save the princely sum of seventeen pounds a year. I have paid the current rent, one hundred and eighty pounds a year, from my own pocket.

Bro has found a more than suitable property, 1, Beacon Terrace, which we may take initially for six months. Bro vows that we will all prefer our new home; it is more sheltered than this from violent westerly winds. My bedroom-to-be is well situated, opening on to the drawing-room, so there are no cold passages or stairs to pass up and down.

Many pettish words pass between Bro and me daily. I wonder whether he experiences this slow death too, or whether it is only I who encounters a sense of drowning after a long slow summer of deck-chairs and parasols.

The morning sun's milky brightness streams through the windows on to Bro's face. He has adopted a strangely rigid stance; hands in pockets, a dishevelled copy of *The Times* poking from under one arm. The sun's glare across his countenance appears bothersome; he is poised in the limelight as though debating what to do.

'Trippy has told Arabel that she will *never* come and visit whilst I am in Torquay,' I say to him, 'and I am sure she never will.' Bro raises his eyebrows and says nothing. 'Henrietta believes Trippy's *better heart* will not permit her to keep this resolution. But Trippy has the fiercest temper and can be quite a dragon.'

'Trippy's emotions, like Papa's, are deeply rooted in the West Indies,' Bro eventually replies, falling into an armchair.

'Last night, after an additional evening prayer, I caught Papa talking to himself. *Again.*'

Bro shakes open *The Times*. Pages rustle and quiver as he flits from one to the next, his eyes scanning the print under the guise of reading. 'Yes,' he says, 'I recently caught Papa saying under his breath, "But there are too many Barretts, too many *called* Barrett. All we related? God! What could be worse!" I am certain Papa was referring to the traces of slaves' blood I think he fears are in our lineage.'

'Does Sam truly have an African mistress? Is that why Papa hardly mentions him? Does he fear Sam will bring more misfortune and brown-skinned offspring?'

Bro emits a feeble sigh and folds the newspaper into an untidy mess. 'Even at a young age you should have deduced from Trippy's stories that a conflict between the body and soul of things exists on our estates.'

'But, Bro, is there no flexibility in Papa's governance, particularly this area of peculiarity: that none of us form close relationships with members of the opposite sex – unless, it would seem, they are members of our immediate family?'

'Papa's theories are hypocritical. The Barrett family can't be held up as an example of purity. With our illegitimate cousins in Jamaica we amount to a multitude as numerous as the tribes of Israel.'

This morning, opening my eyes from morning prayers upon Papa's bowed head, a hostility within burgeoned forth such as I have never felt towards him before. I feel no escape from the countless columns of his moral principles, and it seems a new darkness shapes his beliefs, and that this too will fall upon us. 'Should we never produce children, and remain spinsters and bachelors until the end of our years? No – I cannot believe *that*! What if you were to marry Alexandra Earle?' I pause, and avert my eyes from Bro. 'What if she were to bear you children? You might have to choose whether to continue your acquaintance with Alexandra. Arabel suggested an engagement might be imminent.'

Head angled down Bro drums his fingers on his knee – a taut frayed rope is about to snap – I fear I ventured too far. Bro glances up sourly. 'If you were determined to return to Wimpole Street for the summer you should have done so.'

I am glad it pleases Papa that I intend staying unmarried. *I* shall *never* marry. He can march up and down all he pleases. Being of an intolerably exclusive disposition never have I even wished for marriage and am sure I never will, unless I meet a poet who truly inspires my mind and work and of whom I am worthy.

27 September 1839

> *My dearest Miss Mitford,*
>
> *We go to number 1 on this Terrace, on Monday or Tuesday – & there won't be much risk for me in the removal for so short a distance. My brother means to fold me up in a cloak & carry me.*
>
> *May God ever bless you! – Pray don't throw away more anxious thoughts upon me. If I had any really* bad *symptoms, I wd. call in another physician. As it is do let me enjoy the luxury of being obstinate – perverse as Mr. Kenyon calls it.*
>
> *Your obstinately affectionate EBB*

25 October 1839

> *My dearest Miss Mitford,*
>
> *Dear kind Dr. Barry is no more. A second relapse followed fast upon the first, and you could scarcely have read what I wrote in hope and gladness before all lay reversed, and by a startling decree of God, the physician was taken and the patient* left *– and left of course deeply affected and shaken. He was a young man . . . a young wife & child, & baby unborn . . .*

The same Dr. Barry who forbade me to write. *Anything*. Even poetry! How miserably depressed I am left. Bummy and Crow say, 'Ba, you must pull yourself together,' insisting that it is not my fault he died. Yet I blame myself completely. How can I not?

Dr. Barry, rising from his own sickbed in concern for me, ventured out on a night foul as this, braving cruel torrents of rain to examine the condition of my chest: because of this his second child will never know its father. Although we had thought Dr. Barry would recover, it was an inflammation of the bowels that superseded the fever and weakened his body beyond repair.

How we Barretts are cursed, for this is a curse if ever there was one. Bro first heard the dreadful news on the first of October, just two hours after Dr. Barry's death. That afternoon I watched the flags of all the vessels in the bay hoisted down to half-mast. One very elderly woman, Bro said this morning, walked five miles every day during Dr. Barry's illness to inquire after him. Locally, he was surely a well-liked man.

Crushing waves of grief roll into each other, becoming one great ocean of woe. My new doctor, Dr. Scully, said the storm is almost passed and I am better. But a sea around me rages. I believe I am dying.

Each time I wake, day or night, my eyes fall on the chalk drawing gazing down on my bed, which Papa has given me. The result, he agreed, is very realistic. He said, when he stood back to admire the gift, that he believed it to be the quality of light on the skin that makes the representation near perfect. Certainly, it is the most impressive portrait of Papa I have seen. Pastel colours blended by the artist's fingers create a smooth three-dimensional effect yet, even viewed from this distance, the features appear quite sharp.

Chapter Eight

Sheba

CINNAMON HILL ESTATE
January 1839

Trouble rests on him battered wooden bench beneath shady mango
trees. He have a sort of watchfulness; it makes me uneasy. Stooped
over with tiredness, him body wears no shirt; he never wore no shirt
nowhere, just osnaburg trousers. He also wears spotted green-and-
blue neck-cloth tied in a bow beneath him chin. Strangely, a pink
silken strip's pulled tight, turban-like, over him head, crushing hair.

'Pretty pretty hat,' Big Robert say, strolling by.

Sylvia's perched beside Eleanor on charred verandah steps with
rough edges caved in from fire burns; one tread's half collapsed.
Sylvia say, 'Trouble, crazy crazy.'

Trouble pays no heed. Like he cyaan hear. He spits out grass
seeds he holds in him mouth, treads dry leaves into sandy dirt.

But Big Robert say, 'Im look nice nice.'

Trouble-Too-Much glances at Big Robert fretfully, him crinkled
topknot of hair poking up tall proud as old cockerel's comb at
dawn – though Trouble's comb's black, not red.

Eleanor's whisper say, 'Trouble's hat wos made fram buckra
woman's underwear, one pantaloon leg torn off wen buckra woman
lost its ribbons, so she give it to Trouble's mama and pa. Dat's all
dey leave Trouble-Too-Much afta dem dead.'

Having rested fe a spell, Trouble sets back to work. Already he
sweat through many nights until dawn abeng-blow, humping on
him hunched back wattle hurdles woven from saplings. Stacking
wattle hurdles, rebuilding Eleanor's shack with pure hate and envy
fe what he'll never have, never be, Trouble-Too-Much wrenches

silk hat down tightly over ears, so it looks like him ears must smart and cuss. Like he can hide bad feelings inside him head inside pink bloomer leg. Like it's him been ruined and raped and forced into wrong. Or Trouble-Too-Much's powerful arms build shack up with what? Hope? Love? Black jealousy? Sameway like overseer envies Mister Sam, Trouble-Too-Much builds Eleanor's shack with torments we suffer.

Trouble-Too-Much's suffered too much from sick horror of this place. Me mind takes me days back to when a boy came out from behind Eleanor's half-built shack, behind him red sun sank into golden-blue sea of dusk. 'Trouble-Too-Much ere?' messenger boy shouted, walking through shack village.

Trouble, waving to him, stepped down from Eleanor's verandah, bare chest and trousers smattered with sawdust. 'Trouble-Too-Much ere aright,' he called back.

Messenger boy said, 'Me need to talk wid yu quiet somewhere.'

Trouble climbed verandah steps, disappeared with messenger boy through doorway into shack's darkness.

A long time later, when hoppers shriek in knife-edge grass, their cries mean, coarse, brittle, and stark light falls from moon's full whiteness, led by messenger boy Trouble-Too-Much shambled from Eleanor's shack. He moved weak-kneed to verandah rail he'd been crafting from wood, and spoke into night air in a sorry sorry voice. 'Me mama an pa ded, an-a year pass an nobody care to tell me?' Open moonlight washed him heaving shoulders silver; him body sagged with defeat, though him eyes seemed to fail to believe what he'd just said. 'Dem owe a-lickle money,' he said, 'an fe dat dem starve, fe no work offered to dem by any buckra at any place.' We field-hands grouped on verandah steps, thinking, we owe a-lickle money too, fe rent fe provision ground and we shack.

This make good reason fe Trouble's anger?

After final abeng-blow, shack yards fill up with First Gang. All have empty faces. Painful, pink and angry dusk glow comes. Trouble-Too-Much battles in him heart and head, strutting about too hasty hasty; puffing, panting, pretending like he cyaan care less.

Moving tirelessly fast, in spotted bow tie and pink silken hat as each evening passes, all dawn, all dusk time, like old crazy cockerel that keeps up crowing, Trouble's eyes watch narrowly like he plans to kill somebody – every smile he gives adds to him act – like he cyaan cut and weave wattle; cyaan plaster and whitewash with lime dug from riverbanks, where soft limestone rises, like Isaac and me did; cyaan scythe long summer grasses fe thatching over hardwood beams fast enough to keep off what's tracking him.

Humping wattle hurdles on him back, Trouble passes Sylvia's verandah where me sit at dusk. He all hard from building shack up, from thatching grass and leaves over hardwood beams fe Eleanor's shack roof.

With de gentle comforting clucking of peel-neck chickens rooting in dust round cotton tree's straggling roots, Trouble-Too-Much say to me when me eye offers understanding, 'Yu a-tree, fruit bin picked by too many pickers, too many. Dey leave yu bare. Buckra, e strip de niggar tree. Yu nah cunny like doctor-bird, hard bird fe dead.'

'Why yu do say dis me wanna know?'

'Ask no question, hear no lie,' Sylvia tells me. 'Buckra don't call im Trouble-Too-Much fe noting.' Him eye hunts me face, hunting misery down. Even when we ripping, stripping, straggly weeds with machete blade, Trouble's lips, choosing silence, firmly clamp shut; him don't let out words but him hunting eye tells what hate and envy's in him mouth, on tongue tip.

Some days more weeds than cane, some days none. Some days me use billhook, some days rip weeds out by hand but always me thinking me cyaan work in cane piece no more. *There's no more, there's only less since yu, Isaac, left.* No, me cyaan work here no more fe it happens now. Again. Tiny pieces come too sharp to see clearly. *Slippery red between me legs.* Memory splinters embed in me head, cling to me throat back. Sometimes me wipe Isaac from me mind, slide into feeling again, whatever sharp thoughts slip into me head me heart's spilling out hurt. Buckra looks through me. Into me belly. Them know. Just stare. Cold. Pale. Ill-looking. Mister Richard's one of them. Sylvia say all buckras afraid of slave woman's belly when it bloated smooth like jumblie-tree skin.

Lickle Phoebe and Windsor change too. It shows in Phoebe's weak walk. Sounds in Windsor's soft soft talk. Tears shine daily on Eleanor's face and me often watch she heart collapse since Isaac's murder. Terror rises up right before me when Trouble-Too-Much stands near. *Shuddering, he crashes down, bringing fiery hell minister tell we bout. Me throat tightens. Hands force me waist down, digging me belly in sandy ground. Heavy rustle of osnaburg trousers, belt buckles clunk. Clamping me head down, forcing deep, deeper, filling me with fear, rasping, thrusting like rusty saws.* Coming over shaky, sweat trickles down me nose, and with Trouble walking behind me, me lose footing on rocky paths. And when we reach shack village every night fe days, weeks, months, Trouble-Too-Much's eye sits tight on me belly. 'Dere's no way me'd touch it. No way!' it say.

And now each terrible dusk, and now with night looming ahead, feelings come stumbling over Cinnamon Hill with First Gang and down cane-piece track.

And now sky's burnt red. Red like lobsters in wicker baskets Sylvia weaves fe fisher-boys bringing freshly cooked catch fe selling at Cinnamon Hill. Red like obeah chicken blood. *Slippery red between me legs.* Deep dense and glowing red like obeah cast a spell up there where minister say de heavens are.

Trouble-too-Much plods ahead. Coming to village edge, a shambles of pens, dirty yards, closely packed shacks, he halts until me reach tethered brindled goat him stand beside. Sky's glow stains him richly dark skin red. Him hat's disappeared. He loosens spotted cloth from him neck. Him eye looks all-knowing. Like he sees through my thoughts to ocean open blue. Finally he hiss at me, 'If yu, Sheba, have pickney, yu'll know oo baby-fadda be?' Trouble's words bite. Him eye meets mine; me crinkle up with shame.

Sylvia walks on other side of me. She say to Trouble-Too-Much, 'Don't ask if Sheba know. Leave she alone, man. Go.' Trouble-Too-Much's eye hunts Sylvia's face this time. 'Never trust a Negro,' she voice twists on me sharply. 'Negro swear false, Negro hang thousands to free imself. Torching time yu remember clearly, wen court-house buckra made a studyation to shoot all slave men, an leave all slave woman? Most Cinnamon Hill slave men say, if whites come to take life fe noting dey would run away, not stand together wid slave woman so all we can protect each other. Too quickly we men forget wot Sam Sharpe say "we strength live in unity". Cyaan snap thick tree trunk or hefty bundle of sticks, but tiny twig snap, see. Alone we a tiny twig. Together, towering tree.'

Trouble's done with rebuilding Eleanor's shack. It give to me sleeping place. Wanting to give thanks me offer Trouble a faint smile. Trouble-Too-Much shows me him back. He goes to him own yard, hangs over verandah rail, head bowed. Him eye still fixes on me.

Elbows on knees, me sit on newly laid verandah steps stripped of bark and scrubbed raw yellow. Stooped over, clothes dirt-patched, Big Robert gathers cook-fire wood from trees all we field-hands felled and dragged to village edge. Yard's full and busy now. Sky's grazed red with coral-coloured streaks.

Sylvia sits down beside me. Phoebe sits above my knee.

'Sheba, yu should visit Leah,' Sylvia say. 'Obeah wiser dan yu an me.'

'Leah warn only of bad ting,' whispers Lickle Phoebe. 'Minister mek trouble fe Leah. Leah talk bad, give buckra evil eye, say she'll catch im shadow, mek im die die.' Lickle Phoebe's words lodge in me heart pointed arrow sharp.

Big Robert comes to Eleanor's verandah, he settles, leans against pigeon-pea sacks, legs stretched before him. He opens Bible across him knee, thumbing through torn grubby pages. Eleanor comes to join we, towing two full pigeon-pea sacks, making trails in dirt.

'Hear me true,' Sylvia protests. 'Leah grow herb to heal many sickness.' Sylvia's eye go up mountain peaks where tree fern begins and river's arms reach down to carve rock pools fe janga-fish. 'Leah set fish-pots fe freshwater fishing. She have a cow she hide up dere. Me seen wen she say goodbye to de land at day's end.'

Lickle Phoebe say, 'Sheba get more sick, wot den?'

'Hothouse cost four shilling a head,' Eleanor say.

'Dat wot dey charge yu wen yu last chile die of yaws?' Sylvia ask Eleanor. Eleanor nods. Sylvia fetches she broom made from brushwood twigs fastened to branch handle fe sweeping gritty yard floor.

Lickle Phoebe's small hand stretches out towards roundness of me belly. 'Yu'll grown big fast,' and she almost laughs, stroking me. Me heart never leaves off pounding hard. Me feel hatred swell towards Lickle Phoebe. She head tips sideways and, sameway as old yard-dog, she nuzzles against me chest. Tenderly, she shares food she's gathered when we're fishing or picking red berries, but loathing grows thick from me to Lickle Phoebe, thicker than overgrown tangleweed grass climbing wrinkled tamarind trees.

Moving to stand, Eleanor say, 'Sheba won't get more sick dan she aready be.'

Very well den, me think.

Trouble's ears must hear every word, fe suddenly he shouts, 'If Sheba visit Leah, Sheba won't come back! We need Sheba to work wid we. Saltwater African too many ere. Dem shirk work, swear, feign illness, steal, lie, but buckra pick on we.'

Sylvia breaks from sweeping yard floor. She eye aim at Trouble. 'Trouble-Too-Much, is yu talk buckra talk.' She sits down again, rubs bite-speckled skin on arms and ankles. She turns broom brush skyward fe warding away tiny maskitta dancing about cloud-like in evening air.

Trouble wears him hunting mask. He comes to Eleanor's verandah like being drawn by a string. Me toes curl up. Me feel sick to bottom of me belly. Sylvia's eye tells Trouble to keep him mouth shut.

Big Robert looks up from Bible pages, saying, 'Sheba find Christianity good if it do good fe me.'

'Don't lissen to no minister,' say Eleanor. 'Wot Leah do won't hurt yu, Sheba. God cyaan send nigger to hell. Nigger areadie dere.'

Silent now before me Trouble prowls to and fro, lips snarling, him all teeth and clashing.

Sylvia say, 'Sunday market minister want to end, say we no trade on Sabbath day. Lard want we to starve? We areadie lost pay.'

Tongues clicking, Eleanor, Windsor and Phoebe nod to agree.

'Buckra feed we wid spiteful venom,' Lickle Phoebe say.

Trouble-Too-Much's voice comes again. 'White buckra bwoy sin in de eyes of God, make we distrust brodda, sista,' and he laughs madly at me.

'Why yu say all dis?' Sylvia snaps.

Trouble-Too-Much licks a swollen thumb, staring down him nose. 'Buckra don't know wot freedom is,' he say. 'We sworn to de Lard. To mek trouble's wrong.' Him laugh mocks Big Robert, mocks himself, mocks me.

Me look awry, sliding me eye to earthy yard floor baked hard and dry.

Getting up, Big Robert turns on Trouble, saying, 'It's wrong to do as white men. Mek we bad as dem.'

Me want only to climb from Trouble's eye, from me body, skin, out from yard, shack village, plantation. Life. Hotter and hotter me feel and shivers crawl up and down me spine like frightful chill of mountain stream. Pickney's sucking me belly guts, sucking like red-blue flash from doctor-bird sucking out a flower's soul.

Shelling peas, Eleanor say, tilting towards me, 'Yu gotta git fram dis place.'

Phoebe yawns in readiness fe she sack and sleep.

'Afta cane burning she cun go,' Sylvia say.

Me reach a wall of doubt. Move away from Phoebe when Isaac live in she face? Me must be near Phoebe fe she a strong reminder of Isaac in flesh. But me hate forgiveness Lickle Phoebe shows when me did no wrong. Forgiveness fe wot's left of me. And me love Lickle Phoebe's caring soft ways. Hate turns to love turns to hate; there's nothing in between.

When burning begins me can go where? Despair snatches at me mind, whispering, *Burning soon come.*

Me eyes become heavy slits. Aching tired me eat evening cassava meal Sylvia serve; curl on dry leaf-stuffed sack, wanting to run. But to where? Rain rings sharp on palm-and-grass thatched roofs. Me can dream but cyaan sleep feeling yellow buckra flesh feeding off whatever me eat. Strangled by feelings, me lie half dead. Cyaan run away from what's in me head, what turns and grows in me belly, slides through blood. Sylvia's shack's too dark to see bodies me hear breathing. But Lickle Phoebe's voice travels to me this night, crawls under skin, through flesh, bones, where a living beast sucks. *Leah catch buckra shadow, mek im die die*, Lickle Phoebe said.

Me have a sudden feeling to run. Stealing from sack without thinking further run through smouldering fire-smoke – a wispy milk-white web coiling into rain-drizzle, smelling of burnt sugar and green wood. Run silent path winding long through sleeping village, knowing Lickle Phoebe won't see foot tracks fe at sunrise Harry's broom sweeps between shacks.

Like snake spirit haunting salt marshes, thoughts of Leah curl into me mind as me run through tall grasses, toes sinking into hissing mud, leaving gardens behind, scatterings of cordia flowers, small cinnamon trees, provision grounds passed on from Mama in hills above. Leaving behind Lord Jesus, into looming darkness me head fe vast mountain slope. Lord Jesus creeps up on me trying to take root; Lord Jesus seeping in when me breathe. Me reach place fe uprooting trees fe cook-fire wood; Jesus sinking into me heart as me pass under sky's solid sobbing black roof. *Run past clearing where we held each other, kissed, Isaac, bitten with love's storm. To run me fingers across yu face, Isaac, dat's all me live fe now. Run by Sunday punishment place where you cyaan make market money, Isaac. You were bleary-eyed, you hands and feet cruelly tied. Eleanor helped raise field-stock yoke, weakly heaving you body up. Why we free yu fram field stocks to too soon leave this life?*

Running past cane-piece track. Cotton trees. Leaving restless sea's hum behind. Croaking lizards. Toads. Sweet frangipani. Pimento groves. Trash piles – black against a blacker sky. Running, passing trees where Loa twists and whirls, a great panic grips me. Branches strike me belly. Trunks thump me thudding heart. Spells twirl through hair, round legs, all wanting to suck soul out-a me. Lightning shoots from one tree like shock of pain. Flickering silver, lightning streaks crack clouds. Running through thick-scented jack-fruit forest, on past breadfruit, pomegranate, mango trees. Shadows, charcoal black, leap from behind star-apple tree trunks. Creeping claw of fear of Lord Jesus takes root in me, sinking through me heart to skirt very edge of me soul. Bible pages fall back, fall out, fe me running to spirit gods. Hills grow into mountains. Mountain me climb disappears suddenly cloaked in rain. But goat track leads up steep, picking a path through moonlit streams parted by boulders. Past janga-fish resting in rock pools. Water smooth as silvery coconut oil swirls cold round ankles. Heaven's completely gone when me leap waist-deep in thickets, bushes unknown to me slice cheeks reaching sharply fe bone, sameway as machete blade slashes skin. No Jesus God comes after me through thicket wood so thick me cyaan hack out a path. Water streams from wide banana leaves. Fat raindrops bounce off arms. Me bound so far, run so fast that dripping leaves grow blurred, dim. Scrambling high over mossy rocks, rain-drenched tree ferns soft soft as chicken feathers brush me legs; then sandy-floored clearing me reach.

Bones stick up from a cedar shingle roof, poles rest against shed walls me know must be Leah's. Cockerel feathers clasp a cross nailed to she hardwood door. Me push. Door opens a bit, but it's stiff. Heavily me lean like pushing a great stone.

A shape lies on floor middle. Blinkie-blinkie fluttering in glass jars light wattle walls green. Snoring, Leah turns over. Squawking feathers skim me shin – a chicken flaps through Leah's doorway vanishing into dark forest.

Leah's voice darts out shrilly, 'Oo de hell's dat?' Me heart shrinks in on itself. Walking on feet and hands till she back arches, Leah forces she body to stand upright. Me heart shrinks further than it's ever been, and me feel everything me think me knew of life suddenly disappear after Leah's squawking chicken, over mountains, down hills.

Untidy. Overgrown, Leah's hair's sprinkled with burrs; grass heads heavy with seeds are woven into curls. Standing naked and tall in hut's dark light, 'Me heard yu sick,' she say.

Heard from who? me want to ask but shock of pain from all that's happened surges into me belly; a dull agony throbs in me head, through me heart a deep ache.

Leah's long flat fingers fumble along shelves feeling fe candles. Half she face hidden by hair, a steady gaze she have, putting a candlestick to a rush-light flame's dying burst.

'Wot bring yu ere so late, Sheba?' she ask.

I'm wanting to say, *How yu do know me name?* but me lips get stuck again. Looking hard at me, Leah's African eye holds power like she sees what's sucking soul out-a me, sees into dawn, and beyond. 'Yu suffer sickness every morning? No, dis did yesterday end.' Leah lights two more beeswax candles from de flickering rush-light flame. Moving about she shed, Leah coils cloth she lay beneath about bony pointed shoulders, flat belly, waist. 'Yu have pain in yu back? Chest? Bad dream stay in yu head?' she asks. 'Yu do waan dis wot yu carry?'

'No. Yes. Me not know,' is all me find to say. *It's wot? Cyaan be chile. Chile grow fram love. Dis a bad curse? Or Isaac's heart beats on in me belly? One seed of happiness grown fram me own Isaac soon to be lost?*

'Is only buckra do dem ting,' Leah murmurs. 'Yu betta off widout dis chile.' Flat stone slab she's pointing at sits behind open hard-wood door. 'Yu move rass rakstone?' she asks. She shoves stone slab against door bottom to keep it shut. Leah murmurs again, 'It no more dan wandring duppy.' A smile crosses she face, narrow nose widening as she lips go thin, showing cracked teeth. 'Sit, chile,' she say.

Dirt floor me sit on feels chilly. 'Sit,' Leah's snapping she fingers at me then at she sleeping mat.

Woven rush mat's harsh, cold, till me find Leah's warm sleeping patch. Locking arms round knees at last me ask, 'Dis chile fram Isaac?'

Leah's eye traps me with its heavy grasp. Rarely now do me not feel scared but this fear's different. Terrified by strength in Leah's face and believing me said something wrong all me can move's me eye, awkwardly, me seek a hiding place. In a jar beside me on mat's edge a dry shrivelled snakeskin curls, empty, hungry, wanting a body. Glass beads glint in a shell bowl. Lizards croak on woven wild-cane walls bound to corner posts with withes. Gecko, catching night flies, dart over feathery bundles, under goombay drums, across sacks overflowing pigeon peas, along a hollow reed flute, slithering into Leah's upturned basket of limes.

Shaking a calabash, drawing closer, still Leah don't answer. But she will summon Loa, me know, a link to we spirit world. Me feel Leah's mind work. She drops into me lap a rattling calabash filled with seeds, wound in a pretty web of clay beads painted blue, green.

'Sheba, Loa tek pickney fram yu belly,' Leah say.

Hot tears sting me eye. 'It does know it'll die?'

'Chile's a gift,' Leah say thoughtfully. 'It don't die.'

But sharp she words slice me insides, and me lie wen me say, 'Me know.' *A gift? Dis thing grating in me belly, gnawing at me guts?*

'Me cyaan swear spirit'll go now, understand? Buckra pickney spirit can be strong. But if e do come to be born mek sure yu kill im. Kill im. Keep im fram suffering in we world. Kill im. Kill im,' Leah say coldly. She eye makes four with mine. 'Yu be sure yu understand yu have two choices. Pickney go back to spirit world now, or day afta eighth day of him birth yu kill im fram dis earth. Me give me word so hear me, till ninth day after birth it just like a wandring duppy returning to duppy world.'

But me now feel it a monster me carry, wriggling, squirming, half made. Leah looks far into me mind. 'Yu must mek all thoughts go,' she say. 'Be strong like hurricane.' *Isaac's chile? Cyaan be. How to get up, get out, move, if me buried already?* 'Sheba, yu cyaan hear? Together we reach across, put wandring spirit back. It's still a spirit after birth, lang as yu understand dis, yu free. But first,' Leah say, 'yu must know how much spirit chile worth.'

'Priceless,' me say.

'A-good.'

Shaking Leah's calabash me follow to shed's back door. Me mind ask, *Wot's spirit chile worth?*

From doorway Leah's calling spirit priest by blowing breath between two fingers jammed into she mouth to make a piercing whistling screech. Turning to me, 'Yu come to no harm,' she say. 'Wot me do cyaan hurt. Osun, spirit of healing streams, will walk ere beside yu. Osun will guide yu.' More of she deafening whistles pitch deep into night.

Moonlight falls coolly over Leah's sandy back yard. She yard's no church but a place fe spirits, souls, together. Together we meet in yard middle where creepers climb wrinkled bark of sacred spirit-filled tree, that we salute together. To protect we, Leah draws a cross in blue-black air – not Jesus cross but obeah. Bending low she kisses sandy swept earth, fe from earth all things have death, all things have birth. She then shouts, 'Hee-yu, hee-yu,' again calling spirit priest.

Clouds, arching over moon's path, glimmer dimly as great house white marble and stroke Leah's smooth-skinned calabash rattle. Sprinkling cornmeal from she hand, Leah draws another cross on sand. She lips touch where two lines meet – a sacred place between life, between death. Me lips meet dark bark on spirit-filled tree, then me eye goes into cornmeal cross, fixing on its heart, where future stems from what's past.

Leah shouts, 'Hee-yu, hee-yu,' once more fe calling spirit priest. From far away a goombay drum thunders. Waving she hands in night air, Leah's inviting gods. 'Protect we chillun,' she sings. Feet thud, leaping round obeah cross. Seeds rattle in calabash as me shake.

Dressed beggar-like, a priest man comes running, wrinkly knees poking through osnaburg trousers, coat trimmings flapping behind. He carries two chickens, one black, one white, upside down by scrawny legs, with goombay drums clamped under an arm.

Drums sound loudly in Leah's yard each beat tying we together. Priest bows to Leah. He pushes me onto me knees, swings screeching chickens high above me head, shoulders, bent body, legs.

Dancing, flame-like, at full speed, Leah's twisting, twirling. Never did me see man or woman move so quick. Priest holds both chickens' heads down to Leah's cornmeal cross. Fiercely chickens peck grain but priest works swiftly, breaking chickens' legs and wings.

Priest swings we offering across me belly. Feathers flying, black chicken bashes night-black air with broken wings. Screwing its neck round, black chicken's life he gives to Loa.

Twisting white chicken's neck, priest makes Life cross into Death, fast, so they become One. No blood spills on earth from living sacrifice. Clouds cross de moon. Hunched up, shouting, Leah dances faster than John Canoe dancer; mouth gaping, eyes bulging dangerously. Will of Loa's spirit mounts Leah's back. Priest beats goombay drums. Calabash seeds rattling, me heart beating faster, faster, me cyaan see spirit rider. Leah's soul fights, shaking terribly, as Loa enters she body. Mouth twisting into a snarl, what Leah utters comes from we God. Long flat feet stamp. She falls. She have left she body, Loa makes it move now, she all shake-shivering legs, arms stretched across sandy ground.

Moonbeams light Loa's old wrinkled face. Leaping onto long flat feet, Loa rises, and with great steps, circles spirit-filled tree. Priest's dancing too, swinging dead chickens, offering carcasses up, offering floppy heads up to Loa. Loa's head slants back, she jaw drops, mouth-water dribbles a little from she chin. Leaping round obeah cross, moonlight jumping on withered skin, when wearily Loa falls back, Leah leaps in. Slowly Loa disappears like a queer dream ending.

Blue-grey fingers of light reach across Leah's yard from a dawn-patched sky. Me want to ask Leah, *What now?* Will she walk with me to shack village? Will she walk down mountain sides? But feel too lonely, too foolish, too small.

Silver-grey sun streaks glance between trees, and me check back over me shoulder fe thick red blanket of flowers crawling across

Leah's shingle-roofed shed. All me belly pain gone. Fear turns its face from me.

Bad spirits shrink behind star-apple trees and sweet-scented tamarind and cinnamon trees, and mountain path me make a way down feels moss-springy to tired feet. Spirits creep over boulders vanishing into riverbeds.

'Sheba! Sheba! Where yu bin?' Lickle Phoebe's voice cuts sharp round market track before shack village. She presses me to explain, carrying on she head a roll of woven banana-trash sleeping mats.

Me fumble fe words. 'Market get put fram me mind,' me say.

Lickle Phoebe wears an outgrown blue dress me passed on to she. Cloth clings close to she body like me own stretching belly skin. But Phoebe's skin's shrunk hard against bone. She arms, small pickney hands screwed up with cuts and scratches, hoists banana-trash rolls down from she cotta. 'Me in-a hurry,' Lickle Phoebe say. 'Gotta mek ready fe Barrett Town Sunday market. Yu look betta. Yu bin see Leah?'

'A-good me feel a-good,' but me throat tightens. Cyaan talk more fe feelings come swooping suddenly as if from dawn light, or from Lickle Phoebe's small bony startled face; what's past returns to me, not as memories but as impossible feelings. Misery.

Legs clumsy, bruised body heavy-footed following a flow of dips and hollows in sugar-valley paths, pointing past pumpkin patches and towards shack village. 'Sheba, come back!' Phoebe shouts but me feet keep on down hill.

Chapter Nine

Kaydia

CINNAMON HILL ESTATE
16 February 1840

I open decorated box brought by Mister Sam from London. Pulling out shimmery silk stockings, struggling to put them on, in case no other chance to wear stockings come; buttoning lace-collared dress, pink beaded gloves, I'm dashed about by anger storms. I'm needing so much more than wretched English flannel clothes, too hot for Jamaica, too big for me. 'Mere trinkets,' he'd said, but they'll sell easy when free slaves pass on plantation path after crop-over.

Down narrow creaking ladder rungs – heading for Mister Sam's chamber. Wood panels rubbed with orange peel shine with morning sunlight. From stairwell windows I see tall canes' uncut blades curve under gentle winds.

Opening bedchamber door I don't look at Mister Sam – a sweating bundle twisting its head. I know how him body moves. Pan and towel I've brought for him. He vomits pickney-weak on them.

Chamber door squeaks open. Into dust-swirling sunlight Sibyl's voice comes. 'Mister Sam dying?' She eyes dart round bedchamber. 'Dat why yu wear fine clodes?' Sibyl lifts linen basket balanced on she head up from cotta and lowers it down to yacca floor. Soiled bed shirts, trousers, sheets, topple over basket rim. Mister Sam watches deathly still. He taught me to despise, to wear contempt, bear hurt – but these things I don't know how to put into words. 'Lard God punish im,' Sibyl says. Like she can smell my thoughts. 'Wot yu wantin fram im?' Together we stoop but Sibyl's fingers strain to reach dirty linen bundles, for she pickney bulge never shrink. Friday, she last pickney after May, left she belly bloated big as pumpkin after rain. Joy surges in my belly where life forms from Mister Sam's seed – but only briefly. Bubbles burst when stranded by sea on sandy bay's shoreline – joy bursts sameway. Thinking ahead to another lonely birth sad thoughts begin. Can't bear losing another pickney.

'Afta me do wid washin me miss market an me need something. Yu can go fe me?' Sibyl asks.

'Yu give me money,' I say, 'an me'll go.'

Sibyl roots in skirt-cloth for bitts, searches out a pocket-knot. 'Bring tubs fe washin.' Warm bitts she presses in me hand. 'Coconut oil,' she adds.

'Me must dig up cassava,' I tell she.

Four-poster bed casts long shadows across yacca floor. Grief falls over Mister Sam's face. He sighs deeply. Lids close like he never seen me before.

Sibyl props she shoulder against chamber door. Yawning, she say, 'Why yu busy when she a-come?'

'Oo did come?' I ask. Sameway as clam Sibyl's mouth slams shut. Like she made a theft from me. 'Oo did come?'

'Mama Laslie.'

'Yu seen she? Mama Laslie come ere an me don't know? Me mama? Me miss Mama? Why yu don't call me?'

'Lard have mercy. Yu tellin me to do tings me cyaan do.' Sibyl's eye drops down. Like she heard my thoughts speak. 'She tell me where she live.'

'So?'

'Tek market track. Turn up hill wen yu pass forest.'

'Ow'll me know wen me dere?'

'Flame-heart trees roun she house.' Sibyl arranges cotta straight, bends, firmly sets linen basket atop she head. She walks through doorway. 'Me a-go an wait fe Junius by provision store.' She eye snaps, winking at me.

'Yu look afta Mary Ann fe me?' I shout at she back.

Over she shoulder, 'Ax Old Simeon,' Sibyl say.

I shout after Sibyl, 'Eh? Old Simeon foot bottom broke.' My gut twists round on itself. I run to stairwell.

Mary Ann's curled up on floor below hall stairs. She rolls over, she face still pretty when asleep. She used to skip-play about Cinnamon Hill, happy, before Mister Sam came. Or I'd catch she climbing backwards down sweeping staircase; planting sheself beneath stairwell she'd sit watching she toes wiggling, dreamily.

Halfway I come down stairs. Turning, I'm looking through doorway to Mister Sam. All joy dies, passing into memory – Mary Ann uncurls, crust-sealed eyes unlock, she stretches arms, straightens out folded knees; skirt-cloth works its way up shins notched and scarred from a flogging. Dawn sunlight bleeds livid red across brown skin. Bloated purple stubbornly stripes Mary Ann's leg backs. Eyes closed, she falls back into deep slumber. Perhaps she have bad dreams.

Beneath hall clock, bent over cedar-wood bath, Old Simeon's grey head, ratted hair. One crooked hand grips bath's wooden rim, other's rubbing sides with orange skins. How fast Old Simeon become a stranger after I wrong him.

Coming a little further down stairs, I say to him, 'Yu know bout Mistress Maria's letta?'

He looks up through him one good eye, saying, 'Eh! W'appen?'

I take another step. 'Dis letta Junius de key get yu fe stealing fram Mistress Maria.'

Old Simeon's hand slips from bath rim. Staining air, him face a dried prune saying, 'Letta? Where?'

Nodding towards Mary Ann, I raise a finger to my lips, 'Shsh, yu'll wake she. Yu don't know wot Junius' letta mean? Den me tell yu. Mister Sam cousin told me yu a-tief. Dem kill yu if dey catch yu ere.'

Hungry for disbelief Old Simeon hobbles across hallway, plants himself full-square in hall middle like a stunted palm tree. He looks up cock-eyed. Sadness is on me.

'Me ear bout yu an Mister Sam at busha-house party,' Simeon's hiss-sniggering. 'Yu git any money? We know wot all yu up to. Leah telled ebberyting.'

'Don't touch me wid yu lie,' I yell. Running at Old Simeon, I stumble against him crippled leg. 'Don't touch me, yu stained. Cyaan have chigoe fly hatch under me skin. Yu ear?'

To repay me badness, Simeon says, 'Me mek Charles know wot yu did.'

'Yu did tell Charles?' Under mill-house roof I know Charles' sloshing scum across wood floor. *He does know?* Others done it, I'm thinking – snatch pickney spirit from spirit world – that's what Leah said.

I wrench orange skins from Old Simeon's fist. Old Simeon's clenched fingers match Pa's own blunt hands. Lunging forwards, I strike with my knuckles across him cheek. 'Dis a knife me slice up yu face wid.' My fist's held ready to strike again.

Old Simeon's overall trouser's torn, him old leg blister slants up like two grinning lips.

'Have mercy,' he groans, folding with pain, 'fe me weak bones vexed, an me have vexation of de spirit. Yu young an yu spirit burn wid fiah like yu pa say. Mek me tell yu oo me did tell afta yu bring swimps an cassava. Don't give me no food wid droopy bottom lip. Me cyaan have no bottom lip droop in me cassava.'

Mockingly, I repeat, 'No lip droop in me cassava.'

Mary Ann's awake, making little whimpering sounds. 'Get back to sleep,' I say.

Straightening stiffly, Old Simeon says, 'Lunatic. Yu Ma dirty ooman too.' Him skewed old face chuckles. 'Yu know me teeth bad but me can still eat bellyful-a swimps an cassava. But wot a ugly sin yu mix up in. Give tanks me don't tell minister.' Old Simeon's rheumy eyes run up different ways; one east, one west. 'If minister know wot yu done yu cyaan git marriage certifikate fram im.'

'Wot me do gain fram marriage? Barrett family show woman cyaan hold man dat way.' I grew up in great house, I'm thinking. Lived here all my life. But nothing in it belongs to me.

Old Simeon drags bath out through hall to back verandah. Mister Sam's moaning pulls me dog-trotting up to bedchamber.

'Mister?'

'Water.' Awkwardly he slides onto one side, hot yellow face turning from me.

Bedchamber reeks of rank flesh, of what shouldn't have been. What's past spreads in my belly, feeds off me. Beyond pain's where I live. Beyond fear. But there's no beyond horror. Horror don't end.

I check Mary Ann, for when Mister Sam returned to Jamaica he made all badness happen again and again and again.

* * *

Mister Sam was with she at Barrett Hall. Barrett Hall great house have a big square face. Four windows for eyes. Its shutters, long lashes, some open others closed. Two thin wooden legs support a small square nose jutting from face middle.

Mister Sam leant back in verandah rocking-chair sameway as hog soaks up sunshine – mad for basking in heat I'm sure – he followed Mary Ann through half-closed eyes. I knew because I saw, kneeling in hallway, polishing yacca floor.

Flicking a gold sovereign onto him sleeve, *Heads she wins, tails she loses*, satisfaction crawled across Mister Sam's face. *She loses. Hope's far from this unlucky place.* He walked between great-house legs. House had one eye open. I wanted its legs to buckle and squash him like ants squash under feet in sand.

Blue sea glittered. Barking dogs strained on chains. No wind blew, no other sound but for him boots crunching sand.

Groping with toes, I felt my way down verandah steps. My sight set on Mary Ann, air whispered against my cheek – Barrett Hall's crammed with duppy. Me might have thought them shadows. But shadows can't touch skin, can't be heard inside heads. Shadows don't have voices. Muttering voices. Do they.

On far lake side, Mary Ann, a bold puppy, trotted at Mister Sam's heels past big pig wallowing up to him belly in mud. Leaving coconut brushes under verandah floor, with one eye fixed on Mary Ann, other on Mister Sam, I crept after them, crouching behind tamarind trees, uprooted stumps, branches stripped by hurricanes of leaves. Cane-cutters had hacked back mango grove too, clearing a lake-side place for cattle to feed. Passing blue lake water I couldn't grasp what was happening, everything looked wrong way up. Even me.

Mister Sam led Mary Ann along grove path under blue sky. Trees. Blue sky. Trees. Ivy strips and moss dripped ragged from bark. Mangoes hang thickly there, weighing branches down. Jancra slid from a drooping tree into a sky same blue as glittering sea.

Hovering like Jancra shadow Mister Sam talked to Mary Ann. Most words didn't drift far enough but 'Good . . . are the others, Mary Ann?' reached my ear.

'In cane piece, in great house, Mister,' I heard she say.

Him mouth working, Mister Sam dug deep in waistcoat pockets, drew out a fat white string. Mary Ann nodded. Silvered drops slid into she curled palm; softly blinking, smooth as oyster shell's pearly-white mouth. I watched Jancra peer over she. Coral necklace in she hand. That boy was big but no man. I call him Jancra that boy-man.

They sank down in tall yellow-green grasses, Jancra's stiff white shirt soaking she up. My whole world. White fingers tangled in black curls. I wanted to mash him face with my feet but suddenly my heart gave way, my legs wouldn't work. Crickets screeched in trees and thickets: this fierce jarring high-pitched chirrup became deafening.

Mary Ann rolled aside when he loosened him embrace. Dusting off clothes Mister Sam stood up, looked down – sprawling girl, coarse curls woven with weed-choked grass – he strode away. Glancing back blue eyes said she was never part of him world.

Cattle broke pen fence next day, Mister Sam sent Pa and Friday to cane-piece bottom for driving cattle from canes. My toes slipped between grasses, slid over mosses, following Mary Ann into grove again.

I waited. Mango-tree branches drooping low with fruit, moss and ivy wreaths made my hiding place.

Then Charles found she. Mary Ann's fingertips stuck to she palm. Charles uncurled them. 'Mister wos wid yu?' he asked.

Shame flushed up my neck when Charles peeled Mary Ann's fingers back. Ground shook. Sand shivered, rippled towards Barrett Hall.

'Where yu mama is?' Charles said. Great waves of fear bound me there. Until that day sometimes I thought Charles and me were close, yet strangeness of sand shifting beneath my feet made a mounting and terrible feeling of loneliness wash through my body. Mary Ann's chin trembled. Where sea ended and sky started became indistinct. A bank of mist. Green was gone from mango trees' arms. Coral treasure blinked. Nudge Mary Ann further and she cry. I saw Charles' belly breathing. Him wiry hands trembling. Ranks of trees. She thrashed and reeled to escape whip's lash but now Charles' hand was like a clamp and, with wild rolling eyes of a bull, he cracked cruel leather snake. Tail leapt up to she face then supplejack slashed she back. She face crumpled, body collapsed.

Blue hills became purple, distant. Whip bit she flesh. Small brown birds flitted, danced. Charles walked away. Jancra circled slowly. Jancra's uncle has so many children I lose count.

Lying on she belly, shaking, head twisted up to whispering leaves, Mary Ann's mouth opened, half hidden by black tear-soaked curls. Lids covered Mary Ann's eyes like she long lashes grown too heavy. Skin on she leg backs honeycombed with angry weals, blood-streaked cracks. I untied bandana from my hair, wiped blood from she face. Great house stared. Sad blue sky stared. Ocean stared blue too. Charles walked on to church. Folding Mary Ann's body in my arms, warmth weighing limply on my shoulder – breathing harsh in sharp sunshine – I was hugging she to me.

But she became too heavy for me to carry far. Clinging to my waist, supported by my thigh, Mary Ann and me somehow made we stumbling path back to Barrett Hall. She face came up scarred and swollen where leather slashed from eye to jaw. I saw Charles in it when I dabbed torn flesh with my skirt-cloth.

I took across kitchen garden food for Old Simeon and Junius, great-house store-key keeper. In small square of kitchen window I stood grating cassava into a dish, knowing too well scrunching tread of bare feet was Charles back from church, at last.

I touched indigo bruises. Burning, Mary Ann winced, biting she lip in an effort not to cry. Charles' head passed kitchen-window square.

Slapping dough for white bammie cakes I was promising Mary Ann with my eyes, promising with all my might when kitchen door swung open.

'Me know yu bin wid de minister,' I said.

Charles' mouth was a barrel. Words exploded from it. 'Yes,' he said, 'me wos at church. Ave yu given up yu work fe watch over yu dawta? Where were yu? Yu don't marry.' Charles spat. 'Yu a-sin.' Inside I was screaming *Go go go, Mary Ann.* 'Lard God have mercy,' Charles said, keeping him eye on me what said I remind Charles of him loss. Of all he wants to forget.

Mary Ann limped from kitchen corner.

Charles' hand let necklace free. 'De minister say I must crush dese beads between stones.' Trinkets Mister Sam wrapped in Mary Ann's fingers made a clunk-chinking sound on top of oak dresser.

'It'll reach Mister Sam's ear an mek im shamed.' *Then do as he said,* I thought. *But that won't take away poor shame of beating your own dawta. I'd be afraid to even enter Christ's church. You're behaving white. How can you not be sinner?*

Charles dried palm sweat on osnaburg trouser legs. I could tell Charles had been drinking Jesus' blood. Could smell wine when he breathed. Him eye made four with mine, we both knowing if he did speak of this to Mister Sam, Charles would lose more pay, again. Mister Sam too high and him too wingy to understand Charles' anger. I put on flagstone floor a bowl of ackee, cassava dish, chicken gizzard, feet. And felt Charles' hand soak into my skin. Poison was in my mouth. I was swallowing.

Trapped between another fight and losing Charles or Mary Ann, I search through fear for forgiveness for Charles, finding it somehow in days that have passed between now and then.

Closing chamber door on Mister Sam, I'm wondering how to unpack a bundle of nerves in my belly, for seeing Rebecca Laslie.

In slow chase I'm tracking Sibyl across front lawn. Cotton-tree roots stand up sameway as chicken feet, nubbly and splayed. Sun-yellow logweed flowers stud springy moss-soft path. Lining lane to store tamarind, orange, cinnamon trees, all drenched in scarlet sunrise brings.

'Yu dere!' somebody shouts.

I'm turning my head, glancing across my shoulder a figure behind catches my eye. 'Cyaan see oo is it running up behind,' I say, coming close in to Sibyl. 'E wavin, shoutin.'

Sloping over grass towards we, he slows, becoming a man, becoming Junius, ankle-deep in weeds, shouting, 'Eh! Eh! Yu dere! Yu a-go to market? Buy sum kawn fe me, buy tobacco yard.'

'Yu have money?' I ask.

'Pass by me yard, pretty ooman. Mek we do a-ting.'

'Karri it ere.'

'Me cyaan do dat! Mornin sun hat hat hat.' Junius sidles up to me, savage morning light in him eye, pinching my buttock, whispering, 'Too hat fe me.'

I don't mention Mistress Maria's letter to Junius with Sibyl standing there. She might hear true thoughts in my head.

Sibyl says, 'Kaydia, a-come.' She lifts linen basket from cotta, slumps hard against store door.

Sidling closer Junius hip me hip, him crooked mouth winking says, 'Nothing vencha, noting done. Pass by me yard. Me a-go dere now.' Junius sets off swinging along path from store hut, but him head pointing back to Sibyl says, 'Soon me open store fe yu.'

I cut across driveway overlooking orchard, foothills, wooded slopes. Market basket I fetch from garden-shed fruit rack. Pulling branches low, I snatch ackee hanging in ripe clusters like little red lanterns against dusty blue sky. Basket's soon stacked high with mangoes, freshly dug cassava. Tracks twist through flowering yam to Junius' smart white house. I knock.

'Is oo dat?'

'Is only me.'

'Me a-come.' Wide door swings back. 'Me have a-lickle ting me know yu like to see,' Junius says importantly. Leaving me in open doorway proudly he struts across hut's one room. Solid red mahogany dresser running along back wall overshadows everything. He strokes oiled red wood. Carved into cupboard doors are coral and cresting waves in a palm-tree-lined bay; craftsmanship I see belongs to Pa. Junius opens one door ajar and boasts, 'Me leave Jamaica ana free man in me new home, Ingland, afore freedom come to yu.'

'Pa say yu a-slave again back in Jamaica.'

Swinging cupboard door wide, 'Me *display*,' Junius gives out, him face well pleased. 'Ingland crockeries!' He holds up faded blue china cups he hoards in cupboards, mostly cracked or with handles missing. 'Mek me give yu a-good price.' He steps away from cupboard and, like him scared others hear what he says, moves nearer to me. 'Dese cracked cup specially blessed, broke in Ingland thunderstorm.'

'Wot maggot do afore dog git sore eye?' I ask, taking a cup from him. I examine china decorated with Barrett family crest – a creature in a lion's body, bird's head, great curved beak, outstretched wings.

'Me a servant to Mister Sam's mama in London an at Hope End great house,' he replies. He peers beneath cups. 'But now me money lass.'

I see through Junius when him lie. Him eye can't make four with mine. I pass back him treasured Barrett-crested cup. 'Yu have *any* bitts?' I ask, keeping my open hand reached out.

'Mek me give market money to yu dawta, Mary Ann, dis afternoon.'

'Junius, yu a duppy feedin off cotton-tree root an bamboo thicket, or yu like fig-leaf feeler digging into any tree trunk or nook.'

'Tekeere of de road.' Him eager smile waves me away. 'Yu get kawn, jackass rope tobacco fe me?'

Once a slave always a leech, I'm thinking, wading through weeds ankle-deep. Even sun's too hot for Junius since he sailed from England. But what's in my belly hits hard, giving morning cramps, daybreak sickness, I think. Junius soon slips from my mind.

Following Sunday market women out when chores are done, women carrying tall baskets crammed high with coconuts, plantains, yam. Women streaming sameway as goats flocking from rough shacks onto market path. Coconut-palm mats stroke arms, brush shoulders. We jostle, we shove, stumble over grey boulders rising sameway as small islands; market path moves riverlike, sometimes slow, sometimes fast. Tiny pickney's hands clutch small bottles; big tin boxes balance on heads; packages filled with magic powders leak down necks. Star-white flowers peep from bushes. Banana trees stand taller than me. Bamboos tower. Pimento leaves drip dark green between spicy-scented tamarind trees. Rebecca Laslie fills my mind sameway as flower scent. She found it hard to talk straight when last I saw she. I remember she tear-stained cheeks when she scooped handfuls of dirt to ram down she throat. I know why she did it, to bury searing feelings of aloneness, feelings of bring wronged. She knew I knew too. I read she eye. But we didn't say one word. And my shame flares up at hill's foot when I branch off track rise to fiery red flame-heart trees.

Rebecca Laslie's house stands darkly against forest dressed in brown and red. Weeds swallow my feet. Shabby shutters painted green match wood frills lacing eaves. Weird and grimly windows peer between cottonwood and flame-heart trees. When last did fire glow in your yard? I'm wondering. When were your slatted wooden walls, so creased and cracked from too many idle dry years of sunshine, last licked with de green paint that now peels freely in bold strips? Ants leave trails between thin grasses growing from sandy hollows scattered with tiny yellow flowers before verandah planks.

Cross-legged in verandah shade a man sits on a woven banana-leaf mat beside a cow-head mask. Long time since I seen William Gray, John Canoe-man, who bought himself freedom. He lifts him glistening eye, taps goatskin he tightens to make a goombay drum. Him eye says *Life's still hard up here, even for men like William Gray.*

'Fetch Rebecca Laslie,' I say.

Tucking a river reed into yellow bandana tied tight round him brow, he says, 'Laslie inside.' Smile he gives looks slippery. He remembers who I am? Lips slant down to snarl, then slide into a false grin − cow-head mask, teeming with maggots, looks more real to me and full of feeling than false smile him face wears.

'Oo did build de house?' I ask.

'Old Mister Samuel give money fe Laslie years back an Mama Laslie tek me on to care fe it.' From mouth corners wrinkles pool and ripple out across him brown-skin face like stones dropped in water. Drudgery and grind of slavery's hard-marked into every line.

From doorway shadows thin and high I know that voice that says, 'Is yu, Kaydia?' Face floating from deep gold dust-dirty shade, Rebecca Laslie moves into daylight. *Yu suffered in me belly. In spite of no memory of yu as a pickney, me love yu, an' me sorry*, it says. Sharply she chin twists out over she chest, neck bones poke proud as she walks onto tired verandah planks where weeds make a shady roof for toes. Dull threads like unpolished silver threaten to gleam in Mama's black curls. She pitted cheeks swell out when she smiles and, stepping down from verandah, she swallows, short of breath. She acts well but I know she's not so old. She petticoat edging, cut from coarse linen, looks prettier than ones whites provide. My throat tightens slightly. Silk stockings Mister Sam brought from England; gloves; lace collar; my stiff straw bonnet's what's she keen eye fixes on.

Spinning round sharply, showing sweeping low-cut back of she red dress, Rebecca Laslie, daintily as a cat, mounts verandah steps up to dusky doorway. Rebecca Laslie's house have one long hall holding many doors – my skin prickles, my heart puffs with pride – handwash stand I see; staring-glass; good mahogany bedstead. Mahogany table, chairs. Yet spiderwebs cling to my face, and these walls sing a strange song – neglect, shame, abuse, lies. I walk in on gritty floorboards, market basket's reed handle weaving into my shoulder. Cobwebs smother window-glass, red ants swarm on cracked yacca floor I'm resting basket on.

Scraping she shin with she foot bottom, turning from me, she pours a tumblerful of rum – one spine-shuddering gulp. Rebecca Laslie turns again, she round bold forehead bows towards mine. Beneath each eye dark hollows lie so deep they scoop into she beauty; like wood carvings made by Pa's young hand, they clumsily shape Rebecca Laslie's face and could have been formed by Pa's younger hand. She clamps my face between hot palms, kisses my forehead.

Humming old Jamaica tunes she can't give up hugging me and holding me in she terrible ageless gaze. I watch till I can't watch no more.

'Old Mister Samuel give yu de house?' I ask as she squeezes out my last breath.

Rebecca Laslie's clasping me closer, and she low humming swallows me, I think she'll squeeze blood out-a me.

But she fetches a sturdy mahoney-wood pestle for pounding coffee beans. Mama's club-shaped stick stands tall as William Gray. I remember, like open flat of my hand, Mama's tunes rising pelican-swift, and steady tud-thudder-tud-thudder of wood splitting roasted beans.

'Dem evil white buckra.' Rebecca Laslie batters beans with she mighty smash. 'Mad! An old Myal man oo always wear black, e turn into dog. Mad black dog.' She body sighs, quits hitting. Heat pushes house walls in. 'Wot of young Mister Sam?' she asks. 'E fix yu up in de proper way?'

'Mister Sam wid fever.'

'Yella fever?'

'Im onda bed tree day.'

'Wen tiger git old every dog bark afta im. Catch im, girl, im hot.' She pauses. 'Yu should have better intelligence. Yu not backward as Congo nigger, not tainted wid deir lunacy. Me high cheekbones come fram white Ingland's criminals made to work in dis ere colony,' and, like she feels she must check they're still there, pinched finger-tips stretch up, running across collapsed skin under cheeks. Turning again she pours rum straight from bottle's mouth down she throat; back rigid, but swaying slightly. 'Mek me wash starch out-a bammie,' she says, forgetting to brew fresh coffee.

'Why yu stay away?' I ask.

'Nursin old Mister Samuel in Kingstan. Im tek too lang to die. But now e buried good an ded in Kingstan churchyard. Me have to wait fe money e leave in im will. First e say e leave it. Den e don't. Me plead an plead wid executioners.' Taking a machete up from table-top she tests blade's rusted edge, tickles she thumb, rasping red metal against skin before slicing a yellow pumpkin in two. 'Old Mister Samuel buried twice. Bishop say im body to be dug up fram Kingstan churchyard an buried at Cinnamon Hill wid all Barrett tribe. Yu dig up ded wot yu can expect? Barrett tribe bankrupt. Wot of it? Yu marry Charles yet? E a man dat treat yu good?'

'A man can treat a woman good? Dat's one more ting yu never told me. Many time Charles would've beaten me if me didn't move so swift.'

'Yu git yu fine clothes fram young Mister Sam? Yu git silver, gold?'

Slipping down inside me she words tilt, hope cracks sameway like brittle coffee beans break, split, splinter then shatter. I follow Rebecca Laslie, carrying both pumpkin halves in market basket, through to outside cooking yard. One wooden table stands in yard centre.

Rebecca Laslie says, 'Wen man ded grass grow at im door. Me have young Mister Sam,' she giggles. 'If yu tire of im or Charles, tell me.' She has claws for nails. Wrenching out pumpkin guts she fixes she stony sunken eye on me. 'Yu chile, lose tongue in yu head?'

Pickney sobs I drown in, I don't like it here. Knowing what I have to do I feel older than she.

'Old Mister Samuel juggle in im head fe me money, an leave it up to young Mister Sam, ere,' Rebecca Laslie says.

'Yu did get it?'

'Me did not. Young Mister Sam owe it me. Things changin, an

young Sam Barrett have no manner fe caring fe im uncle's old ooman. Old Mister Samuel build dis ouse but me cyaan live ere wen me work fe im in Kingstan.' Rebecca Laslie's tongue clicks, 'No.' Turning on me she says, 'Yu eye wata?'

'W'appen, Ma? Yu cyaan elp me?'

'Mek yu gimme ackee.' She hand, slithering forwards, reaches into market basket. 'Seed peepin out-a pod.'

'All Mama Laslie ever do's waan waan waan fram me. Wot yu done fe Mary Ann an me?'

From goatskin drum outside comes William Gray's ragged finger pulse.

Rebecca Laslie screams, 'Yu have no rite, no rite to come calling me Mama!' Remembering she swipe have strength of driver beating yard ox, I take back one step. 'Yu no care, yu no good, yu –' Hands strangle my throat. Table-top smacks my forehead. Fingers crushing *crack* wring my neck with power of great white ox pulling cart full-a cane stack.

'Yu no good cockroach.' She throat grip tightens. 'Yu no dawta. Yu waan dis, dat. Yu don't know – too much grief. Yu have life too easy. Me *had* to give yu up!' she shrieks. 'Old Mister Samuel cyaan let no ooman keep no pickney. Not if im its baby fadda. Yu not normal. Leah, she telled me. Why yu waan buy horse fe Pa, good milch cow – e cyaan tek care o'imself? Pa not yu fadda. Why yu give im any money? Is me money dat yu give.'

Drum outside moving louder.

'No, yu lie! Yu lie!' I'm shouting, shaking, feeling she and me lose we grip. Clutching she belly Rebecca Laslie buckles, keeping she eye on me what say I remind she of she loss. Of what she don't want to remember. Of what she thinks I gain.

'Yu punch up me belly till me all pumped up,' is what I think she says but words disappear into squawks. Sweat beads she back. Shrinking over table-top, she cradles she belly and bundles up in she faded backless red dress. Thickly down she leg a red path dribbles, staining sandy floor where my feet trod. From verandah goombay din comes like Mister Sam's funeral's here already, marching up house path. Rebecca Laslie's feet shuffle to cover slimy red pool. Dead pickney's what it is.

Staggering through hall darkness, I follow she into bedchamber darkened by closed jalousie blinds. Stretching across a coverlet, soaking cream lacework red, she sobs. Dust swarms round she body in sunlit shafts. I squeeze she shoulder. It tense up.

She claws my arm. 'Yu jus try to kill me!' Lunging out she screams, 'Yu not me chile! Too white! Too white! Because of yu me lose me pickney!'

'Yu a-no good mother,' I scream back.

'Me hope yu die poor an slowly.' She brow's rutted as dirt track I'm wanting to be on. 'I'll tell Charles wot yu done, bout Mister Sam yu baby fadda.'

'Charles areadie knowed it, Mama.'

'Me hope yu spend yu life alone. Yu messed up. Yu deserve no one. Come, lissen.' Grabbing my collar, grasping my neck, forcing me nearer, nearer, tearing English collar lace, Rebecca Laslie hiss-whispers, 'Me never talk wid yu again. Old Mister Samuel, e yu pa. Me give yu money to Sibyl yesterday. Sibyl's Pa's dawta. Not yu!'

Wrenching my neck free from she grasp, running through cobweb-strung chamber, inside I'm seething. Whipping up market basket, William Gray's drum marks my heart's beat. Spilling over basket rim, mangoes smash. Ants teeming thickly and swiftly, dark like a wool blanket, welling up from holes in hall floorboards. Daylight punches my face. Drum. Drum. Drum keeps rolling. Hitting stony path splits my yams. Wings my feet have, flying down hill track. Melon pips and flesh scatter scarlet on dusty stones. Running, running, running from Mama's words inside my head.

She keeps up bawling, 'Cyaan ebber come back! We don't waan yu ere no more! Cyaan come back now! Yu! Gwan!'

Brightly printed scarves on freed slaves' heads stop my haste hitting market track, dirt flies all around me like golden waterfalls flowing up.

Beggars squat-huddle beneath bamboo branch tunnels. Shade sits on beggars' wrinkled ash-grey skin. Mangy black dogs whimper, tied to wrists with string. Naked pickneys sucking mangoes crawl about like little beetles on their bellies.

One worry-flecked face trips me up. 'Beg yu a cotch fe de nite?' beggar asks. 'Me a-come fram Kingstan.'

Down I look into small brown pools for eyes, but Rebecca Laslie's voice comes screeching from flickering sunlight freed by waving bamboo bursts. *Pa not yu fadda.* Pa's not my Pa?. *Too white! Too white! Me* had *to give yu up! Old Mister Samuel, e yu pa. Because of yu me lose me pickney. Sibyl's Pa's dawta. Not yu!* Pa isn't who he is.

Hurrying on I'm gone with others, joining beggars dressed in tatters, rush-walking fast as flames to grass shacks, heading for Barrett Town. Dirt, I'm thinking. Dirt. Rebecca Laslie's face's carved from golden dirt.

Market's a hot jostle of naked pickney screaming. Stench of unwashed bodies, clothes, leaves my belly reeling. I'm shrinking, shouldering past trays balanced on gay shawls tied round women's heads. Stale stench from foul slurry flowing in open gutters I'm leaping over, mixed with high reek of rotting meat. Passing pens crammed with bleeting goats, barking dogs, squealing pigs, I find a stall for Sibyl's shopping. 'Me waan coconut oil,' I say to stall-holder.

One nigger-black slave woman canters, dog-like, around stall where I'm standing. We eyes, like paths, cross. Who she is? A bunch of lilies she carries draws my gaze. Flowers for what? I'm thinking. To celebrate crazy life? Death? Birth?

From stallholder's mouth filth rolls out, waving brass-ringed fingers, clinking bangles jangling. Bottom rolling, she shouts, 'Wots wrong wid de red nigger girl?' She a field-slave, me think, for she tiredness disappears on Sundays.

Nigger-black slave woman stands stone still. Can't see thoughts behind she gaze. What stands between nigger-black slave and me? Air? A sea of confusion? Mister Sam moves between two worlds, England and Jamaica. Islands can drift together, but I don't move. She eyes search urgently. Like I must listen to some suffering. Listen to she wanting. In my head I'm following. Following an urge to reach out.

Wrapped in some terrible secret, she does nothing but stare. Slave's mouthing my name. A hint of remembering – *Sheba*, my head-tongue says, *yu a field-slave fram Cinnamon Hill plantation –* she face's stayed sameway. We eyes still crossed, I cannot speak. My feeling of wanting, to touch, to pull my hand from my chest is so strong. All my life. All my worth. All of what I am like dead blossoms wilts to nothing.

Gold light from a cloud streams, sunlit eyes search mine. Sunbeams offer a halo but Sheba's no angel. Can't see wings. Scent of lilies hovers above rancid smell of market, of decayed flesh. I peer over basket rim; three bitts left; one guava; one hand of bananas. Sibyl's bitt must've fallen with fruit and yam and without me down Rebecca Laslie's hill, or Rebecca Laslie stole it. Two bitts I throw to Sheba. Cheap glory come from small bitty-money, I know.

'Kaydia! Wot yu did do?' Charles' eye dismember me body but him voice stays proud. Can't bear him in my sight. Can't swallow, throat's too tight. Can't breathe, air's too hot. But my head turns back to a world I know.

Pushing through growing market, growing heat, I slide sideways, mingle with pickneys flocking behind nigger man on fine bay buckra horse. He swigs long from brindled goat-hide water flask then, head down, twists him moist beard between finger and thumb. Charles' narrow face I'm looking up at. Charles looks down on me, cold brown eyes hatred-filled, seething.

Mister Sam tugs on my mind. 'Wot news yu have?' I ask.

'Ride. Me a-ride to Mo'bay, den on fe a-work in Spanish Town. Mister Sam fever badda dan ever. No good.' Bay horse Charles' perched on stamps, tossing its head, tail swiping flies. 'Kaydia, come, yu cyaan save im. Come, move away fram Cinnamon Hill wid Mary Ann an me. Is betta Doctor Demar tek on all im care.' Market heat's stronger. Slanting forward, Charles reins horse back.

'Wot yu doin on Mister Sam horse? Eh? Ow come?'

'Mary Ann's where?' Charles asks. 'Wot yu done wid she?'

'Is yu oo touch she,' I say; I feel a guilty sense of glory. Mister Sam's baby's snug, safe inside my belly. 'Don't yu touch Mary Ann again,' I say.

Charles bellows, 'Is betta fe Doctor Demar come.'

Leave Cinnamon Hill? Go? Where? Sickness in my belly swells from unborn pickney. *If Mister Sam's uncle's me pa, an this new pickney's Mister Sam's – it's too too white-skinned. Me know Charles'll know whose new pickney is. Me cyaan leave Cinnamon Hill with him.*

Striking out, Charles' heel cuts into my belly. My body disappears in spikes of pain. Pickney around we stop chattering. All eyes turn sharply on me. Pickney crowd's backing off. What's become of my baby? Charles' foot stabs horse's ribs. Charles lets one tear escape. Gathering slack from reins he says, 'Me wi see yu on Chewsday. It tree, no two day times. Yu cyaan live no more in de great house.' Mister Sam's horse walks swiftly away. Ripping inside me don't stop. Sealed off, Charles rides on. Thick with fury my tears come.

I'm shrinking from sun's brightness shouldering past women bartering jerked pork for fresh cow's milk, past grain stalls with sacks empty and folded from low rainfall.

'Sum kawn fe me?' I ask a woman's humped back. She rests against piles of pigeon-pea sacks. Smoothing oily wet hair, twisting round, Leah's skin's taut sameway like bulging bag draped over she arm. Splitting me apart she says, 'Yu wid chile yet?' She questioning eyes gleam, like I'm a known enemy. 'Me eye say yu owe me money to keep pickney dere, or it born dead, or born as black dog.'

'Say wa? Only one bitt left,' I say.

'Yu cun give dat an yu crop an gloves an hat.' Leah pulls me closer by she low growling voice. 'Yu waan black pickney-dog?'

Leah's black dog scuttle-hops up to me, one paw won't touch stony ground. Dog's belly sags like empty corn sack swinging from its scrawny back. Coromantee's long sad notes twist from a black reed flute played by Leah's nose blowing down its hollow body. Thinking black dog must be Myal man, Rebecca Laslie or Mister Sam's pickney flopping along, backing from snarling, bristling, dog I realize no, him laugh at me. Laughing. Laughing. Laughing.

I drop my last bitt into Leah's hand. 'Mek me give yu all me money. Guava. Banana.' Then scattering squawking chickens across old men's skittles games me run away from market place.

Rebecca Laslie's humming flows into tamarind forest, following as I run. Birds singing free beautiful notes. Deep inside my belly aches. One thought only circles in my head. *Mister Sam.* Past flame trees I run, through fierce and fiery sunlight. Branches' crooked fingers point and scratch savagely.

By coopers on plantation path I meet Sibyl, Friday and Mary Ann. Skin beneath Sibyl's eyebrows sags, hanging in heavy folds near temples at she eye corners, giving each eye a slanted look. *Look like life hard as we make it.*

'Coconut oil? Tubs fe washing?' Sibyl asks. *Is she face always haggard this way?* 'Yu did see Mama Laslie?'

I say, 'Mama says yu have me money.' Sibyl says she gotta protect sheself from people like me. *Who to believe? Who not?* I say, 'Yu're half. Me half, dat way we should share.' *Because he feel shame fe it Pa won't speak to me?*

'Yu have coconut oil, tubs fe washin?' Sibyl asks.

'A fe me money,' I say. Clutching rattling tin, Mary Ann reaches up to my face. 'Junius give yu dat? Nutten in-a dat. It full-a rakstone.'

Rapping my chest with rattling tin Mary Ann bawls, 'Yu cyaan come back widout tings fe we.' She headbutts my neck, tin knuckles beat my grey skirt; fists hammer my chest. My breast holds no comfort for Mary Ann – Rebecca Laslie milked me dry of comfort. Of love.

'Yu have Junius' jackass tobacco rope?' Sibyl asks.

I shrug. 'Junius put cramp in me head.'

'Kaydia,' Sibyl says, 'lass night de cockerel crow, an hens a-cacklin afore dawn. It tell me something cyaan be rite. Tell me yu a-curse. Sand an rice me must sprinkle outside an roun me sack tonite. But yu cyaan lose me bitt, fe true. Yu pay it me. Yu a-bad curse.'

I'm making to punch Sibyl's floppy belly, bawling, 'Mama Laslie give yu me money! Me she dawta too!'

Friday sneaks behind Sibyl's bulky body. Sibyl's viewing me through narrowed eyes. Like I'm mad. *Yu don't know what's wrong till yu done it.* Mary Ann clings, Sibyl peels my daughter from my skirt. Walking on up plantation path they go, shadows slither behind them drawn long by a setting sun.

Bursting into Mister Sam's chamber I run.

Stretched across four-poster bed, arm's flung out sameway as washed-up starfish, 'Papa,' Mister Sam whimpers. 'What have I done? My dear, poor Papa.'

'Yu fadda in heaven won't spare yu,' I say, levering open jalousie blinds. Only calm thing I see's blue salt water; inside me an ocean roars. 'Wen minister come yu must repent of yu sin, Mister Sam, or be stuck in hellfiah.'

Mouth hanging open, throwing himself forward, dead crab stink in Mister Sam's wet breath, 'Is he not come to pray with me?' he pleads. Sinking into pillows again Mister Sam's throaty voice whispers, 'Is he not come to pray?'

Drying mouth corners I say, 'Soon me a-come, mek me go to do kitchen stove an me a-carry fe yu cool water.'

Window grids forged from cast-iron bars form a wall from ceiling rafters to kitchen flagstone floor. Old Simeon lurches down great-house track, him shape fits one small iron square. Red streaks hover as a doctor-bird flits across another square. Long scissor-tail feathers a-quiver – colours shrieking with light disappear into flower heads threaded through wood trellis outside.

Stuffing a pipe with tobacco, Old Simeon hobbles up to kitchen doorway. My toes crawl into golden sand spread across flagstones by evening breezes.

'Fe wot yu look at me like dat?' Old Simeon asks me. 'If put on Kingstan freak show yu bring in big money.' Hobbling across kitchen, 'Wen yu gonna cook?' he adds.

Emptying oven ash into bushes I'm glimpsing Old Simeon over my shoulder. 'Why yu don't shut yu mouth?' I shout back.

'No church service bring Mister Sam back,' he returns. He lifts night lantern from kitchen shelf, him one good eye glitters spite-fully; other eye's clouded milky-white. 'We have funeral afore minister rive ere.' Leaning back, Old Simeon scratches him crooked spine against iron window grid sameway like old mule shoulder-scrubs a post.

'Mister Sam not buried yet,' I say.

Old Simeon's pipe's lit. White whiffs of smoke he breathes into dark sky-blue dusk. Smoke weaves round him aged face, and ears big like crinkled conch shell's rim.

Sweeping hearths I breathe out despair, lost in feelings for what's in my belly. Filling iron kettle from stone water jar, a terrible face something like Mama's peers up from dark water. I hear Rebecca Laslie's voice. *Me cyaan find a name bad enough fe she.*

I go by gentle smell from sleek horses sweating, slow-mixing with wood-nut smell of stable-block hay. Why I must search for Mary Ann, I'm thinking, I passed she on plantation path? But my eyes search front garden, follow plantation path sweeping round and down past sugar works' red-tiled roofs to smooth blue stretching sea.

'Mary Ann hide in Mister Sam's chamber?'

Old Simeon chuckles, 'Mary Ann hide ere in kitchen block.'

'Yu a-crazy ass. Yu a-case,' I snap back.

Old Simeon pauses from lantern lighting. Crossly he glances at me. 'Me no case, no trunk, no box!' Old Simeon's tongue clicks sharply. 'Yu rage wound yu pa's heart. Minister, e not clebber but e know everything bout Mister Sam settin fiah to slave shacks. E know bout yu stealin. An what yu carry in yu belly.'

'Ow minister know? Yu telled im an Charles an Pa?'

Old Simeon sucks on him pipe. He draws in again, breathing out only air. Chuckle-coughing, he shrugs, taps burnt tobacco flakes into a cupped palm, dusts tobacco from him hand. He shuffles with lighted lantern to kennels to let out Mister Sam's dogs.

Mary Ann whines, 'Me waan candle.'

Wedged between stove side and empty rum barrels, I see Mary Ann. 'Yu go fetch a-candle. Git to yu chores.'

Sawdust trickles from she fist, drowning a rat-bat dead. Rat-bat's flapping its cloak-like wings in dying circles on flagstone floor. Mary Ann's face uplifts to mine. 'Me cyaan,' she says. 'Me cyaan go now, me busy. Don't ax me.'

'Yu must see yu Mister Sam?' I ask mockingly. 'No! Yu go now.'

Minister's voice finds me, shouting, 'Kaydia! Kaydia!' till again I'm going back on my step. Black gown fluttering about ankles, minister strides towards kitchen block.

Smoothly Jancra circles naseberry tree. Anger comes like ropes tightening round my neck, shivers run up my spine. Sameway as cold air creeps through cracked and crumbling stone walls, under doors, round cotton tree. Trailed by hungry dogs, Old Simeon goes to a bench below cotton tree. I follow minister to Mister Sam's chamber.

'I spoke with your, you, your . . . Charles on the coast road from Montego Bay,' minister says.

'Me know.'

'Kaydia, why is Charles so deeply perturbed? He is beside himself, I mean I . . . As you, I am sure, are aware the leaf hasn't turned over, so to speak, but is there anything else? Anything I should know?'

'Me don't know, sir.'

'I think Charles thinks you are with child.'

'Me?'

'Then you must tell him. No, I will go to him. I'll tell him this isn't so.' Swiping at air minister says, 'There's a mosquito in here.

For goodness' sake close the shutters, anyone would think you were trying to kill him.' Desire flickers, flaring into fierce yearning. Like he have funny thoughts a little smile crosses minister's lips. I raise Mister Sam higher on lace pillows. 'Stay with your master all night,' minister says.

Mister Sam's trembling hand yellow-white as chicken feet reaches out to minister. Clasping arms round minister's neck Mister Sam draws minister to him, kisses him hands; eyes brimming, tears leaking.

Mister Sam's words to minister come soft, bitter, clipped. 'Please . . . You must . . . write to my father. Please, tell him everything. Should I die, write to my sister, Henrietta. Send her my endless love.' Mister Sam falls back again sighing and snivelling.

'Wait outside,' minister says to me. 'Oh, and Kaydia, I appreciate that due to your duties you will be absent from the service tonight but I trust your daughter will be present.'

I close jalousie blinds. Groaning, Mister Sam writhes. Bed moans under him shifting weight. I wipe wet forehead skin; lower lip; cheek; chin. Curtains fall in heavy loops as slowly I drag blue velvet across windows. I dip in tallow rush pitch. Then I'm gone from Mister Sam's bedside.

Leaning my ear against chamber door I stand outside. Voices sound muffled through solid wood like shadows look blurred under water.

'. . . for God so loved the world,' minister says, 'that He gave His only begotten son, that whosoever believeth in Him should not perish, but have everlasting life . . .'

I walk across gloomy lawn towards kitchen block. Sky holds a faint red glimmer above dark blue sea.

'Sam fever worse?' Rushing down my spine, Pa's laughing catches me. 'E not noticin wot yu do fe im,' Pa pitches testily. 'Yu cyaan see dat girl?'

'Where yu bin?' calmly I ast. 'Pa?' Pa sucks him teeth, him eye matches hell's fire. 'Yu me pa?' I cry, wiping tears from cheeks.

Moon makes shining leaves blue. Breezes chase leaves, brushing in and out of gaps moonrays passed through. Pa turns. Sweat brewing. But he cause me no more trouble now. Him gone.

Minister walks to him horse in stable-block. Pa scents victory, rays of him laugh flit between trees back through Cinnamon Hill gardens, reaching across black chamber into sea's glittering blue deep as love depths.

I fetch cassava from storage jar and from sack, yam for boiling in water. Moonlight beams over kitchen flagstones.

'Mama! Mama!' Mary Ann calls. 'Mister Sam bawling!'

Mister Sam's face, a white mask, bends over chamber pot, vomits onto floorboards. And Mister Sam's gagging, vomit gushes from him mouth. He retches again, it racks him body.

Getting onto my knees what strikes me's how Mister Sam also weeps, forlorn face yellow-white, too weak to speak.

Softly him hand slips from him chest. 'Papa,' he moans.

Rocking forward, back on my feet, 'Forget yu fadda,' I mumble. I pinch Mister Sam's shoulder. 'E won't know yu cyaan work. E cyaan know all wot yu dun.'

My wish for any place away from here's bigger than anyone's. But Mister Sam's no longer with me. Already him thick with sleep.

'Jesus, lover of my soul,' I'm singing, sinking onto hard yacca floor. 'Let yu to thy bosom fly. Mister Jancra fly up high. Sugar cane, water roll. Hide me. Save me. Save me.'

Chapter Ten

Elizabeth

1, BEACON TERRACE, TORQUAY
24 November 1839

My dearest Mrs. Martin,
    . . . Since the first of October I have not been out of bed – except just for
an hour a day, when I am lifted to the sofa, with the bare permission of my
physician, who tells me it is so much easier to make me worse than better . . .
    Dearest Papa is with us now – to my great comfort & joy! – & looking
very well, & astonishing everybody with his eternal youthfulness! Bro &
Henrietta & Arabel besides, I can count as companions – & then there is
Bummy! We are fixed at Torquay for the winter – that is, until the end of
May: after that, if I have any will or power & am alive to exercise either, I
do trust & hope to go away . . .

Agreeing with Papa is not possible in this instance: he has confessed
to dismissing a Wimpole Street servant for forgetting to lock the
door after dusting 'Mama's room'. Since Mama's death Papa treats
her possessions as objects of reverence, and disallows anything to
be re-arranged in 'Mama's room' or for the door to be left unlocked.
There is no movement from Papa on this, even though we have
left one house for another. Even though Mama's feet never walked
Wimpole Street floors. His devotion remains immemorial, even
though she has been dead for nine Octobers.

Disagreements with Papa are bad spirits sniping at me in this
room. They clomped up the stairs, stomped up to my bedside as
though stamping on the souls of us more earthly folk. Beards of
smoke rise from the fire and hang about my chamber. I wish the
curtains of stale air would clear. If only Crow would unlatch a

window. But one breath of wind will increase my sickness so that, if it so pleaseth God, I may live only another day. Pains which were ghosts of sensations are now revealed fully in flesh. And I am haunted all week by leeches and blisters though I sometimes know not which doctor comes.

I sense Papa's worries and feel that the decline in his good spirits is due to more unrest on his estates, poor sugar yields and, worst of all, Dr. Barry's death and the decline in my health all coinciding with the anniversary of the loss of dear Mama.

The woman has returned. I believe she knows that in the dark world in which I live I can no longer spread or even open my wings, as I once did, galloping from hilltop to hilltop, cantering through valleys, the wind satin-smooth, a blue-white mist hanging over distant chimneys. At first I'd wanted to be rid of her, then could not bear us to be parted. Her face, streaked sometimes with distress, often seeps into my thoughts; cotton-soft as summer breezes the black folds of her garments slip past my sleeping eyes. Although I occasionally feel her touch whisper across my skin, two months have passed since she sat by the fireside, and now with horror I see a vision most grotesque.

She nurses a newly born baby the size of the wax doll with flaxen hair that is propped against Henrietta's window-sill in Wimpole Street. But this baby's complexion isn't peachy-pale, her dress doesn't mirror silk the lemon shade of buttermilk fringed with foamy lace. This baby's round eyes aren't blue but a bright clear brown, the dark bare skin copper-coloured, shiny. The baby's face crumples up; its cry turns into a wail. Worst of all the little neck swells becoming scarred and red, the face blood-spattered. My heart begins to race. Could this be an aberration of light? A Negro baby, here, in my room? Surely it isn't kin of mine.

I do not fear the future. It is the past that scares me. It is impossible to reconcile the past. Impossible. All my life I have been haunted by ghosts. The past constantly visits me. I believe souls live on because I can feel the spirit world.

When I find it within me to look back the baby has disappeared. A young boy stands at the woman's side now. His attire, like that of little Ibbit's, is tailored to suit the latest fashion. Long dark

-173-

wavy ringlets tumble to a shirt collar edged with the best London lace and the shoulders of a light blue felt waistcoat trimmed with navy cord and matching velvet buttons. The yellow trousers stop just below the knee; bright white ankle socks and closed sandals. Somewhere, in the maze my mind has become, I have seen the gentle curves of this child's face, the swell of the forehead, the coral bloom to his cheeks. He is not aware of me, only the woman. He hands her a square-shaped board. But no, no it isn't a board, it's a piece of needlework exquisitely stitched. A tapestry stretched across a wooden frame depicting the picture of an old house. The picture stops the woman crying. She begins to unpick the design. The stables are still there but the buildings I recognize as the home farm cottages begin to disappear, as does the clock tower, the lake and Alpine bridge: the lily ponds fringed with bullrushes are quickly unravelled. Threads pulled out she winds around her delicate hand, and then throws all that I once held dear in a loose ball into the blazing fire. Lastly she attacks the house, unpicking domes, spires, leaving not even the shape of a memory, simply smooth cream-coloured cloth.

A frightful pain slices the left side of my body. Were it not for the coldness of the draught from the windows I would be content to lie back against these pillows, out of harm's way, out of air's way, and continue with the two things of which I seem a little capable: being ill and writing poetry.

25 November 1839
This morning the waves are quite calm. Oysters, fresh from their watery bed, have been harvested in gigantic nets, and now dear Papa is next door in the drawing-room contentment is not far from my reach. But every joy turns to sadness. Even the hushed crash of bursting waves grows tiresome. The bay. Screaming gulls. Sea and sky as one.

I feel as though I live in the sea. I have before me another full five months at sea. The mixture I take of opium and brandy does little to calm my nervous state. I wish to see no one. I have no compassion for it, but now Dr. Barry is gone, I *must* write.

I *must* write.

What grand thoughts these are – I *cannot*. Papa's heavy knock is at my door. He walks in in a blast of sunshine and with a biting wind from the drawing-room windows.

There is a strangeness in the way his eyes search my face. Fearful, he takes my hand in his – almost as reluctantly as the sea's heart he swells with sadness. And when I smile . . . When I smile, Papa says he lives for when I smile . . .

The savage fingers of this immortal wind glance between cracks in the sash-window-frames. Whilst Papa says he is struck by how many people still stroll on the beach, and amazed by the scores of swooping swallows, I am thinking Italy's climate and romantic scenery will suit me better than any London or Torquay. Gulls, like torn scraps of paper, soar on each veil of wind. Sand studded with pebbles recedes, returns, unsettled in the restless, relentless swash of crashing waves.

When at noon Papa sat at my bedside holding my hand, I said, 'Fetch me a shell, Papa, a clam shell, that I might feel the clusters of miniature barnacles.' I was longing to be with him striding across the beach. Tonight the prevailing winds are weak, and within these walls sour memories prevail.

Water reflects on the ceiling turning this into a blue chamber. I wish that just for one minute the crashing waves would cease. And the sea be completely calm, quiet, smooth as the paper on which I ought to be writing.

Dr. Scully told Papa whilst standing over my bed this evening he thinks there is hope. But I wonder whether I shall last the winter – whatever His will is.

11 December 1839

Before he left to catch the stagecoach dearest Papa said he could see how tiresomely lonely I have become, but that my suffering is a brilliant example of pious resignation and humble submission.

'I will write to Sette,' Papa suggested, 'requesting that he tell all in London to have more conversations with you on paper.'

'Sette is a wonderful correspondent,' I replied. 'And the depth of his kindness shows in his letters.'

Miss Mitford has sent me a copy of *Finden's Tableaux* via Arabel. But apart from that, now Papa has left, as is the way, I haven't heard from Sette since.

Despite the grief Papa has suffered, with fine carriage and sparkling eyes he last entered my chamber, his arms over-flowing with presents, baubles, trinkets, such great armfuls of gifts I blushed deeply. All spring long he will surely have the worry of whether Bro or Sam should have returned to Jamaica with my beloved brother Stormie. But Papa's strength never falters. See how he has protected us until the end. Papa follows the Lord's word. His trust and true love are my salvation. That he stayed constantly atten-tive at my bedside for one full month is proof of this. And when, being so overcome with emotion I could not speak, he took my hand, we prayed together. 'Papa,' I said, 'I understand you have many to care for in London and that you must soon leave.' 'Ba,' he replied, 'to make you happy, that is my reason for being on earth.' He speaks with such clarity and determination. *He* challenged *me*. Imagine *that*! It is no small wonder he is one of the most popular men in London – if not *the* most popular. In my heart I felt that dear Papa cannot, will not, *must not leave*. He vowed he would not. Then he did. My dive into the greatest depths of sorrow, loneli-ness and despair must upset dear Bro, who occupies the chair in which Papa sat at my bedside.

10 January 1840
Bro looks more than discontented gazing from the window into the mist cloaking the sea. 'Last night, shortly after leaving your bedside,' he says, 'I announced in a letter to Papa my intention to marry.'

I refrain from giving voice to the words stirring in my breast – *I wish to provide for you financially* – I so dread upsetting Papa, my lips are tightly fastened, my hands seized and tied.

Bro is in love, deeply, he tells me. This comes as no surprise. Would Papa deny Bro marriage? At thirty-three years of age Papa had eight children and had been wed to Mama a good thirteen years. The wounds of my heart would never heal; therefore I hardly dare to dream of love.

'Papa asserts firmly that we must fix our minds on the Lord,' I say, with a fake gaiety. 'It would be folly to raise this matter with him once more, and should he fear *I* intend marrying his wrath would grow greater, his condemnation more intense.'

Bro begs me not to speak a word of this attachment to anyone, which is quite contrary to my feminine nature. But will he listen to me?

My sight drifts from Papa's portrait back to Bro. Bro is the easier to love, to be sure. Inwardly I shiver. Biting my lip, looking hard at Bro, I say, 'I am being cowardly, I do not deserve you as a brother. What do I want with my inheritance? Since October I have neither dressed nor moved for stale bed sheets to be changed for fresh. Nevertheless, I was fearfully shocked by your outburst at dinner not a month ago, which I heard through closed drawing-room doors, and equally startled by Papa's reply.'

'"A grandchild is a dead child,"' Bro reiterates. '"God's will is that each of you – *all* of you – remain celibate".'

'Papa's conviction strengthens with time. I am terribly worried, Bro, that you might enter into a battle with him, the consequences of which would be beastly, would rip you both apart and rupture the family.'

He does not like to leave me, dear Bro, although I doubt he would be happier in London with Papa.

Lying flat on the blistered skin of my back, a war breaks out from within. Gilt-framed, Papa's smile no longer serves as an anodyne. I stare at the ceiling, my heart beating fast. I must tell Bro to ring for Crow but feel too tight-chested to move, to speak, too many tribulations bearing down on me.

Clouds of colour dance before my eyes, a vivid seascape, scarlet waves, mauve, acid green, strangely wonderful they seem, varying in shape and size. Strands of light ripple like waves upon the ceiling. The forms of mermaids rocked and bent by waves, a golden net of curls splays out across the sea. Blue-greens once dressed my room, just as they once dressed me – I had a girlhood penchant for wearing leafy greens. My green bower was the warmest room at the top of Hope End. It was carpeted and draped in emerald soft as the moss-cushions of the forest. Curtains trailed gracefully about my bed, opaque and willow green. Hangings of hills dotted with sheep like so many distant scudding clouds; secret valleys; stags in the deer-park. I remember every veined ivy leaf framing my open window through which a fragrance of honeysuckle and roses blew in. From here I gazed upon the gardens; woods stretching to meadows of wild flowers and the blue Malvern Hills where I rambled with the wild wanderings of youth.

A mermaid has swum past, her hair . . . I am tangled in a net of waving black curls. Is it easier to sink, or walk, or swim?

15 January 1840

Dearest Miss Mitford,

Shame on me to have let you write again, without any words of mine, in grief & sympathy for your illness, coming in between! . . .

. . . Do you walk enough, & lie down the rest, almost all the rest of the time? Have you not learned to write in a horizontal posture as I do? . . .

Before leaving for London Papa presented me with Shelley's most recent collection. Now that I have mastered the art of horizontal writing, I will, with pencil notes, inscribe each volume of Shelley's stacked amongst the note books I keep at my bedside. I am most particularly interested in *A Defence of Poetry*, and Shelley's speculations on physics and morality, and the translations of Plato's *Symposium, Ion, Menexenus*. But have found, even at a glance, that I take great exception to Shelley's ideas on religion, especially Christianity, and rather fear I won't be able to help myself from deleting all these passages I am flicking through and entering my own opinions. Shelley lacks an accurate command of Greek. Some of his translations are little more than nonsense. I am pausing only here and there on passages which strike me – the carelessness of this version is remarkable. That this is a posthumous volume edited by his wife, Mary, is no excuse. Though a great poet, Shelley cannot translate Plato, we have more than sufficient evidence. His understandings are insufficient to say the very least!

17 January 1840

This morning Bro reads to me an article in *The Times* stating that the old franking system has finally been replaced by the penny post, and payment is to be made by the sender.

'This means,' Bro explains, 'that for the cost of one penny, you may write to your heart's desire without the worry of burdening any of your dear friends or family.'

'It offers wonderful liberty,' I say.

Bro agrees that it is surely the most successful revolution of the day. 'Right,' he says, 'I shall go and brave the winds on the clifftops.'

Tucked in the cleavage of Torquay hills I lie ensnared by my long-possessed secret – to be swept off my feet by a dashing poet prince. Each day, when letters arrive on the silver server, I fear I pay highly in disappointment, for they bring no such news.

28 January 1840

This morning I was surprised to see Hugh Stuart Boyd's seal upon a letter. That this elderly sightless man with whom I was blindly in love in my girlhood has not forgotten me altogether is a very pleasant notion indeed. Through the kindnesses of Nelly Bordman I recently heard Mr. Boyd was settled in Hampstead, though his exact whereabouts she did not divulge. And nor has *he*.

29 January 1840

My dear friend Mr. Boyd,

... Yes! Indeed! You DO treat me very shabbily – I agree with you in thinking so. To think that so many hills & woods shd. interpose between us. That I shd. be lying here, fast-bound by a spell, a sleeping Beauty in a forest, & that you who used to be such a doughty knight shd. not take the trouble of cutting through even a hazel tree with your good sword, to find out what had become of me! Now do tell me, the hazel tree being down at last, whether you mean to live at Hampstead, whether you have taken a house there & have carried your books there, & wear Hampstead grasshoppers in your bonnet (as they did at Athens) to prove yourself of the soil! ...

3 February 1840

I wish, more than anything, that I might be back in London for the Queen's wedding day, but the spitting of blood increases with these cold February winds. Dr. Scully's daily visits have merged this week into a stream of agony – he subjected me to a dynasty of blisters. Blister-torture, I call it. Blisters applied on the chest every three days for two to three hours. During visits Dr. Scully tells me all the scandals of the neighbourhood, from the local landed gentry cheating at baccarat, to a steam packet exploding recently in nearby waters (which explains why the post is rather erratic, I suppose), to the disgraceful behaviour of Lord-something-or-other while in wedlock. Such gossip gives me pleasure, and even *I* talk, but very little. My poetic voice is wasting to a whisper.

This past week my knees have ached – I am confined again to bed – except when lifted, baby-wise, to the sofa when they make the bed, but then I am inclined to faint from the exertion of movement.

6 February 1840

My dearest Sette,

We have not heard from Jamaica, which is a shame. Bro went out to the Hopeful, through such a foaming sea, that I shd. have been terrified if I had known anything about it before his safe return. Dr. Scully told me he tried to persuade him not to go – all in vain. We have tremendous seas & winds – & a chimney on the other side of the house, 'nodding to its fall'. But nothing makes me fail to perceive the great advantages in point of shelter & warmth of this number 1. My room particularly is quite a nest of a room – there being nothing at all like it, according to Dr. Scully, in the whole of Torquay. During our short attack of frost, he used to stand before the fire every morning rapt in admiration, whilst Crow reported the state of the thermometer.

The rock wall is falling to pieces. Indeed, great rocky fragments have been hurled, in the manner of avalanches, so near some of the houses facing the quay that their inhabitants have fled – Papa's artist, Mr. Mills, escaped crushing, just by six inches & a half . . .

15 February 1840

Ever dearest Miss Mitford,

Can anything grow anywhere or anyway with this terrible wind? . . . I took two draughts of opium last night – but even the second failed to bring sleep. 'It is a blessed thing!' – that sleep! – one of my worst sufferings being the want of it. Opium – opium – night after night! – and some nights, during east winds, even opium won't do, you see! . . .

20 February 1840

. . . Now, my dearest Miss Mitford, write and tell me all about yourself and dear Dr. Mitford! It would revive me like an inward spring, to hear a great deal of good about you. Is it to be heard? God grant that . . .

A windy day *again*. Seagulls, like strips of white cloth, are blown high over endless rolling grey sea. This week's physician forbids my escape from this room – should I say tomb? – how am I to be calm within when there is such turbulence without? How, with all these stresses and strains, Miss Mitford thinks I am to be a poet, I know not. I know I must keep on in this dreadful place yet fear I cannot, that some part inside me is cracking.

And how can I call Miss Mitford a dear friend when my correspondence is inconsistent? Nay, dreary?

. . . Papa has not come yet – but I am not as silly as Dr. Scully fancied, when he found me with tears running down my cheeks because of a 'fortnight's absence', and sat down with a kind of despair at my bedside, with his 'Well, Miss Barrett – there is no reasoning on such subjects!' I know very well that these 'fortnights' are apt to grow. That was a fortnight before Christmas! Dearest Papa has so much occupation, and so many to care about and discipline in London, that it is very difficult for him to go two hundred miles from it – though Styx be 'nine times round him' with promises . . .

This evening's melted jelly did not digest agreeably. Twice daily I take a glass of wine, one spoonful at a time. All I managed when the Hedleys visited last night was a few minute sips of beef tea.

Crow has 'just come to remind ma'am there is a visit planned by the Hedleys for this evening'.

'Jane will, I hope, bring her darling daughter, Ibbit, that we might have an angel once more in our midst.'

'I trust she will, ma'am,' Crow replies.

I long to be that child; running and skipping, just as I did, in a little white muslin dress and frilled pantalettes.

When I reach out she escapes me, running too rapidly, leaping too high.

. . . There never was a more absolute flirt than Ibbit. Indeed, her love for 'jeloms' as opposed to 'waddys' is honestly divulged upon every fitting opportunity – & her indignation too, wherever she cd. say of mortal man 'he never speaked one word to me'! Nay! The very trick she has of catching the light with that lovely golden hair of hers, which hangs like a net of curls from brow to waist, is instinct with flirtation! . . .

2 March 1840

I was on the edge of collapse when Dr. Scully just now visited. It is with the greatest sufferance that I permit this treatment for I swear the blisters he applies serve only to distract me from the cough continually wracking my body. In Dr. Scully's company I am intensely nervous. Does he regard me well? I think not. Is that why he talks unrelentingly? The touch of his hands, the points of his fingertips prodding my wrist as he feels for my pulse are hard, cold. Fat black tentacles feed off my veins: these wriggling, bulging leeches suck from me the will to walk. Although the last draught of opium went some way to relieving the agony within my stomach, being so weak and frail, my hands tremble. This afternoon I cannot write. I cannot sleep and, I fear, never will.

I must ring for Crow. She shall bring another draught of opium. One more will not hurt.

Hope End surfaces. Dreams, like grains of sand are swept asunder, swallowed by raging salt water. Somewhere, thick with dust in the Wimpole Street attic, is the parchment on which Cousin Richard wrote for me tales of the 'bad mad' runaways. I feel very nervous about it – far more than I did when my *Prometheus* crept out of the Greek, or I myself out of my shell in the first *Essay on Mind* – I struggle with the shape of verses and become thought-tied. Should I attempt to tell a slave's tale with my own breath I shall be in two panics: whether I can write it, and whether I shall want it published.

As my eyes close again I look upon the black slave woman, Quasheba. Would she have been considered a beauty in Africa? A beauty with black skin? Can black represent beauty?

I shall not turn my sight from all that was but look deeply upon the deserts we Barretts have created, and think what can be done.

Let tides of peace flow into my mind. Give to me the gift of reverie. The resourceful man uses imagination. To see, hear, taste, smell, touch. How powerful a tool is this! Quasheba is fighting. Fighting for liberty. Had she a lover, a black cane-cutter? In the sunny ground between the canes, said he, 'I love you,' as he passed? When the shingle-roof rang sharp with the rains, heard she how he vowed it fast: while others shook, had he smiled in the hut, as he carved her a bowl of the cocoa-nut, through the roar of the hurricanes?

Mysteriously, I am beginning to experience an intense bond similar to sisterhood – a unity with the runaway's cause. I too have a longing for freedom. A longing to flee, soul-forward. I know not how or why Quasheba took flight, but if she was treated as one might presume Cousin Richard treated Negro women indentured for life . . . Such tales have long resounded in my ears; the rape of a young woman fresh from childhood. Strangely, feeling so strongly, deeply – I feel it in my bones, in my very soul, that the missionaries were not the root of the slave uprisings nor the fall of the apprenticeship system, as Sam claimed, and that extreme violence perpetrated by women, the terrible acts of which Cousin Richard spoke, such as Negro women killing their own children, must have meant something. Something sickening. Must have been due to evils within plantation life. I *do* have a mind to write on this. And to publish. How to go about such a task I must not forget. How to not sympathize but empathize. Imagination is like the act of remembering, without memory being in the consciousness – I have heard this before. I have been here before. I have lived this already.

I am black, I am black! And yet God made me they say: but if He did so, smiling back He must have cast His work away under the feet of his white creatures, with a look of scorn, that the dusky features might be trodden again to clay.

This is where spirit meets flesh.

Imagine Quasheba, a wretched black soul on bended knee, a Christian, pleading for her right to live. Did her white masters whip her lover to death? They dragged him . . . where? . . . She crawled to touch his blood's mark in the dust . . . How much grief, I ask, must her soul bear? 'Mere grief's too good for such as I,' comes the woman slave's reply, 'so the white man brought the shame ere long to strangle the sob in my throat thereby. They would not leave me for my dull wet eyes! – it was too merciful – to let me weep pure tears, and die.'

Cousin Richard said of Quasheba that she probably strangled her own child, and must be without her faculties. He defined her by what she was not. Though I sometimes fail to see her clearly – it stands to reason that this runaway slave was neither bad, nor mad – if I focus on what she was, then perhaps I can wear the cloak of change.

She wears a child upon her breast. An amulet that hangs too slack. And, in her unrest, cannot rest. Thus they go moaning, child and mother, one to another, one to another, until it all ends for the best. For her offspring is of its mother's flesh yet not of her race.

How her belief in God and His throngs of angels must be tried. Though she may not be looked down on by the tall windows of a church, she must have hope. Must have faith.

What might compel one to destroy the very beautiful creature that through one's suffering was created? Can the joy of the first-born child bring the deepest grief? What of my intimate friend, Trippy? Orphaned at a young age, penniless but for the legacy of two slaves who were sold to pay her father's debts – is Trippy not the offspring of a slave and a white West Indian planter? What does she think of dear Papa? What did she think of Cousin Richard?

Can it be that when black one is always a fugitive? How a God-fearing slave woman committed infanticide begs the question, is she any more unnatural than dear Papa? Papa's conviction, that none of his offspring should marry, surely goes against all that is natural. Countless times have I heard of infant deaths on plantations. But is Papa *killing* his grandchildren by preventing their births? Is this not some kind of murder?

It is one thing to choose, quite another to be forced to be barren for the rest of one's days. Forced to be barren like me. Or forced not to be. On many occasions have I heard of a dark child, much darker than its white parents, suddenly appearing with Negroid features. Why it happens I now know – this is a crude justice; the tragic reminder to all is the offspring's skin colour – I am certain. It is God's will.

Would Quasheba then not wish to rid herself of Cousin Richard?

Of it? Be driven? Could she bear to look upon a face so white? If Papa fears dark offspring, would Quasheba not fear a white child? Would the reminder not be sickening to her also? The master's look, that used to fall on her soul like his lash, or worse.

3 April 1840

The *Hopeful Adventure* let down her anchor this morning. The bay waters are jagged and bristly but there have been no exploding ships. Bro, with his brown wind-blown hair resembling the wreck of Hesperus, reads Papa's letter aloud.

"'Negroes attending church last Christmas on Cinnamon Hill and Cornwall estates, and those refusing to attend Sam's 'busha-house dances', or refusing to accept Sam's extra Christmas bottles of rum were, the Presbyterian minister Hope Masterton Waddell says, treated unfairly by Sam, and even denied their usual sugar ration." According to the minister, Sam is guilty of another, greater folly.' Bro arches his eyebrows. 'Sam has banned African field workers from participating in abstinence societies!'

I am praying for God to forgive Sam, to help us all *please*: to bring humanity together not only in mind and in flesh, but in spirit. For ever. 'Do we not all long for freedom?' I ask. 'Long for grass greener than that on which we tread? Freedom to love? To live? To die? Oh, how that longing must increase ten-thousand-fold if one is imprisoned not simply by social etiquette but literally enslaved by a system of severe floggings, treadmills and other tortures imposed by an alien race.'

Bro says he too fears that although slavery is ended, the cruelty that went with it is not.

My beloved friend,

I am as well today as possible after a sleepless night. The weather is very trying – & I have not been suffered by my Liege Lord physician, to have my bed made, for above a month. But altogether I bear up tolerably. What they mean to do with me this summer is a matter of fidgeting. Here, I am sure not to stay, if I can move – my own longing being for London, & my physician's, I see too plainly, for the torrid zone. Do not mention this to anybody, dearest Miss Mitford . . .

4 April 1840

What is behind Papa's conviction – the divine right he believes he has to rule and control our lives? Papa's father had a string of mistresses and illegitimate children, seven in all, I believe; his emotions overflowed everywhere. He abandoned Grandmama, leaving the family in disgrace. Papa is the opposite of him . . . *How I remember the coming of that letter to apprise him of the loss of his fortune, and just one shadow passed on his face while he read it . . . and then he broke away from the melancholy and threw himself into the jests and laughter of his innocent boys . . . and in all the bitter bitter preparation for our removal, there was never a word said by any one of us to Papa, nor by him to us, in that relation . . . he* suffered more, *of course, he suffered in proportion to the silence . . .* We never knew what was going on. Everything was rumour or stumbled upon. So it remains. And when Papa sent for Bummy to look after us whilst he was on business in London from June to December that year, her lips stayed hermetically sealed.

Sadness created an agonizing melody in Papa's breath, when after luncheon he walked into my room, held my hand and paused between each line of prayer.

If Papa *were* to find it within him to change. Imagine – *that* would be a dream come true.

. . . The weather is unbending – & altho' the east wind returned yesterday, we are not likely to be long molested. By favour of its absence I had my bed made three days ago – the first time for six weeks – but the moving to the sofa produced great faintness & exhaustion – to which however I shall not yield the point about trying again. Indeed we – Dr. Scully & I – are beginning to talk of transferring me by the said sofa, & additional wheels, thro' the one intervening door into the drawing-room – let but the weather be settled, & one of us something stronger . . .

Memories. Everywhere. I am tormented by this storm. The curtains, not yet fully drawn back, thinly disguise the sun. Sam's pallid face comes to me; impatient. Vexed. I fear he looks unwell, and that I must blame myself for this. Sam leans, headlong, into the gale, his sickness full-blown.

Dr. Barry died for my sake. I was instrumental in Sam returning to Jamaica. And I persuaded Bro to remain in Torquay. I fear a great disaster looms as a consequence of my bold, selfish, stubborn stupidity. Were Bro and Sam to leave this world for the heavenly stars, Papa would have lost both his first and second sons. How am I to bear the truth about myself?

I look across the restless sea. It might provide an answer. From a grey foreboding sky the mist of grief falls, whispering over turbid waves, across the stretch of barren yet fertile earth visible from my window. In Sam's eyes I see death. And Bro?

White waters froth like a fresh bed sheet waiting for Bro to slip beneath. The water holds his body-shape. His shirt is saturated. My heart beats, but Bro's breath drowned by water does surcease. Entangled by weeds he sinks below the tempest; white transparent skin; arms bloated; riding the swelling currents of the tide of the deceased.

In sheer terror I lie unable to sleep. Can condemnation be removed by repentance for one's sins? God's love is too great to bring upon Papa such tragedies. Beloved Papa has suffered so. That the Lord God will spare us the horrors I have witnessed with my very own eyes is one simple truth I know. Not for my sake but for *his*.

I taste the sadness with which Papa is surrounded. Sam's expression was sadness. Sadness is the silenced slave. I have a freedom, and yet with that surely comes a curse; for it is true I am cursed. To be ruled by self-doubt and inner-conflict surely is. When I think on my inheritance a cold wind sweeps this body I so despise. I am no more than a useless machine that cannot fight back. I am useless, helpless, worthless. Scarcely worth taking care of. Unlovable.

Chapter Eleven

Sheba

BARRETT TOWN MARKET
May 1839

Yu lunatic, me head say. *Yu liar. Yu promise, like lunatic, yu going to run an here yu are, walk walking a-side Lickle Phoebe. Pickney strapped to yu chest drains wot yu drink, eat – cornbread, roast fish, bammie. Yu fear if yu mek noise someone will hear. Will know. So yu walking on silent feet. Speaking silent to yuself.*

Market days passed fast until this one came. Coldness grips me, and me cyaan find meself no more. *Yu know wot yu have to do but yu fraid to do it. Fraid to kill it.*

Owl-eyes in Lickle Phoebe's hungry face fix on pickney bawling and butting me full hot breast. Every strike of him feet's a knife stabbing.

A woman stumbles against me. Curses. Me seen she face at Cinnamon Hill; eyes grief-filled. She do housemaid work fe Mister Sam, Sylvia did say, and now Mister Sam flee to England she live at Cinnamon Hill all by sheself. In a violent rush of passing pickney she's whisked from me sight. Inside me flare, too long imprisoned, storm-like, it a anger of anguish briefly uncovered. Holding out me pickney, begging she'll take him, me must think of something to make she hear, make she see. Words run from me mouth, 'Yu, fram Cinnamon Hill!' me craving shout. 'It me, Sheba!' She name? Kaydia, me remember. But already she's lost in a flood of market sellers. Vainly me eyes search fe she face. Blow-winds come soft as shadows off salt-sparkling blue sea, a thirsty heat licking skin dry.

Silently looking to Phoebe, me clutch pickney back to me breast, clench hands into fists, and feel more alone than one palm tree on lonely windswept beach.

'Yu did mek ow many bitts?' me ask Lickle Phoebe.

She fishes in a pocket. 'Two.'

'Me carry yu bitts, keep em safe safe. Sylvia telled me to. Me do it fe she.' Lickle Phoebe hands money over, around it me wrap me tight fist. 'Me give yu me yellow candy,' me say.

Guiltily me weave behind Lickle Phoebe, weaving towards coast road through crowds of women holding on their heads trays of saltwater fish, crying, 'Fi-ish! Fi-ish!' Trays of freshwater shrimps go by, women calling, 'Jan-ga! Jan-ga!' Baskets of avocado, crying 'Ripe-peer! Ripe-peer!' Pig trotters, yellow and nubbly. Flat white bammie cakes stacked high. Pickney gather round rising sour dough smell from scorching fresh baked bread. Sunday market quenches thirst, fills moaning bellies. Black dogs bark. Old women with faces dark purple as star-apple, warty as soursop, sit neatly cross-legged before small herb bunches, lettuce heads, lima beans, duck eggs, ackee yawning open red to savagely hot sunbursts.

Walking backwards on stick-thin legs, Lickle Phoebe's staring at free-black slave's fancy waistcoat trimmed with bright red ribbon. Best best petticoat lace frills out beneath dress hems.

Going towards stinking mud-fish stall on market edge, Lickle Phoebe say, 'White-nigger have cray-fish, duck, salt-marsh plover.' At stall corner fe tethering pack asses, donkeys loaded with pannier baskets peacefully swish tails around sucking foals' flanks. Rows of women with dung-caked feet shout, 'Yam fe cleaning donkey yard! Yam fe cleaning donkey yard!' Dung juice seeps through baskets' wicker weave; baskets piled up with muck upon heads. Brown slurry juice dribbles behind ears, drips down grinning babies sucking on yielding breasts, leaves trails down necks, bald raw patches.

Me eyes flick from black nigger women to white nigger women and back. Scornfully Lickle Phoebe looks at white nigger, she brown eyes merciless as baked-hard earth holding a mixture of horror and hate. Turning, walking backwards to look on stinking mud-fish stall, Lickle Phoebe say, 'White nigger, Mama say, more filthy dan black nigger fe buckra treat white nigger worse dan we. White nigger aint just slave, dem street-beggar, escaped fram prison, not paid fe like we.'

Stony red sand track we're coming to clings to yellow-white coastline. Cyaan walk fast fe sharp stones bite even we hard feet. Pickney's hand's tapping and prodding me rock-hard breast, head rooting under burning swollen flesh. Temptation draw me to break him neck. *Yu lunatic, yu forget to run!* Red sun slants down to coast-line and coast road we're on, each step bringing closer me dread. *Mek sure yu kill im,* Leah's voice say.

Soon market's a dot, bay's yellow-white curve hugs warm flat calm sea, and fish stench gets swallowed in a shy sweet honey smell stealing into late-afternoon breeze.

Chattering to sheself like she does, Lickle Phoebe quick-steps ahead, hopping, snatching at flies, criss-crossing red stone track. Me treasure Lickle Phoebe, treasure she voice, treasure each song, but all day truly me almost running to get away fe me feel so unclean and move clumsily on heavy unsure feet. Sadly me think of cane burning and sundown. Deep within feelings flutter and stir, bad feelings about taking Lickle Phoebe's bitts. *Yu a coward,* me head-tongue says. But me want to be far from Lickle Phoebe to think and to plan when me should dig a grave fe me pickney. When me should bury pickney's future – eighth day? Ninth day? How do me remember with too much hurt inside me breast? Red clouds sweep too fast across blue sky; me search in me heart. Onshore winds blow warmly in from sea's quiet face – a ready strength, a deep peace – sea's blue heart surges like some great beast, rises, falls, fe this's where Loa lives, a spirit world where dead slaves' souls go. Salty tang blow you touch to me, and me want to smile feeling you, Isaac, everywhere. Clouds move freely, sea, salty air. Sun sinks slowly red and although me feel you, Isaac, me cyaan see you anywhere. Me feel how you hot mouth once covered mine; me skin sizzling under you touch. Fe you me love's more fierce than any blazing suns.

Giving a broken trampled look, 'Wot if me run away?' me ask Lickle Phoebe. 'Yu'd shout afta me?'

Lickle Phoebe sings, 'Yu cun run if yu waan. No one come afta yu.' She's skipping to and fro, halting on stony track like a goat kid then leaping across boulders and back to rubbed smooth sandy places where track's beaten by many tired feet.

'An yu won't raise de alarm? Yu'll cover yu mouth?'

Lickle Phoebe keeps skipping. 'Yu cun run if yu waan. No one come afta yu.' Slowing to a walk she say, 'Ow yu wanna know? Me won't tell no one if yu go, so ow yu wanna know?'

Pickney isn't made of bones, skin, flesh, blood. Kill it. KILL IT afore ninth day. Osun, spirit of healing streams. Osun, yu know, will guide yu. Me remember now all Leah said.

'Yu hungry?' I ask Lickle Phoebe.

Lickle Phoebe say she's not but she sucks loudly on me yellow candy stick, sharp cheekbones showing through skin. Skin scarred with cane sores, deep scratches, cuts from tending pumpkin and squash plot, no more Lickle Phoebe's a light, loose chile. Wide-eyed as a cud-chewing cow Lickle Phoebe works on me yellow candy twist. Skin crusty, clothes needing patching, she's scratching, scratching flaking scabs. Me think she turned sick with something. That's why me feel bad about taking she bitts.

Flowers stray onto red stony track. Mango trees lean over like tall women with not enough in their pockets to buy what they want fram we stall. You towered over me. Strong arms. Words. Branches, spread life's wisdom to me fe me die when they took you, Isaac, and you leave me at plantation.

Single smoke strand stretches across evening sky smudgy above mountain ridges but a clear sign fe parting. We come plodding up a low hill, every step bringing me closer to running.

Pickney's red crying face turns up to mine. Standing still, letting him suck what he can, me struggle to let out a word. Part of me body's trapped in him face – all me want to do's forget. *Cyaan name im. Me cyaan love im. Lickle Phoebe cyaan love im.* Burning bagasse and molasses stink hangs stale in orange sky, pecks and prickles me nose too. *It's de running time.*

'Pickney tirc?' Lickle Phoebe ask.

Sleepily him head moves sideways, banging me breast. Him eye, a lantern dimly shining, makes four with mine. Me breasts will burst. Snake of true hatred runs through me blood. Clamping on again, sucking from nipple tip till it bleeds, pickney drains what goodness me have. Flames we see from hilltop sweep orange-grey to black through cut stubble, hunting out coney, snake, boar, sleeping pickney. Smoke curls back on itself from fire's red blaze, a wall of air trembles and shivers like sugar furnace. Boldly raging flames pour smoke up into dusk-blue sky leaving a sooty path; soon there'll be nothing but trash, and a sea of smouldering ash.

Coming over hill's wide shoulder me pledge to pay back Lickle Phoebe's bitts some day. Me gave she me last candy twist. Me did that fe she.

Flames reach over big hill's brow, making afternoon air ripple like freshwater streams.

'Dem must finish burnin afore brown dusk settle on plantain grove,' Lickle Phoebe say.

Old Simeon from Cinnamon Hill stands upon a grassy hummock under a clump of trees. He rests on a spade, body looking stunted like clouds have pressed him down. Behind him, violently shaking its head, stands a mule, and behind grey mule minister's cloak billows, great bat-wings shadowing a shiny-smooth mahoney-wood coffin.

'Somebody dead,' Lickle Phoebe say.

'Cyaan say. But coffin's real enough,' me say, wanting to run, now, as we trudge over dunes.

Lickle Phoebe's drawn spent face scarily mirrors sharp-shaped rocks on mountains ahead. 'Is Mister Richard Barrett dem bury,' she say. 'It puzzle me fe tink where im shadow go afta im dead.'

'Mister Richard Barrett? Ow yu know im dead?'

Lickle Phoebe gives a strong smile. 'People say Leah mek poison fe im.'

'Mister Richard Barrett, dat one, Mister Sam cousin?'

Me head-tongue say, *Mister Barrett, yu me pickney fadda. Bury de fadda, bury de son.*

Minister's cloak flaps whipping around legs like it's trying to push them from under him, and Old Simeon's skin gleams funeral satin black as him elbow slides off spade handle. Though him skin's aged him muscles swell richly as burnished mahoney wood – Simeon's turning back to him job. Red sandy earth clods flump on grass. Each thump say, *Reach across, put wandrin spirit back. As lang as yu understand dis yu free.*

Pickney's feet start up jabbing breasts again. Silent as Jancra wing-tips slipping blue-black into evening sky, Leah's words come on feeble winds, and cord tying red pickney and me together withers, finally. Old Simeon's spade scrapes raw rock stone, smashes into rock-hard earth.

Not looking back me run. Me head thumps with what Leah said: *Yu must make all thoughts go. Yu must be strong as hurricane.* Wind have fingers; hands; fists; howling, living breath; and if me stop now me'll be afraid, afraid of what chile might do. It knows it's returning to spirit world? Me cyaan bear to tell fe true.

'Sheba! Sheba!' Lickle Phoebe bawls. Me cyaan answer. There's too much hurt to understand, too much to explain. Taking grass path, swamped by a knowing pain, wanting to shout *Phoebe! Cover yu mouth!* me run. Branches grasp at arms, spiked wooden fingers cruel hard-burying into skin. Me mind say, *Pickney's soul isn't born. Peacefully it'll go back to where it belongs.* But fear clings to me. *Keep running. Don't ever turn back.* Over rocks, through streams evening sun spills copper-red across, run, leave no tracks. Pickney's head knocks on me breast. Screeching bird shape cuts forest. Still. Hot. Dead.

Clapping on sand, slapping stone, me feet sound stiff and risky against sure but faint sounds of Phoebe shouting. Grasses slowly rush past. Lickle Phoebe's eye looks after me. Me know she's standing, shouting, though no answer comes. And even when Lickle Phoebe's calling's stopped and shouts fade to silence, me know she eye bawls fe another glimpse of me back, running away.

Scrambling on tides of fear me dare not one peep at struggling, wailing red-skin chile. Moving through underbrush me don't run now but stop, looking way way below like me can see into dust of me life that's past.

Me eye follows uneven bristly-bush path leading to ledges, up and across leafy skies. Now me see a safe safe hiding place where jagged rocks overhang a hollow bare pink cliff face.

Bamboo clumps burst over rocky edges. Tree ferns, thinly green, reach into blue. Air plant's grey roots streaming like hair kept alive by what? Red rocks' thick fingers shoot skywards. White streams plunge from cracked rugged crags to a bowl of swirling quivering water beneath. Grooves scooped trough-like into rocks make paths to soothe tired feet. Lolling on me breast's him head. *Me did make such a face?* Oh, to sail de winds, to fling meself up and out, flapping great wings and be free free free. But him wispy hair holds fast on me neck like grasp of him hand on me finger, and presses on a sticky hollow under me chin.

Brushing aside creeper curtains, sticks snap light as tiny bones beneath cautious feet. From cave roof a rank rat-bat stench fills me nose. Me fingertips unlatch lips dragging down me nipple. Me lay pickney down, without belief in what me doing, on powdery, feather-soft rat-bat dropping bed, without belief in Osun, without belief in God.

Fingers uncurl from tightly clenched hands like tiny brown tree ferns unfurling; searching fe me voice pickney's head moves blindly. Cyaan hold him tenderly like it Isaac's chile. Isaac's chile it cyaan be, fe Isaac's face me should see. Should be Isaac's skin me stroke, dark richly smooth; eyes, full bright moons.

Side by side we sleep then as dusk grows colder me body wraps warm round pickney's tiny softly breathing curves. He snuggles, elbows nudge me belly.

Me mind begins to race. Me see Lickle Phoebe's pale black face; drawn with sadness she eyelids close. Why me did leave shack village? me wonder – Eleanor, Sylvia, owl-eyed Lickle Phoebe. When me listen to me heart me know that part of me life's long gone. And when me shut eye still me see thicket, hair-like creeper strand, banana bunches, brilliant wiry flowers palm-climbing. Vines strangling tree ferns. Ackee. Bare pink cliff face, as if pickney and thick forest journey have been carved into me eyelids.

Light fades from cave's coldly dark mouth. Me think, *No longer sun will yu scorch pickney wid yu fiah*. Tight and close me draw me bandana, protecting pickney from tomorrow's hot spears. Fastening a hand round him neck me wonder, this how to soothe spirit chile to sleep?

Tenderly rubbing him back, me lay pickney over me knee. *Dis more hard dan cane-piece work*. He struggles to breathe on him belly. *Yu can put spirit back, if yu waan to yu know yu can*.

Him body jerks, mouth gurgles, soaking cloth with spit. Me smother him face tighter with bandana. Panic writhes through muscles, through crackling foaming bubbles frothing from him throat. Him head struggles hard.

Bandana lifts from him nose and sucks into it with each breath. Never did flesh die so hard. Never did me know such power in so small a body, such small fists. *Pickney cyaan fight forever, can he?* Wishing me used creeper-rope to hang him, not this strangle-hold, me loosen bandana, slowly. Bloody white blobs form in a lather round him mouth, round nose. Him body thrusts forward and up then falls floppily. Cyaan look again though chile don't flinch. *Him flesh return to water?* Me won't risk uncovering him fully yet fe me feel pickney's spirit soar. Hear me now, even when cloth was drawn tight me felt him eye upon me. Me think he'll keep breathing. Suddenly me realize, no. We free.

Slowly me untie bandana though tiny thumping feet suddenly fight again savagely. Blood leaks from him nose slanting down across him cheek and tiny perfectly rounded chin. Me tears don't heal, they seal what me done.

Rugged mountains cast long cold shadows. Moonbeams slide down rocky slopes. Down steep mountain-goat path me walk numbly and stiffly, picking a way through trembling grasses, a limp bundle of a body cradled in me bandana, thumping dully against sorrow-filled chest. Sand, whitened by sunshine, lights up under moon's silvery touch. Me feel him warm, still twitching, feet. Black branches' shadows point like fingers to moonlit seawater. Running through thick wood forest me go, toes slipping between sleepy flowers' droopy heads, running through mangroves; trees, perched on roots like ready-woven baskets, trunks twisting skywards. Night winds stroke shady pimento groves freely before a white sand bay.

Me eye rest on me pickney – a lead-heavy shell. *Wait fe dawn den bury wot yu done.*

Sky turns a deep mango colour, red-purple streaks flare across. A feeling fills me body of holding you at night, Isaac, safe safe safe. But even this leaves me nowhere stranded. Sadness stained.

Pelicans glide, bills sagging. Me filled with a cry but all sound's missing. Red sun rolls up from cool blue sea. Gently me lay pickney down having carved sand aside till fingertips touched chilled stones. Wind gusts hold their breath. Me feel white with fury fe me have no wrap fe him body bare; only cold sand to clothe him. No funeral drum beats dawn air but me heart throbs strong to soothe him.

Watching red sky splinter with gold me cyaan look true at him fe fear him stare can cut me down.

Me lay out tiny hands, arms outstretched like branches, him

darker cheeks, bulging tongue, bruised neck, face so sad me want
to offer relief, offer to him comfort forever, as fire drains from dawn
sky. Me don't have no lock-up fe cell bars these hands, cell walls
him cloud-soft skin. Sky held its blue breath when me crouched,
waiting fe pain to swell. Kneeling forward me whole body shuddering and rocking in huge waves, agony with spirit chile came.
In Sylvia's shack me animal-cries brought no one, fe all field-hands
were out working. And labour lasted so long me believed something was wrong. It were more like a battle than a birth. Between
waves me rested till next pain crest, scared pickney wouldn't fit,
afraid me split, tear apart. Soft, smooth, warm, a pale copper
monster's born, wriggling, squirming, howling. Memories float
leaving my mind – *This curious limp thing could feel, cry, stretch him
spine?* – there's a bleak deathly gleam to him wretched copper face
now. Me did make an kill such a face. Me watch meself fade in and
out of it.

Yu must make all thoughts go. Yu must be strong as hurricane. Lower,
lower me sink heavy with woe, spreading coarse gritty sand over
him body till me fingertips burn. Breezes whistle through mangrove
branches – him voice discovers a way out, wailing across water like
angry nesting morass bird. Feelings cyaan be dashed, crushed.
Wanting to rip feelings out, me drag me eye from me pickney spirit
grave, step across sand and away from him. *Spirit's no longer here.*

Sky glares slippery red. Sea's angry sparkling blue eye's staring
staring staring. Cupping hands over me ear me stare back, searching
fe Isaac. Longing.

Pelican-wing shadow roams across many fine lines left on sand
by waves lapping. Past enters me head. It happens now. Again.
Tiny pieces come but them too sharp to see clearly. *Slippery red
between me legs. Hot. Cold. Pain.* Night's darkness enters each day.
Me see buckra's white face. Me cyaan find a path from Mister
Richard Barrett, cyaan remember way out so stop, and stoop. Smooth
sea-washed abeng shell me cling to me ear sings of dashing over
sand, dropping canoe Isaac and me carried, painted black, dug from
a cotton-tree trunk. You laughed, Isaac, scattering squawking
chickens into palm-thatched fishermen's huts, a clutter of nets,
cowskin sails against bamboo walls. Cyaan feel seawater, cyaan feel
warm morning sun breathe on shoulders, only you, Isaac, and

morning before abeng, and warmth of you arm round me shoulder;
lying, lip to lip; you body warmth, salt of you breath, and kissing
you sleeping head.

Wading out to sea, salt-streaked cheeks brushed by now whispering gusts, tired, heavy me is, wading into distressed waters, de
salt smell sting.

Chapter Twelve

Kaydia

CINNAMON HILL ESTATE
17 February 1840

From yacca floor I look up through dark blue bedchamber window. Morning star lost its shine. Mister Sam lies tombstone stiff.

Mary Ann wriggles between my knees, saying, 'Gimme breadfruit. Mek me gib lickle bit fe yu.'

Dividing she hair into bunches, I say, 'Me cyaan eat now,' *Mister Sam's pickney fills me belly.* 'Chile, sit still. Yu cyaan mek chair out-a Mister Sam. Yu cyaan touch im.'

'Why?' Shuffle-scudding on she bottom she tries to struggle free. 'Mister Sam don't move.'

Conch-blow bellows *Fuuuuffuu-ffuu.* I stay silent till monster stops moaning. 'No,' I say, 'e a-sleepin.' I drag Mary Ann close into my belly.

What's this dawn I see? Freedom? Victory? Blazing sun can't find its strength but Mary Ann keeps up battling. She scrambles from my clasp, swiftly she run-hide fleeing through Mister Sam's chamber doorway, along landing, slipping down stairs, across hall, front lawn.

Swelling up I reach out to touch Mister Sam's hand, cheeks, chin. To tease flaming gold hairs from him chilled dank brow; dead white skin. Him spent and gone. Pale, half-closed eyes turned dull; cloudy like marble with no blue flicker. Even him faint yellow eyelashes seem curious now to me. *Mister Sam cyaan let no ooman keep no pickney. Not if im its baby fadda.* My blood too? *Cyaan see yu as brodda. Me see yu as a curse fe pile of grief yu cause. Noting but pity me feel fe yu. Pity an shame. Cyaan tell no person, not even bedchamber, wot me do to try to raise money fe Charles, fe Pa an me dawta; wot me do to try to claw Mary Ann fram yu. Me waan no person to know wot happened, not even bedchamber – but all me know have memory an dem live on afta me an yu.*

Pelican flaps through my thoughts landing on sea. Dawn breeze mutters over Mister Sam's lifeless form; moon-like face bled of colour. Breeze isn't a stranger. Stranger's me.

Gazing between jalousie blinds I see no hope, no tracks, no lanes across blue sea. Fear, like sneaking dawn light, creeping into me. Candle-flame breeze blows upon suddenly dies.

I move to verandah where two months past my master stood, sweating rum, I was struck by a screaming sun, a flashing, glittering sea. My hand in apron pocket clutches buckled metal skeleton of earrings – missing jewels crushed between rocks somewhere in front garden below. Matching sister necklace of false pearls lies shattered some place near Barrett Hall. Leaning forward, resting elbows on verandah rail, my eyes slant down. Any guilt for what I've done begins to fade. All my thoughts confused with finding my own way to freedom from Cinnamon Hill.

Mary Ann's disappeared. She laugh comes back to hit me. *It's she me waan to guard. Not Mister Sam.*

Rattling into my thoughts cart wheels come, rattling up plantation path. Heading through hall for kitchen block, 'Mary Ann! Mary Ann!' I'm shouting. Framed by hall doorway, Dick's cart passes gate at drive's end. Cart's piled high with rum-filled puncheons balanced on bundles of guinea grass, pimento sacks bulging over tailboard.

Cracks between kitchen flagstones emerge. *Flagstones Pa's grandpa unloaded from a flotilla.* Guard dogs let out shrill whines. Friday, snoozing in Mister Sam's cloth cot, opens one eye. A horse's sigh shoots into sky's brooding greyness, and stable-block's curiously changed by hissing sounds of lizards sliding through hay, smashing through dawn silence.

Then bushes become busy with birds. But like tiny pickney in my belly I'm trapped in silent stillness.

'Kaydia! Kaydia!' Dick's bawl sounds like a lunatic in my head, waking me in an unknown country. Loudly I hear Dick calling now. 'Kaydia!' he bawls. 'Me need yu elpin in still-house. Yu'll do dat fe me?'

I shout to Friday, 'Friday, yu big nuff fe workin wid Dick.'

Cradled in hammock cloth Friday nods loosely, swinging sameway pickney-like, green birthday shirt Pa give him soiled, dirt-creased. Stinking of rum Friday tips himself over hammock side, flops down at my feet, him gleaming face grins wide as watermelon slice. Cordia flower twisting open skywards to sun's cool gaze.

All my love for Mary Ann comes flooding back. My head-tongue says Mister Sam's death brings a glimpse of how close mother and daughter might be. I feel terror at my own pain. I'm saying to Dick as Friday and me reach cart horse, 'Yu see Mary Ann dis mornin? She pass by dis way?'

Tugging at pimento sacks buried under thatching grass, Dick tests load for steadfastness. Cart's whole load wobbles. Shaking him head Dick says, 'Work gettin harder an me floggin meself gettin crop in.'

'No yu aint,' I say. 'Yu aint worked fe days.'

Dick yanks up grey horse's head from feeding on lush grass. He holds horse steady. Swollen skin round horse's eyes breeds raw pink patches, he stamps an unshod hoof. Fitfully cart's load shudders. Slapping horse's hollow sweating neck, 'Horse wid fever,' Dick adds, 'him coat sweat.'

'Cart's overloaded,' I say.

Friday say, 'Lickle ol fashion but it work,' him eyes glazed over.

'Cart weary, but e last,' Dick says. 'Me must go down plantation path to wharf, unload puncheons, pimento sacks, drop off feed sacks by slave shacks on way back up.' He checks short chains clip firmly from horse's collar to shafts, jangling them. He pats horse's pitted dappled chest. 'Any fool cun git puncheons to stay on top. Friday cun tie dem.'

I'm saying to Dick, 'It look easy,' but pushing forward in my mind I see Friday – my eyes skim crazy stack on guinea thatching grass; curved wood making cart-horse collar ache with age – my heart says no.

Sun's blazing eye comes piercing through clouds, showing hotter than hot day. Bending low Dick grunts. Him hands mould together to form a stirrup for Friday to mount cart. Sweat brews on Dick's broad bare back, Friday's little foot weighs on stirrup hands. Leaning against cart side Friday hoists himself up like him shin up coconut tree.

'Me gonna chuck dis rope up,' Dick shouts to Friday. Sweat trickles like raindrops down Dick's shoulders, soaking osnaburg trouser-cloth. He throws up rope, it snakes through blue morning air.

Pa walks round track curve where treetops join like arch he carved for Cinnamon Hill church doorway.

My eye keeps wandering for Mary Ann.

Pa's standing level with me, chewing coffee beans mighty hard. 'Yu see Mary Ann dis mornin?' I ask him. 'She on path to Sibyl's hut? Yu'll watch out fe she?'

'Me watch out fe she.' Pa's chewing savagely. 'W'appen?' he asks.

'Friday workin fe Dick, Pa.'

Pa's jaws snap shut. Him eyes follow mine. Easing him body forward Friday straddles puncheons nesting in thatching grass, him feet a-walk in air. He feeds rope round puncheons' belly.

Dick looks vexed. Cart can't keel over, I'm thinking.

'Lard hab mercy.' Pa sighs, and spits crushed coffee beans onto driveway. Friday, shaking, clutches top puncheon rim. Him faith-filled eyes flash a look at long drop down.

Spitefully Dick yanks both reins, bringing horse's old bony head sharply round. 'Me try turning cart up an round in driveway, heading up afore going down,' Dick says. Cart moves maddeningly slowly, wheels juddering forward; back. Shallow morning heat getting deeper.

'Friday big nuff fe workin wid yu, Pa. Yu tink e'll be a-carpenter?' I ask.

Squatting on heels, rapidly cracking fingers, him eye full on me, Pa says, 'Say wa? E a-lickle pickney. Dis too risky. Yu cyaan see dat, girl?' He turns out trouser pockets, into one hand he empties fluff, coffee grains, filth. Pa's fishing for more beans. 'Wot's dis yu dangle fe Charles? E butcher yu if e know,' he says, and chucks a small coffee bean catch into him open mouth.

Dick shouts, 'Beast! Beast!' Horse's muscles tighten, swell, pulling forward up drive slope; coat matted with sweat, hooves slipping on dusty stones. 'Beast! Beast!' Dick shouts. 'Cyaan pull de load up to turn cart back.'

'Yu see Mary Ann on plantation path?' I ask Pa again. He says nothing. Cart's wooden sides creak. Blood seeps from horse's cracked lips. Cart's jerking wheels stop. 'Pa, why yu —'

Pa says, 'Shut yu mouth.'

Cart bottom makes tearing sound like osnaburg cloth ripping. 'Don't, Friday – go on!' Pa bawls.

Sun's screaming on Friday's spoiled birthday shirt. Sky's hot. Empty. Blue. Road's empty too.

Stained by shrieking sunlight banana leaves shine.

'Mister Sam ded dis mornin?' Pa asks me.

'Yes.' I don't feel any worry lift now Mister Sam's gone.

Dick shouts, 'Beast! Beast!' pulling reins taut, almost wrenching bit clean from horse's long brown teeth.

'Oo de ell's dat comin round back way on Sam's horse?' Pa says. 'E cyaan elp?'

This time I know it's Charles before I see him. Minister follows on trotting black mare. I hide behind Pa. Truth slaps me brutally in my face. Charles knows what I carry. Knows what's already growing inside. He knows Mister Sam not fully gone.

Pa sings out, 'Cotch de cart it full-a feed! Friday, come down ere! Yu drunk on rum. Any fool cun see.' He bawls to Dick, 'Lame horse weak! Yu idiot. Yu cyaan tek harness off? Tek machete an cut it afore de horse fall.' Cart rolls backwards. 'Wedge rakstone!' Pa bellows. 'Cart slide backwards fore de horse!' Spitting out coffee bean jots Pa snatches reins from Dick, grabs bridle with such force bit part's sliding from horse's bleeding mouth. Horse's brown eyes roll back to half-moon whites. Hurling himself against horse, sweating shoulder rubbing sweating shoulder, Pa shouts, 'Git up! Git up!' Groaning cart bottom splinters. Pa bawls at Friday, 'Git down.'

Friday stretches up over rum puncheon, him belly's slithering back towards cart tailboard.

'E too scared to come down, Pa,' I say.

Pa shouts despairingly, 'Jump! Jump!' He keeps on goading Friday. 'Jump out-a deway!' Leaping to one side Pa's jumping shows Friday how.

'Yu stay! No, move on up!' Dick shouts, pushing cart from below and behind now. Dick's pressing, straining, leaning full against cart tailboard. Cart halts, rum puncheons rock. Dick springs clear of tailboard. Stumbling onto bony knees grey horse screams. Puncheons tumble over cart back, Friday topples from him perch.

Wild pig squeal – Friday shrieks and shrieks in awful agony. Puncheons battering him body, head, spilling over pimento-stuffed sacks, bounce-rolling down plantation path; split. Smashed. Rum gushes downhill. Rum flows red. Slumped between shafts horse rears up front hooves, mane splaying out in yellow-white flames.

Pa have a zombie face. He just stands there. Lips shaking.

Friday's bloody rum-soaked body wedges awkwardly beneath puncheons, torn sacks spewing pimento atop cart's wreckage.

'Yu aright?' Dick asks Friday. Clambering up pimento-stuffed sacks to guinea thatching-grass bundles, crawling over splintered puncheons, Dick shouts, routing for Friday. No answer comes. Then I see Friday's bleeding head; sameway like broken chicken's neck twisted unnaturally it defy any kind of faith in life, limply falling back dead. In my mind him still squealing like pig with machete to him throat. I sharply feel yoke of guilt slant across my shouders.

'Friday never aright afta dat,' Pa says, him voice broken. He joins Dick to pore over messy stack. Pa's trembling hand reaches out, grasps rope loop like it's a line leading to hope. Searching for ways to free Friday, he tilts up a puncheon, ripping out grey-green shirt shred.

Turning, I see myself through great-house windows, rushing along landing – how I got here I don't know – down hall, across front verandah. Cinnamon Hill great hall's empty. 'Mary Ann! Mary Ann!' I'm yelling. Flying up stairs, I yell, 'Yu not gawn to Sibyl's yet?' Blocking Mister Sam's chamber doorway a shape black as a shadow moves. Panting hopelessly, 'Friday. Is Friday,' I'm saying. 'Me tink Mary Ann aright, but me cyaan find she.'

'It's Monday, Kaydia, what's wrong?' Minister shoves him hands in deep black gown pockets. He must have come in by back door, I think.

Frantically my thoughts spin back. 'Is Mary Ann. Rum. Friday. Gone.' My burning eyes scour plantation path sweeping round, eye-watching drive for Charles.

'How much rum was lost? How many puncheons?' minister asks, moving to window to see. 'It's a mercy the consequences weren't more serious.' Minister hisses under him breath, 'This horrible, cruel weather.' He asks again, 'How much rum was lost, damnation? You must answer clearly. I can't understand if you keep blubbering.' But minister shudders. Like he smells something else wrong. Smells more than spilt rum. 'You will send for Junius to find someone to clear up, clean up any mess. And get Friday to water my horse, she's hitched to the cinnamon tree by the cut wind.'

'Yu pass Mary Ann on plantation path?' I ask. Turning into Mister Sam's bedchamber minister, muttering prayers, closes door on me, turns chamber key. I shout after minister, 'Yu ride wid Charles dis mornin?' Fury flares hot within my breast. Over and over my hand's banging hardwood door. Breaking through my pangs of loss I feel thin ray of hope – at least Mary Ann's alive.

I can tell it's Pa thudding into great-house hall. I break off from door thumping.

Sticking to stone wall, quaking, Pa's all pain and rage. 'Wot's dis yu dangle fe Mister Sam?' Leaning back, hard breathing, Pa's head batters stone wall two, three, four times. 'W'appen, Kaydia?'

'Someting wrong.'

'Speak out. W'appen?'

'It a-accident.'

'Dere're no accidents!' Now Pa's bawling, him body shaking violently. 'Puncheons brik. Friday . . . killed. Always someone's fault. Always someone's blamed.' Pa's head's battering stone like skull's about to crack.

'Don't, Pa. It me telled Friday go on.' Pa comes to a standstill. Air reeks of anger. 'Where Mary Ann?'

'Don't blame yuself. Isn't yu fault,' Pa speaks kindly now.

'Me cyaan care wot you say. Wen it appen me was dere.' She *choose* to go with Charles? Me cyaan hold onto she?

'Don't blame yuself,' Pa says.

Walking into great-house hall Sibyl strokes she swollen belly, caresses broad thighs that seem to grow out, unavoidably, fill up too much anxious space.

My eye can't make four with Sibyl's. Asking like she knows, Sibyl says, 'W'appen, Kaydia? Where's Friday?'

'Yu see Mary Ann dis mornin? Yu see where she gawn?' I say.

'Me not know. W'appen to cart back dere?'

'Friday's lickle bwoy,' Pa says accusingly. 'E shouldna work in distillery.'

Shivering, Sibyl mumbles, 'Friday. Lickle Friday.' She shudders – disbelief – too swamped by loss to speak she whines hoarsely.

My eyes go under hall stairs to Mary Ann's empty sleeping place. 'Mary Ann,' I shout, running outside to coarse lawn grass. 'Mary Ann!' Can't take my eye off looking for she. Can't shift what's done.

Old Simeon's bench stands empty. Dull clop of unshod hooves gallop full pelt from stable-block; air's filled with quivering sounds of my footfall on beaten ground. Knowing I'm seeing Charles astride Mister Sam's bay horse, Mary Ann in front, I run run run head-long down driveway past upturned cart. Before me she goes. Turning back, Mary Ann's look catches me, scorches my heart, though fire in she eye's long died out.

'Charles,' I'm bawling. 'She me dawta, yu cyaan tek she way fram me.' *Me cyaan bear witness to dis.* I'm shouting, 'No. No. No,' my voice a jagged gash. Mary Ann's face screws up, hair blowing free. I sing out *Wayah!* Mary Ann's little screwed-up face locks in me mind. Along drive I follow, flying like wicked duppy's chasing.

I need someone alongside me so I don't lose sight of why I'm pelting down plantation path, headed seawards. But even dawn breeze desert me.

'Mary Ann! Mary Ann!'

I'm screaming, speeding down hill under shrieking sun. Running through gushing rum, blood, making plantation path a swamp, my feet slither, giving way beneath my belly. Dashing on slushy sand, screeching sky scorches blue. Galloping horse turns into sunlight. I holler. Toppling over, rolling. Smashed. Running upright again but frantic rush of dread holds me back. My belly groans. Jerking forward, back, I wobble. Can't bear losing another pickney. Can't take that risk. So I run away from Charles, from Mary Ann.

Feeling warmth of smooth-stoned coast road I branch off other way, swerve from Montego Bay. Run away. Coast road to Falmouth's empty. Open. Rising. Rum flowed red. Screaming gone. Dead.

The Runaway Slave at Pilgrim's Point

Elizabeth Barrett Browning

I.

I stand on the mark, beside the shore,
Of the first white pilgrim's bended knee;
Where exile changed to ancestor,
And God was thanked for liberty.
I have run through the night – my skin is as dark –
I bend my knee down on this mark –
I look on the sky and the sea.

II.

O, pilgrim-souls, I speak to you:
I see you come out proud and slow
From the land of the spirits, pale as dew,
And round me and round me ye go.
O, pilgrims, I have gasped and run
All night long from the whips of one
Who, in your names, works sin and woe!

III.

And thus I thought that I would come
And kneel here where ye knelt before,
And feel your souls around me hum
In undertone to the ocean's roar;
And lift my black face, my black hand,
Here, in your names, to curse this land
Ye blessed in Freedom's, evermore.

IV.

I am black, I am black,
And yet God made me, they say:
But if He did so — smiling, back
He must have cast his work away
Under the feet of His white creatures,
With a look of scorn, that the dusky features
Might be trodden again to clay.

V.

And yet He has made dark things
To be glad and merry as light;
There's a little dark bird sits and sings,
There's a dark stream ripples out of sight;
And the dark frogs chant in the safe morass,
And the sweetest stars are made to pass
O'er the face of the darkest night.

VI.

But we who are dark, we are dark!
O God, we have no stars!
About our souls, in care and cark,
Our blackness shuts like prison-bars!
And crouch our souls so far behind,
That never a comfort can they find,
By reaching through their prison-bars.

VII.

Howbeit God's sunshine and His frost
They make us hot, they make us cold,
As if we were not black and lost;
And the beasts and birds in wood and wold,
Do fear us and take us for very men; —
Could the whippoorwill or the cat of the glen
Look into my eyes and be bold?

VIII.

I am black, I am black,
And once I laughed in girlish glee;
For one of my colour stood in the track
Where the drivers drove, and looked at me:
And tender and full was the look he gave!
A Slave looked so at another Slave, –
I look at the sky and the sea.

IX.

And from that hour our spirits grew
As free as if unsold, unbought;
We were strong enough, since we were two,
To conquer the world, we thought.
The drivers drove us day by day:
We did not mind; we went one way,
And no better a liberty sought.

X.

In the open ground, between the canes,
He said 'I love you' as he passed:
When the shingle-roof rang sharp with the rains,
I heard how he vowed it fast.
While others trembled, he sate in the hut
And carved me a bowl of the cocoa-nut,
Through the roar of the hurricanes.

XI.

I sang his name instead of a song;
Over and over I sang his name:
Backward and forward I sang it along,
With my sweetest notes, it was still the same!
I sang it low, that the slave-girls near
Might never guess, from what they could hear,
That all the song was a name.

XII.

I look on the sky and the sea!
We were two to love, and two to pray,
Yes, two, O God, who cried on Thee,
Though nothing didst thou say.
Coldly Thou sat'st behind the sun,
And now I cry, who am but one, –
Thou wilt not speak today!

XIII.

We were black, we were black,
We had no claim to love and bliss –
What marvel, ours was cast to wrack?
They wrung my cold hands out of his –
They dragged him – where I crawled to touch
His blood's mark in the dust – not much,
Ye pilgrim-souls, – though plain as THIS!

XIV.

Wrong, followed by a greater wrong!
Grief seemed too good for such as I;
So the white man brought the shame ere long
To stifle the sob in my throat thereby.
They would not leave me for my dull
Wet eyes! – it was too merciful
To let me weep pure tears, and die.

XV.

I am black, I am black!
I wore a child upon my breast, –
An amulet that hung too slack,
And, in my unrest, could not rest!
Thus we went moaning, child and mother,
One to another, one to another,
Until all ended for the best.

XVI.

For hark! I will tell you low – low –
I am black, you see;
And the babe, that lay on my bosom so,
Was far too white – too white for me.
As white as the ladies who scorned to pray
Beside me at church but yesterday,
Though my tears had washed a place for my knee.

XVII.

And my own child – I could not bear
To look in his face, it was so white:
So I covered him up with a kerchief rare,
I covered his face in, close and tight!
And he moaned and struggled, as well might be,
For the white child wanted his liberty, –
Ha, ha! he wanted his master's right.

XVIII.

He moaned and beat with his head and feet –
His little feet that never grew!
He struck them out as it was meet
Against my heart to break it through.
I might have sung like a mother mild,
But I dared not sing to the white-faced child
The only song I knew.

XIX.

And yet I pulled the kerchief close:
He could not see the sun, I swear,
More then, alive, than now he does
From between the roots of the mango – where?
I know where! – close! – a child and mother
Do wrong to look at one another,
When one is black and one is fair.

XX.

Even in that single glance I had
Of my child's face, – I tell you all, –
I saw a look that made me mad,
The master's look, that used to fall
On my soul like his lash, – or worse,
Therefore, to save it from my curse,
I twisted it round in my shawl.

XXI.

And he moaned and trembled from foot to head, –
He shivered from head to foot, –
Till, after a time, he lay, instead,
Too suddenly still and mute;
And I felt, beside, a creeping cold, –
I dared to lift up just a fold,
As in lifting a leaf of the mango fruit.

XXII.

But MY fruit! ha, ha! – there had been
(I laugh to think on't at this hour!)
Your fine white angels, – who have seen
God's secret nearest to His power, –
And gathered my fruit to make them wine,
And sucked the soul of that child of mine,
As the humming-bird sucks the soul of the flower.

XXIII.

Ha, ha! for the trick of the angels white!
They freed the white child's spirit so;
I said not a word, but day and night
I carried the body to and fro;
And it lay on my heart like a stone – as chill;
The sun may shine out as much as he will, –
I am cold, though it happened a month ago.

XXIV.

From the white man's house and the black man's hut
I carried the little body on;
The forest's arms did around us shut,
And silence through the trees did run!
They asked no questions as I went,
They stood too high for astonishment, –
They could see God rise on His throne.

XXV.

My little body, kerchiefed fast,
I bore it on through the forest – on –
And when I felt it was tired at last,
I scooped a hole beneath the moon.
Through the forest-tops the angels far,
With a white fine finger in every star
Did point and mock at what was done.

XXVI.

Yet when it all was done aright,
Earth 'twixt me and my baby strewed,
All changed to black earth, – nothing white, –
A dark child in the dark, – ensued
Some comfort, and my heart grew young;
I sate down smiling there, and sung
The song I told you of, for good.

XXVII.

And thus we two were reconciled,
The white child and black mother, thus;
For, as I sang it, – soft and wild,
The same song, more melodious,
Rose from the grave whereon I sate!
It was the dead child singing that,
To join the souls of both of us.

XXVIII.

I look on the sea and the sky!
Where the Pilgrims' ships first anchored lay,
The great sun rideth gloriously!
But the Pilgrims' ghosts have slid away
Through the first faint streaks of morn!
My face is black, but it glares with a scorn
Which they dare not meet by day.

XXIX.

Ah, in their stead their hunter-sons!
Ah, ah! they are on me! they form in a ring!
Keep off, – I brave you all at once, –
I throw off your eyes like a noisome thing!
You have killed the black eagle at nest, I think;
Did you never stand still in your triumph, and shrink
From the stroke of her wounded wing?

XXX.

(Man, drop that stone you dared to lift! –)
I wish you, who stand there, seven abreast,
Each for his own wife's grace and gift,
A little corpse as safely at rest,
Hid in the mangoes! yes, but she
May keep live babies on her knee,
And sing the song she liketh best.

XXXI.

I am not mad, – I am black!
I see you staring in my face, –
I know you staring, shrinking back, –
Ye are born of the Washington race!
And this land is the Free America, –
And this mark on my wrist, – (I prove what I say)
Ropes tied me up here to the flogging-place.

XXXII.

You think I shrieked then? not a sound!
I hung as a gourd hangs in the sun;
I only cursed them all around
As softly as I might have done
My own child after. From these sands
Up to the mountains, lift your hands
O Slaves, and end what I begun.

XXXIII.

Whips, curses! these must answer those!
For in this UNION, ye have set
Two kinds of men in adverse rows,
Each loathing each! and all forget
The seven wounds in Christ's body fair;
While He sees gaping everywhere
Our countless wounds that pay no debt.

XXXIV.

Our wounds are different – your white men
Are, after all, not gods indeed,
Nor able to make Christs again
Do good with bleeding. We who bleed, –
(Stand off!) – we help not in our loss,
We are too heavy for our cross,
And fall and crush you and your seed.

XXXV.

I fall, – I swoon, – I look at the sky!
The clouds are breaking on my brain:
I am floated along, as if I should die
Of Liberty's exquisite pain!
In the name of the white child waiting for me
In the deep black death where our kisses agree, –
White men, I leave you all curse-free,
In my broken heart's disdain!